Life After

Stories of Life, Death, and the Places in Between

Life After

Stories of Life, Death, and the Places in Between

Robert J. McCarter

Little Hummingbird Publishing
Flagstaff, AZ

Life After
Stories of Life, Death, and the Places in Between

Version 1.0 October 2015
ISBN: 978-1-941153-94-9

Visit Robert's website at: www.RobertJMcCarter.com

Published by:
Little Hummingbird Publishing
P.O. Box 23518
Flagstaff, AZ 86002
www.LittleHummingbird.com

Little Hummingbird Publishing is a division of Arapas, Inc. Find more about Arapas at: www.Arapas.com.

For my ever courageous and amazing Aleia!

CONTENTS

Stories of Life, Death, and the Places in Between

Robert J. McCarter

INTRODUCTION

EVERYTHING IN THIS BOOK IS A LIE. ONE HUNDRED PERCENT fiction. I don't have a special connection with the afterlife. I don't have paranormal abilities. I'm a writer. These are stories. I made them up.

That said, there is truth in everything in this book. It's the nature—and job—of fiction to take us places we can't normally go, to expose our humanity in ways that are clearer and easier to understand than in our day-to-day lives. Lying to tell the truth, if you will.

As you might imagine from the title, the focus of this book is lives on the brink—either right before or right after death: a ghost trying to solve his own murder, an old man in a care home fighting for meaning at the end of his life, a holographic husband helping his wife through her grief, a couple living their lives knowing exactly how they are going to die.

That line between life and death, those places before and after are interesting territory. If you've read any of my novels (like *Shuffled Off: A Ghost's Memoir, Book One*) you know this is territory that I am drawn to. There are a lot of fascinating things to explore here, questions that don't have easy answers, problems that aren't really solvable. These stories are thematically along the same lines as *Shuffled Off*. In fact, one story, "Detecting Haley," takes place in the ghostly world of that book.

From science fiction to paranormal fantasy, from very short stories to a long novelette, from a far distant future to our real world, these stories cover a lot of ground. They will entertain, and if you let them, they'll give you something to think about, something to talk about.

For those interested in such things, I've added a brief bit about each story at the end of each one—the story behind the story. Thoughts on where and how these things came to pass and notes on the history of the story itself.

Thanks for exploring this territory with me. Feel free to drop me a line over at my website (RobertJMcCarter.com) and let me know what you think.

Enjoy the adventure!

Robert J. McCarter
July, 2015
Flagstaff, AZ

Stories of Life, Death, and the Places in Between

Robert J. McCarter

SHOGUN DREAMS

JEFFERY SMITH WAS A WHOLLY UNREMARKABLE MAN. HE was neither old, nor young; neither short, nor tall; neither skinny, nor fat, although he did have the appropriate middle-aged bulge around his waist. He dressed unremarkably in jeans, which he looked slightly awkward in, and a long-sleeved white dress shirt buttoned all the way up to the top. Even his phobias were entirely unremarkable: spiders, airplanes, and intimacy.

Jeffery Smith was the kind of man that would go to a party and no one would remember he had been there. When he left a job, it often took his coworkers several days (or even weeks) to realize that he was gone.

Jeffery Smith was dying, but in the most common way. Stage 4 non-small cell lung cancer had just been discovered. Statistically speaking—and being an accountant, Jeffery knew statistics—he didn't have much time.

But today, on this Monday in March, Jeffery Smith felt remarkable. The previous week he had gone in to see his doctor for a cough that would not go away. He was surprised by the call from the office to come in (he thought he had the flu, or maybe even bronchitis). He was even more surprised when his doctor solemnly told him of his diagnosis. There would be MRIs and more tests to type the cancer and determine the treatment, but the doctor was sure of the diagnosis.

And, perhaps most surprising, is what Jeffery did after the appointment: he went to his place of employment, the accounting offices of Richards, Parson, Thomas, and Gosling, and promptly gave his two weeks' notice. When he told his boss, Alan Gosling, the news, Mr. Gosling promptly sent him on to HR, and HR, seeing that he had nearly one hundred days of vacation and sick leave accrued, told him to pack up his cubicle and leave. Now.

And so he did, filling a banker box with his few meager possessions: a tiny flag of Japan; some anime action figures; a few manga; a Final Fantasy IV poster; and other miscellaneous office flotsam.

Jeffery was dazed by the suddenness of it all, although he was not surprised; he knew he was just a salaryman, an easily replaceable cog in the workings of Richards, Parson, Thomas, and Gosling. He stood outside, banker box in hand, for a full five minutes wondering what to do. Then something remarkable occurred to him, so he walked to the bus stop and took the bus to the mall.

JEFFERY SMITH, BANKER BOX IN HAND, STOOD AT THE front counter of Dream Makers. He had stood there for some three minutes, but the receptionist hadn't noticed him. This was normal. He studied her, as he often did when people didn't notice him. She was young and thin and beautiful with blonde hair, very white teeth, and was showing a slightly more than tasteful amount of cleavage. Unremarkably, Jeffery did not mind waiting.

When she finally looked up and noticed him standing there, she said, "Welcome to Dream Makers. How can we make your dreams come true?"

"Umm..." he began. "Ahh..." he continued. Jessica (which is what it said on the receptionist's name tag) just sat there smiling evenly, showing off her dazzling smile and perfect teeth. "Well... You see..." Jeffery continued to stammer and start. "I want to dream."

"Excellent," Jessica said. "Just one moment and I will have one of our Dream Specialists come speak with you."

Jeffery Smith sat across from Dream Specialist Mindy Miner. She too was beautiful, with a dazzling white smile, and plentiful cleavage on display. But she was a brunette, not a blonde. *Something for everyone*, Jeffery thought.

"Would you like some coffee?" she asked.

Jeffery paused, normally he only had the one cup in the morning, but today was different, today was special. "Yes, please."

"How do you take it?"

"One sugar with cream."

When Jessica had delivered the coffee, Mindy smiled at him and said, "What dream can we fulfill for you today, Mr. Smith?"

Suddenly over being shy about his dream, Jeffery let it come tumbling out. "Japan! I want to experience an epic adventure in the land of the rising sun. It should take place in the 17th century and start off like the miniseries *Shogun*, but end happily with the daring English adventurer finding love and embracing the new culture as his own."

Jeffery Smith had watched *Shogun* with his father when he was eight years old (over the strenuous objections of his mother). It was then that he had fallen in love with the Japanese culture. Much of his adult leisure activities revolved around Japan: manga, anime, aikido, faulting attempts to learn the language, and tending to his three bonsai trees.

"Very good, Mr. Smith. We can do that. I presume you have seen the miniseries numerous times?"

"Oh yes, at least twice a year since the DVD came out."

"Very good, that will help. And I suppose you would like our deluxe package, which includes: extended REM; advanced hypnosis—"

"Yes, yes, all of that. It will feel real, right?"

"Absolutely real. Guaranteed."

The interview went on for quite some time with Mindy asking specific, and often embarrassing, questions about what he wanted to experience. Nudity? Sex? How much sex? How explicit should the sex be? Even what positions he liked and attributes of his preferred sexual partner. Jeffery Smith answered these questions, slowly, with his face beet red. He came to the unavoidable conclusion that the typical Dream Makers client wanted to dream of sex and romance.

ON TUESDAY, JEFFERY SMITH WENT TO SEE THE DREAM Makers physician, Doctor Chahel Sen, for a physical. Doctor Sen was a beautiful man with shiny black hair, smooth brown skin, and kind brown eyes. Jeffery was worried that his health condition would cause problems. When he told

Doctor Sen of his diagnosis, the doctor asked, "Are you currently being treated?"

"No," Jeffery answered. "Not yet. They still have more tests to do before a treatment plan can be determined."

"Then it will not be a problem, sir. Many of our clients come to us as after a diagnosis such as yours."

Jeffery Smith felt sad to hear this. He thought for once in his life he was doing something remarkable. It was upsetting to hear his reaction was common.

On Wednesday he went to the Dream Makers psychologist, Doctor Karen Thompson. She too was beautiful, with long brown hair and shining blue eyes. But, much to Jeffery's relief, she was not displaying any cleavage.

They started with a brief hypnosis test (to make sure he was a good candidate) that left Jeffery with a brief and shining image of him fighting Darth Vader with a samurai sword. Maybe it was her affable manner, maybe she had done something while he was hypnotized, but soon she had him talking with ease about his parents, his childhood, and how he felt about his diagnosis.

As he was leaving she asked him one last question, "Why don't you just go to Japan, Jeffery?"

"What?" he asked, surprised by the question. He couldn't imagine that particular question was Dream Makers approved.

"You long to see Japan; you could just get on a plane and go see it."

"Well... I... You see..." he stammered. "I don't have much time. I want the epic adventure." He didn't mention what was, perhaps, the real reason: his fear of airplanes.

On Friday he received a call from Dream Makers telling him that he had passed his exams with flying colors and that development of his program was well under way. Was he available for a Monday evening appointment?

The rest of Friday and the weekend passed with excruciating slowness. He spent his time watching *Shogun*, Godzilla movies, *Memoirs of a Geisha*, *Cowboy Beebop*, *Ghost in the Shell*, and many other of his favorite Japanese movies. Interspersed with his movie watching, he went to the dojo twice to practice aikido (or "falling down and getting up" as Sensei referred to it), ordered and ate Japanese takeout, and danced around the room singing: "Turning Japanese, I think I'm turning Japanese, I really think so."

ON MONDAY AT 6:00 P.M. SHARP, A LIMO ARRIVED AT Jeffery Smith's apartment and took him to the Dream Makers sleep facility. There he was greeted by Doctor Alan Michaels. The doctor wore glasses, a white coat, and was rather unremarkable looking—Jeffery Smith found this very comforting.

Jeffery was seated in a small room with a bed, two chairs, and some medical equipment. "How does it work?" he asked.

"Our approach is three pronged," Doctor Michaels began. "First, we use a mild psychotropic that will make you more open to suggestion and make your dreams significantly more vivid. Second, we use a proprietary drug that will deepen and lengthen your REM sleep and enhance your recollection of your dreams. And, thirdly, we use hypnosis before and during your dream to create the experience you want."

"What if something goes wrong?"

Doctor Michaels smiled. "We monitor you the whole

time. Relax Jeffery; I've done this thousands of times. You are going to love your shogun experience."

Jeffery Smith sat across from Mindy Miner for his post-dream interview. He felt like a new man. He hadn't shaved in several days, and the top button on his long-sleeved white dress shirt was left undone.

"Samurai swords, epic battles, beautiful women. It was... It was amazing." He paused, his brow furrowing. "I am still having dreams; really, really vivid dreams."

Mindy smiled, typing on her keyboard. "That is what we like to hear."

"But..." Jeffery began, before a coughing fit overtook him.

"Is it your health issue?" Mindy asked.

"Maybe, I don't know. I think I may be having some reentry difficulties. I finally did something remarkable, and now my life is just not interesting anymore. I mean... I quit my job and blew a ton of money on this. What am I going to do now? Wait to die?"

Mindy nodded and frowned. "You know what? Your plan comes with a follow-up visit with Doctor Thompson. Why don't you go see her? Here's her card."

As he got up to leave, Mindy said, "Oh. One more thing, Mr. Smith." She handed him what looked like a mini samurai sword about six inches long. "Open the flap on the end of the pommel; it's a USB drive with copies of the images we used in your hypnosis. You may find them useful in remembering, and reinforcing, your dream."

Jeffery left in a daze and went to the dojo to practice. Even that had paled; he was limited by his own skill, his own ability, unlike in his shogun dreams.

JEFFERY SMITH DIDN'T GO TO SEE DOCTOR THOMPSON until a week later. By that time his shogun dreams of Japan had faded and he had fallen into a deep depression. Lung cancer; pending radiation treatments; parents dead; no relationship—where was the adventure? What was he going to do?

At first, he had decided not to go see her, but then he remembered what she had asked: *Why don't you just go to Japan, Jeffery?*

It stuck in his head. Why didn't he? Well, he was deathly afraid of flying, there was that. What if he wasn't? What if he could fly? He had enough money in savings to go, what else was his money good for now? What if he could get treatments in Japan? What if he could study aikido in Japan? What if he could study *Japanese* in Japan?

These thoughts swirled around his head during a long, sleepless night. In the morning he called Doctor Thompson's office and found there was a cancelation for that very afternoon.

JEFFERY SMITH DID NOT LOOK HIS NORMAL SELF. HE WAS dressed in sweats and a T-shirt, his hair was messy, his face unshaven, and he had dark circles under his eyes. He sat slouched in a chair across from Doctor Karen Thompson.

"What is on your mind, Jeffery?" she asked.

"I want to go to Japan," he replied.

She nodded and smiled. "Good, I think that is a good step."

"But..." Jeffery began before going silent.

After a lengthy pause Doctor Thompson prompted, "But what?"

Jeffery shook his head. "Ohhh. There are so many buts. But, I am afraid of flying. But, I have stage 4 lung cancer and have to begin treatments soon. But, I have a cat. Who's going to take care of my cat, Batou? But. But. But." Jeffery slunked lower in his chair.

"Listen to me, Jeffery, there are challenges here, but none of them insurmountable to you going to Japan."

"What about flying?"

"What are you scared of?"

"Well, crashing, of course. And, you know, crashing in the ocean. And then the sharks." Jeffery watched her closely, but not a hint of a smile was betrayed. He thought it silly, but it also seemed logical to him. If you survive the crash in the ocean (which would be bad enough), you have to survive the sharks. "I don't suppose you can just hypnotize me so I can get on the plane?"

"Yes, Jeffery, I think I can."

Jeffery sat up straighter, a smile spreading across his lips. They talked for the rest of the hour, and at the end Jeffery was hopeful.

"Umm..." Jeffery began before leaving. "Do you help non-Dream Makers patients?"

She smiled and said, "Yes, I do. I would love to help you with this. Give your insurance information to my assistant and I will have her see if they will cover your visits."

JEFFERY SMITH'S FAREWELL PARTY WAS HELD AT THE dojo. It was, really, the place he felt most at home, the place he felt he most belonged.

He had only planned to go for three weeks; there were

still so many uncertainties, and his oncologist was having a fit about him waiting so long to start treatments.

When Sensei had brought up the idea of the party he had demurred, but Sensei had insisted, telling him, "If the last few weeks have taught us anything, Jeffery, it is that life is uncertain. If you don't want to call it a farewell party, call it a celebration of your upcoming adventure."

There were about fifteen people in attendance, which surprised and pleased Jeffery. About half were his dojo-mates, three were accountant friends, three were manga/anime friends, and the last was his sister Amy Smith-Warner.

He was touched that she had driven from Dallas to Houston to attend his party. He would be driving to Dallas early in the morning to catch his plane and could have said good-bye to her then.

Sensei insisted that he and Jeffery do an aikido demonstration. Normally, Jeffery would have refused to do such a thing in front of friends and family, but Jeffery was not feeling normal any more. So together they demonstrated the fine art of falling down and getting up.

His friends praised his skill, and attested amazement, which felt good. He knew that even after nearly twenty years of practice he was merely adequate, not excellent. But, he thought, perhaps to those who did not know aikido, what they had seen him doing *was* amazing.

To a person, his friends all congratulated him on his journey, many with a trace of envy. Although he was seriously ill (and some of his friends could only see that), he was doing the kind of thing that many of them had only dreamed of. He was doing something remarkable.

His sister kissed him on her way out and said, "I am proud of you, Jeff."

JEFFERY SMITH BOARDED THE BOEING 777 WITH A SMILE on his lips, happy despite the persistent cough that would not let him forget his illness. The fear that had always stopped him from flying wasn't gone, it still nipped at the edges of his mind, but he had seen himself fly (and survive) so many times now that this seemed almost normal. Completely unremarkable.

The flight attendant greeted him with a smile, "Welcome aboard Japan Airlines."

"Domo arigato. Glad to be aboard!" Jeffery replied.

As he walked down the aisle people noticed him. Sometimes a quick glance, sometimes a small smile, sometimes a muffled chuckle. Not only did Jeffery Smith not care, he loved it. He was dressed unusually: he wore black aikido gi pants (he knew they would be comfortable for the long flight), and a black T-shirt with the flag of Japan emblazoned on the front.

He settled into his window seat next to Hana Endo, a Japanese native returning home. "Ohayo gozaimasu," he said to her. It was morning and he knew enough to know that it was the proper greeting, as opposed to more commonly known "konnichiwa."

Hana smiled at Jeffery and replied, "Good morning."

Jeffery introduced himself and they chatted amicably until the plane started accelerating down the runway. Then Jeffery gripped the seat, closed his eyes, and used the visualization that Dr. Thompson had taught him. Over and over he saw himself enjoying the flight and safely getting off the plane in Tokyo. He did this until the fear had passed and they were well on their way.

Later, after explaining his quest to Hana, he pulled out the glossy prints he had made of his shogun dream images and showed them to her. At one, a beautiful picture of a Buddhist temple, she said, "I know that one! It is the Fugen-in Temple on Mount Koya, and it is shukubo."

"Shukubo?" Jeffery asked. "What is shukubo?"

"They rent rooms to foreigners, you could stay there."

JEFFERY SMITH SPENT SEVERAL DELIGHTFUL DAYS SEEING the sites in Tokyo before boarding a train to Osaka. Once in Osaka, it took a subway, a train, another subway, a cable car up Mount Koya, a bus, and finally a short walk to get him in front of the Fugen-in Temple. He stood there in awe, taking in the grace of the traditional Japanese architecture, the beauty of the finely sculpted topiary, the sweet smell of the cherry blossoms, and the wonders of the delicate gardens. The beauty of it took his breath away and brought tears to his eyes.

He felt transported back in time to 17th century Japan. Just as he first experienced it as a boy with his father watching *Shogun*.

This was better than movies, or anime, or manga, or even his memory of the temple from his shogun dreams. This was Japan, for real and in person. This was *home*.

JEFFERY SMITH WAS DEEPLY TROUBLED AS HE SAT IN HIS small room at the Fugen-in Temple. He was meditating, zanzen style, as the monks had taught him. His three weeks were at an end, and if he was to return to Houston he must go catch the bus in less than an hour.

He felt death all around him. Death if he returned to Houston; while the radiation treatments might extend his life, what about the *quality* of his life? Death if he stayed; while the quality of his life might be higher for a time, it would surely be shorter.

He returned his attention to his breath, letting go of his worry, yet again. *One, inhale; two, exhale; three, inhale.* He counted silently, as he had been taught, to help keep his mind from wandering.

But, how could he leave? To his great delight he had discovered that some of the monks practiced aikido, and that Buddhism—which he hadn't seriously studied up until now—dovetailed perfectly with the martial art. How could he leave Mr. Kishi, the gardener, who had so swiftly taught him more about Bonsai than all the books he had read?

One, inhale; two, exhale...

But how could he not return home? There he had insurance that would cover his treatments and make sure he would be cared for at the end, if it came to that. Remarkably he didn't feel much different than when he arrived. The cough was not gone, but it was not any worse. Maybe this lifestyle was changing him; maybe he would live longer here.

One, inhale; two, exhale; three, inhale; four exhale...

And what of longevity? He could die on the walk to the bus, or at any time, for that matter. But he couldn't completely abandon himself to the ancient practices, it just didn't seem wise.

One, inhale; two, exhale; three, inhale; four exhale...

His mind finally calmed, he quietly completed his meditation and rose. His path was clear now, he was certain.

JEFFERY SMITH WAS A WHOLLY REMARKABLE MAN. AT THE age of forty-nine, after being diagnosed with stage 4 non-small cell lung cancer, he left Houston and moved to Japan.

He sought refuge in a Buddhist temple on Mount Koya, and there he found his true home. He meditated, practiced aikido, gardened, studied Zen Buddhism, and eventually became a monk.

He combined modern medicine with Kampo (Japanese herbal medicine), and a Buddhist lifestyle to dance with his illness. And "dancing" is what he called it. He could not hate, or fight, that which had brought him to his true joy in life. His lung cancer eventually went into remission and he enjoyed many years of good health.

When the telltale cough came back at the age of fifty-seven, Jeffery Smith was not scared, merely curious. He went to his oncologist and discovered that the disease had come back, and that it was time to dance with it once again.

Jeffery Smith died a good death several months later at his beloved Fugen-in Temple.

Jeffery Smith was a wholly remarkable man.

BACKSTORY—SHOGUN DREAMS

MY FIRST PUBLISHED STORY, "THE PATH OF THE FAERIE King" landed in a collection called *100 Stories for Haiti*, and I really got into the idea—writing for a cause. In fact, I've had six stories published that way at this point.

This story was written for, and first appeared, in *New Sun Rising: Stories for Japan*, a collection raising relief funds for the March 2011 earthquake in Japan. The call for stories came with a stipulation: the stories had to celebrate Japan and its culture.

I live in Arizona and have never been to Japan. Have limited parts of the culture I understand (the *Shogun* miniseries was my biggest introduction to the culture as a teenager). And I wanted to have a sci-fi element to the story.

That is the beauty of constraints, they channel your energy and actually empower your creativity.

I am also aware of how a fatal diagnosis can change someone. My wife runs a non-profit that helps people navigate this tricky territory, which all started with helping our best friend live with (and eventually die from) a brain tumor.

After pondering the constraints of the story, the opening line "Jeffery Smith was a wholly unremarkable man..." popped into my head and we were off and running (with quite a bit of research on Japan, of course).

I missed the mark on this one in my first draft—I stopped as soon as Jeffrey got to Japan and didn't follow it through.

My wonderful beta readers helped me see the issue, and I was very pleased when this story was picked for the collection.

Life After

Stories of Life, Death,
and the Places in Between

R
I
P
?

Robert J. McCarter

WHEN MISTER GRIM
CAME CALLING

When Mister Grim came calling, he always presented his card: a crisp white rectangle with just the two words "Mister Grim" in bold black letters. He kept them in a slim sliver case with a monogrammed "G" on the lid. He was frightening: tall and gaunt; white hair and clothes; pale, almost translucent skin; and long bony fingers.

The first time I met Mister Grim was after I had a heart attack, he was standing over me in my hospital bed. "Who are you!?" I asked, shocked by his presence and his visage.

"I am Mister Grim," he answered with a rictus grin, handing me his card. "I will be your guide, when the time comes, for the journey." He talked slowly, spacing each word out, with a dry crackling rasp of a voice.

"My what?"

"I was just next door taking care of another pilgrim and thought I would pop by. It wasn't clear if you would be traveling today. I thought we could get to know each other." His manner was oddly formal and incongruent with his appearance.

We talked for a time. It was very uncomfortable for me, but Mister Grim seemed oblivious to my reaction to him. He was interested in my past, my childhood particularly. He wanted to know if I had ever seen ghosts, or fairies, or other "spiritual" beings. I answered his queries using as few words as I could, like a child trying to get away from the interrogation of a parent.

He eventually left, or I fell asleep, and the next thing I knew I awoke with a tube down my throat surrounded by my family. I dismissed it as a dream until I came across that card underneath me in the bed. When I touched it, a shiver ran down my spine, and I thought I could hear that rasping voice echoing down the hallway.

After I got home from the hospital I had a dream, well, more of a memory, about my father—he died of a massive heart attack at the age of thirty-seven, two years younger than I was at the time. My mother and I stayed by his bed-side in the hospital for days on end. One night when she was out, he woke up briefly, with eyes wide, and grunted something unintelligible—in my dream it sounded like "gggrrrriiiimmmmm." That was the last sound he uttered. He died less than an hour later.

I woke up in a cold sweat, crying and incoherent; my wife thought I was having another heart attack. After that I was driven, haunted even, by my dad's last word and the image of Mister Grim standing over me. I taped Mister Grim's card to my treadmill and got busy getting healthy: I gave up smoking, lost forty pounds, started eating better, and paid more attention to my wife and kids. I even told my wife the whole story. At first she thought I was crazy, but when she saw the changes I was making she became my most enthusiastic supporter.

THE SECOND TIME I MET MISTER GRIM, I WAS ON AN expedition climbing Mount Rainier. My new fitness level and zest for life had transformed me into an adventurer. He appeared inside my tent at base camp, his skeletal form haloed in the dawn light. In that now familiar rasping voice he said, "Are you ready for that trip yet? It is best to plan in advance when embarking on an extended journey."

"No!" I shouted. I struggled to get out of my sleeping bag, but couldn't—I only managed to extract one arm. The zipper was stuck and I was locked in there like a mummy while Mister Grim hovered over me.

"Everyone makes the journey sooner or later," he said, his bony hand slowly reaching towards me as he placed his card in my one free hand.

I woke up screaming with that damned card clutched in my hand. I told everyone in the expedition that I had a gallstone getting ready to pass and got off that mountain as quickly as I could. Later that day an avalanche buried half the expedition, killing two—if not for Mister Grim visiting me, it might have been three.

When I got home, I put that second card on the refrigerator and redoubled my efforts: I got even more fit, ate better, took up meditation, worked harder on my marriage, and started researching and investing in anti-aging technologies. I also focused on accumulating wealth, reasoning that the more money I had, the better my chances were of survival. I didn't know where Mister Grim wanted to take me, but I knew I didn't want to go.

THE THIRD TIME WE MET, I WAS EIGHTY-SEVEN YEARS OLD and in a clinic waiting to get my first life extension treatment. One of the companies I had invested in had finally figured out how to extend the human life span and not a moment too soon for me. I was torn about going through with it; my wife hadn't made it, and I wasn't sure I wanted to go on without her. However, my resolve hardened as soon as I saw him standing there.

"I am beginning to get the feeling you don't like me," Mister Grim said, handing me his card, his voice sounding like the rustling of autumn leaves.

I screamed, and it was not a dignified scream—I screamed like a little girl. Seeing him, yet again, caused an instant panic attack; not at all good for a man of my advanced age. Mister Grim, though, seemed completely unfazed by my outburst. "Please don't be offended," I said, when I had recovered from my initial fright. Wanting to placate him, I added, "Actually, I owe you my gratitude."

"You don't say?" he said, raising one thin white eyebrow on his emaciated face.

"Without your visits I would have been dead long ago, you are an effective...," I said, struggling to find the right word, "ahh... motivator."

"My pleasure, I have enjoyed our little chats, as not many can see me before their time comes."

"Can I ask you something?" I asked, finally working up my nerve after all these visits.

"Please." He seemed delighted at the opportunity; his face forming a stiff grimace that I think was meant to be a smile.

"Where is it that you want to take me?"

"Why, on your journey to the other side, of course."

"But what, exactly, is on the 'other side'?" After all my running from him, I had to know.

"So sorry, but I don't know." He frowned, an expression that fit more naturally on his face, unlike his previous attempt at a smile.

"You don't know? How can you not know?"

"I am but a ferryman, if you will, guiding souls across the river Styx. I don't go with them, I just make sure they get to the other side—it is up to them from there."

"But... Is there heaven? Hell? Reincarnation? Oblivion?" I asked, my voice breaking in desperation. "You must know. You must!"

"I am afraid I don't. I only catch a glimpse of them as they move on. I can tell you this though: everyone seems to have a different experience once they get to where they are going."

I survived the extension treatment, barely, and thankfully. His words were no comfort at all. That third card I pasted to the bathroom mirror. To palliate my worry, I started researching and investing in companies working on extending human consciousness beyond the body.

THE LAST TIME WE MET WAS ONE EVENING ABOUT NINETY years later in my study.

"Are you ready to take the journey yet?" he asked, handing me his card. "You have run the course with your medical interventions."

His appearance was not a great shock this time; I had been expecting him. "No," I answered as I stood up. "I won't be going!"

"Oh?" His tone was surprisingly even; my defiance did nothing to ruffle his grim composure.

"Technology now exists to transfer my neural pattern into an artificial life-form; I am going in for the transfer in the morning."

"You assume that your soul and your mind are the same thing. They are not, one is eternal, the other finite."

His words stopped me short. "But if a soul can attach to a biological body, why can't it attach to a technological one?"

"Perhaps it can, I don't know, but whatever kind of body you have, it is not eternal. The journey must be taken."

"No. The artificial body will have a much longer life span, and by the time that is ending, I will be able to switch to another body."

"You fear the unknown, believe me, I understand. But your fear will not stop the inevitable. Alas, the point is moot," he gestured to the chair I had just been sitting in.

I looked down at my body, limp and lifeless. "No!" I cried. All this time, all this effort, and still I had not escaped. I fell to my knees weeping, and in desperation I asked, "Some way, there must be some way out of this. Please!"

"There is one way, but the price is extreme."

There was a way? I was shocked, intrigued, and repelled all at once. "What... What is it?"

Mister Grim proceeded to tell me the tale of how he became Mister Grim. He had been a British infantryman in the American Revolutionary War and crossed paths with the previous Mister Grim many times on the battlefield. Like me, he could see his Mister Grim before it was his time and attributed his long survival to those sightings. He had hoped to escape the war with his life, but was injured in the Siege of Yorktown, and died several days after Cornwallis's surrender. In the end he was made the same offer Mister Grim made me.

"I tire of being the ferryman and long to continue on my journey—I am ready for what is next. You can take my place by taking this." He extended his silver case to me, and in my desperation I grabbed it. The case felt cold and heavy in my hand, oddly substantial.

Mister Grim smiled and said, "At last..." He let out a long exhale that reminded me of a spring wind, as the color returned to his skin, hair and clothes, and his face and form filled out. When the transformation was complete he looked like a young man dressed in a British military uniform. "Thank you. Your first task will be to guide me to the other side."

At the same time he was being restored, I felt myself transform into the albino, emaciated form of Mister Grim. Without thinking, I handed him a card from the silver case and said, "I am Mister Grim, I will be your guide," my voice a hollow rattle. I took his hand and escorted him to the other side. I have been doing the same for souls, just like you, ever since.

It was so kind of you to inquire about me, but now that you know who I am, we must be about our business. Here is my card. I am Mister Grim, and I will be your guide.

Robert J. McCarter

BACKSTORY—WHEN MISTER GRIM CAME CALLING

BACK IN 2009 I WAS PART OF A SMALL WRITERS GROUP here in Flagstaff, Arizona. We were all friends and wanted to write—we had fiction, nonfiction, and children's books in the group.

We didn't last all that long, but it was a wonderfully, protective cocoon to get back into writing. We often met at the little Flagstaff airport terminal, on the second floor in this open, airy space overlooking the runway and the pine trees beyond.

The genesis of this story was the image of the grim reaper as an old-fashioned gentleman that always gave you his card when he came calling. I remember reading it to the group in that room at the terminal. Everyone was quiet as I read and there were some shivers when I finished.

It was a good way to get this writing thing rolling.

This story was originally published in Issue 1 of *Azure Keep Quarterly*.

DETECTING HALEY

A Walter Anchor, Ghost Detective Story

Chapter 1

I HATE BEING A GHOST. DON'T GET ME WRONG, I'M GLAD to have consciousness and all that, but it's the little things I miss. Like the taste of a tender, juicy steak and a cold beer. The sound of an audience clapping for me. The feel of a pair of dice in my hands. The rough texture of a cat's tongue. The searing heat of the Tucson sun.

But so what? I'm a ghost and I've got a murder to solve. *Mine.*

We ghosts usually have unfinished business, and since I haven't heard the "call," I figure my unfinished business is my murder—that's what's keeping me earthbound. The "call" is that glorious event when a ghost moves on to the next stage of their afterlife. Opinions on exactly what this is varies, but I'm ready to be out of here.

Not that I'm qualified to solve murders or anything. I was a dentist by trade and before that an out-of-work actor.

These thoughts rumbled through my mind as I stared at the dead body on the grimy carpet below me.

"Well?" Emily asked. She looked at me with her ancient green eyes that inhabited her round baby face. She has short, curly blonde hair that reminds me of Shirley Temple when she was a kid. Emily died when she was four years old, but now she's eighty years dead. There is a lot of wisdom packed in that adorable little body. But I gotta tell you, it's more than a little disconcerting.

"What?" I shrugged, looking at the dead body and her ghost. She was in her late twenties with long brown hair. Her blood had pooled and congealed on the light-blue carpet. Her ghost was gape jawed and clearly in distress, the thin silver cord that attached her soul to her body still intact, going from belly button to belly button.

"You've got to do something," Emily insisted.

"Why?" I asked.

"The poor thing is suffering," she said, pointing at the wispy mess of a ghost, its mouth open wide, a pitiful moan escaping from its throat.

"You do something," I said.

"I am. My plan is to whine until you do something." Emily may be eighty years dead, but there was still a lot of four-year-old left in her.

I sighed. "This is a distraction, Emily. We are here track-ing a clue to my murder."

"Yeah, and that clue took us here. To her. I think we need to investigate."

I nodded, stooping down and looking at the body. "Maybe we can snoop around and get Banquo to come take care of the bardo-brain." The bardo is a place we ghosts often find ourselves when things don't go so well and this ghost had all the signs.

"Should I go get him?" Emily asked, her voice going all high when she said "him." The girl has a great big crush on Banquo. He's kind of the ringleader of our graveyard community, and Emily has had a thing for him since he first came there around ten years ago. He is an expert, as much as anyone is, in helping these distressed ghosts.

I looked closer at the corpse, getting down low so I could clearly see her face. I felt a tingle of shock flow through my ghostly form. I knew this woman. She temped at my dental practice the month before I was murdered. And now she lay here also murdered.

Even though I wasn't experienced at the detective thing at the time, the knife sticking out of her back gave away the "murder" part of the equation.

My name is Walter Anchor. I solve murders. This is my first case.

Chapter 2

"YEAH," I SAID TO EMILY, "GO GET HIM." WITH A GIRLISH squeal and a "pop" she was gone, and I was left there with the dead dental assistant.

I looked around the grubby little Tucson apartment. A small bedroom, a kitchen with dirty dishes everywhere, a cracked LCD TV in the living room. I then looked at the victim again. Tall, slender, dressed in designer jeans and a pastel blue blouse stained with her own blood. Her nails were well manicured and the makeup on her face expertly applied.

This was not her apartment.

Being a ghost detective is all about observation. It's not like you can question witnesses, or root through their garbage, or run a background check. What you can do is watch and observe, twenty-four hours a day, seven days a week.

The ghost groaned and I got up and looked at it. Her ghostly appearance was nothing like her physical appearance. She had a diffuse vapor-like form, her eyes wide, her limbs vague stubs. She was lost, trapped in her own personal hell, a place known as the bardo. This torturous state is not uncommon for us earthbound spirits, and even less uncommon for the murdered.

I have never been in that state. I have Emily to thank for that.

The ghost moaned again and I listened carefully. The one great advantage of being a ghost detective is that you can sometimes talk to the dead.

"Haley," I said, remembering her name. "It's me, Doctor Anchor. Can you tell me what happened?"

"Blaaa," she hissed, her eyes meeting mine briefly. "Blaaaack Shooooes."

"Black Shoes?" I asked.

"Blaaaack Shooooes," she moaned again. In fact, the need to listen carefully was overkill. Haley just kept saying it over and over again, the moan of it becoming a kind of eerie mantra as I went back to examining the body.

The knife was thin and long, buried to the hilt between two of the vertebrosternal ribs. It had pierced her heart, she hadn't been alive long; the person wielding the knife had known what they were doing.

I made a slow sweep of the apartment and found out several things. Someone named Roger Coptic lived there, he was a slob, a drug addict (the used needles in the trash can were a dead giveaway), and hadn't been home in quite some time (the wilted marijuana plants in the bathtub helped with that).

Which led to the question, what was a nice girl like her doing in a place like this? And, what did this Roger Coptic have to do with my own murder?

Chapter 3

MAYBE I SHOULD PAUSE AND GIVE YOU A LAY OF THE LAND. Like when I was alive and a patient would come in for a procedure. It seemed to always help for me to sit down with them and tell them what to expect, warn them of the difficult parts, and make sure they understood both the risks and the rewards. Especially the unpleasant procedures like a root canal or an extraction or root planing. Ah, hell, who am I kidding? I was a dentist, most of the "procedures" were unpleasant.

I would put on my deep actorly voice and tell them the toughest pieces in the calmest, most reassuring voice possible.

So here goes.

The world thinks I committed suicide, which I frankly find depressing. I know, suicide is pretty high in my line of work, but I was a happy dentist. Seriously, I was. I loved my job, I loved my staff, I loved my patients. My life wasn't perfect, I had been divorced for several years and found myself a bit phobic about relationships (could explain why my best friend as a ghost appears to be a four-year-old), I had a bit of a gambling problem (okay, okay, by a "bit," I meant "massive"), and I hadn't talked to any family members for a few years.

So yeah, there was the good in my life and the not so good. Just like any other human on the planet, you peel back the layers you're going to find some nasty stuff. Me, I was lonely. I worked too long because I didn't have much else to do, except for gambling. It's hard to feel alone when you're throwing the dice at the craps table and people are cheering you on.

Anyway, where was I? Oh yeah... lay of the land. So about six months before finding Haley murdered, I had been working late, finishing my charting, avoiding going back to my big empty house, when I was murdered. It wasn't anything spectacular, I had just sat down in one of the dental chairs and closed my eyes for a moment—I must have fallen asleep. Next thing I knew I was a ghost hovering over my own body.

It was a shock, to say the least. Looking at my body, a hypodermic still sitting in my slack hand, a drop of blood where the injection had been made in my arm. It looked like a suicide, but I know it wasn't.

I spent several months in the dental office—and not by choice, I must say—watching. I guess you could say I was haunting the place. I didn't "do" anything but creep people out occasionally, but I watched and waited and listened.

My partner in the practice, Doctor Wheeler, kept things going and soon people started talking about me. Specifically, talking about me like I wasn't there.

So let me give you a piece of advice. If you find yourself a ghost, get away from the people you knew if you can. This shouldn't come as a surprise, but folks don't see you the same way you see yourself. There are misunderstandings and your intent is not always apparent. The experience can be disturbing to say the least.

So, one brief example germane to this story. When I was alive, one of the office girls, Annie, couldn't get her car to start after work, so I drove her home. It was the right thing to do. I loved my people. But to hear her talk about it after my death it was like we both "felt" something that night and if she had just let me know that she had "felt" something too, then everything would have magically changed and I wouldn't have been some lonely loser and not taken my life.

So, I was stuck in my dental office, and as the picture of the events of that day became clear, I decided I needed to find my own murderer. One clue at a time, one step at a time.

It's not like I had anything else to do.

Chapter 4

WHEN I HEARD TWO POPS, I LOOKED UP FROM HALEY'S body and saw Emily and Banquo. Emily was beaming and looking up at the big-bellied man. Banquo stepped forward, his eyes on me and then the ghost.

"Good evening, Walter," he said.

"Banquo," I replied. Look, I give the guy his props. He knows a lot and does a lot for our little community, but I just ain't in the fan club. Not one of his students.

Now it could be that he is also the leader of the Midnight Circle—the nightly gathering of the ghosts at the grave-yard—and that irks me a bit. Sure the guy's an English Lit professor, knows a lot of Shakespeare and other plays by heart that he leads the circle in. But maybe they should give someone with acting experience a chance every now and then. Someone like—

"Have you tried to reach her?" he asked.

I snorted in response. I knew he knew the answer. He just wanted to hear me say I couldn't be bothered.

"I know you can help her," Emily said to Banquo, her little lispy voice higher than usual. She's one of the reasons I don't feel the need to faun over Banquo—she does it more than enough for both of us.

"My boy," Banquo said to me, "you really should take the time to help those in need."

I straightened up and met Banquo's gaze. "I am," I said, pointing at myself with both my thumbs. "Who else is going to solve my murder?" I moved away into the bedroom to see what I could see there. I left Banquo, Haley's ghost, and Emily to do their thing.

ALL THAT TIME I SPENT HAUNTING MY DENTAL PRACTICE I learned many things, but most of them not useful to solving my murder.

Mostly what I learned watching and listening was the messy reality of humanity: unhappiness, affairs, depression, petty bickering, addiction, and the like. I also saw the good stuff (kindness, love, and generosity), which I had known was there too. But, it was the quantity of the not so good stuff that surprised me.

Ultimately I did find a clue to my murder. There was something off about Midge, my office manager. It was the guilty look she kept getting on her round Midwestern face when no one was looking. She knew something.

When I could finally leave the dental office (that's a

whole 'nother story), I started following her everywhere and eventually came the day when the letter arrived. It was a plain white envelope with her address shakily written in blue ink. She had rushed into the bathroom with it, avoiding her husband and daughter, and opened it.

It said, "If you need to reach me again about your financial problems, drop a note at this address." It was followed by the address of the gross apartment Haley died in.

Midge's hands shook as she slowly tore up the letter and flushed it down the toilet. At first when I saw that guilt on her face I had been angry; seeing her scared like that softened that feeling. She knew something, but whatever she had done, she had been coerced.

I shook right next to Midge, my ghostly form turning diffuse, my vision tunneling in, a crushing depression descending on me.

Conspiracy... had there been a conspiracy to kill me? Was Midge part of it? It looked like my death was part of something larger. I was nobody, just a failed actor turned dentist. Who would want me dead?

I would have fallen into the bardo right then and there if it hadn't been for the little voice that said, "Not cool, let the lady go to the bathroom in private. What kind of sicko are you?"

I saw the little ghostly form of Emily, her hands on her hips, her mouth a sneer.

Seeing her shocked me back to myself. "Who are you?" I asked.

Chapter 5

As I looked around Roger Coptic's bedroom with its unmade bed, its piles of dirty laundry and unopened mail, I tried to tune out Emily and Banquo. Her voice was an octave higher than usual as she said things like, "Oh, I so know you can help her," or "Did anyone ever tell you you look like Lawrence Olivier from when he played King Lear at the West End in London?" or "What are you doing later tonight?"

Banquo's replies were curt but courteous. And then at some point things got quiet out there, which was fine by me.

"I had a thought," Banquo said to me, from the door of the bedroom.

I looked up from the grease-stained pile of mail, not answering, but giving him my best "can't you see I'm busy doing important things" look.

"I think you should try to pull her from the bardo. She might have some information for you about her murder and that might help you along."

Emily stood behind him and to his left, her eyes all doey as she stared up at him. "Walter," she gasped. "Isn't that a brilliant idea? That was brilliant, Banquo."

And it was a good thought, but I certainly didn't want to say that in front of Emily. "I guess," I replied. "But, I have no idea how to—"

Banquo's face lit up like a kid on Christmas morning. "I'll be happy to show you what I know, my boy." Banquo loves to teach, it's really his thing. And while I appreciated the thought, I can't stand it when he calls me "my boy." I'm not his boy.

BANQUO IS CHUBBY, BALD, SIXTYISH, AND GREY HAIRED. He slowly paced around Haley as he lectured, his hands clasped behind his back. Very much the professor.

He started by explaining the bardo—I know what the bardo is. It's that place ghosts often get stuck where they are reliving the worst of their past, stuck in their regrets. It's hell, quite literally. Haley was there, no doubt. Her eyes were wide, her mouth slack, B-movie-ghost groans coming out of her mouth. And I felt for her, I did, but it's not like there's an easy foolproof five-step plan to get someone out of the bardo.

"The essence of it," Banquo said, "is finding something more important to her than her suffering."

"Oh," I said in my best dry sarcastic tone. "That's all."

Banquo stopped and looked at me. He has this penetrating gaze that, if the rumors around the graveyard are to be believed, can see directly into your soul.

"People like to suffer," I said by way of explanation, his eyes focusing on mine. I really didn't want him looking into my soul. That grunge and disorder that has its home there is mine, all mine. Emily looked at me too, her little brow furrowed. "Really, they do," I continued. "Look at anyone you knew when they were alive. How many ways did they make their life harder, how many things couldn't they let go of that would have made them happier? How much—" I cut myself off when I saw Emily's face, her lower lip was quivering and she looked like she was about to cry. I knelt down in front of her and said, "What is it, honey?"

As little girl tears rolled down her ghostly face, she said, "My mom, after I died. She couldn't let it go, she suffered so much. I..."

I carefully modulated my ghostly form (a must for a

ghost to touch another ghost) and pulled Emily in for a hug and let her cry. She was in the past, and when she was like that she was much more the four-year-old girl and much less the eighty-year-old ghost. I caught Banquo giving me a "look what you've done now" look.

After she was done crying, she growled, "Get your mitts off me, you perv."

I didn't take it personally. It was Emily's way of telling me she was all right.

"Now," Banquo said, clearly about to resume his lecture, "you knew her, what might be more important to her than her suffering?"

"Knew her?" I said. "She temped for me for a month. We weren't exactly bosom buddies."

"Nevertheless, you knew her best. What might be more important to her?"

And thus began my first lesson with Banquo. And I will admit he was smart, knew his way around the ghostly world, and was generous with his time. But, that doesn't mean I suddenly became one of his disciples, hanging on his every word, kowtowing to him. I listened and I learned.

We tried everything, it took hours and hours. I kept hoping someone would discover the body so we could, at least, get out of that disgusting apartment. But no such luck. The sun set, night passed, and the sun rose before I finally stumbled onto something. It came from fatigue, not thinking.

"Hey, Haley," I said. "You look good today. You know I really appreciate you coming in and helping us out, but I'm kind of torn. I have a policy of not dating any of my staff, and if you weren't... well I would... you know." I used to be an actor, so I sold it. Being all shy and coy, my ghostly cheeks flushing red. I am not sure what possessed me to try it beyond fatigue and what I had learned haunting the office—more than one of the girls and at least one of the boys had had a crush on me.

There was a sharp snap, as the silver cord connecting her spirit to her body broke, her eyes came into focus and a smile formed on her lips. "Doctor Anchor, why, I had no idea." She blinked rapidly a few times, her eyes widening, her mouth opening, her form firming up a bit, looking a little less bardo-ish.

"I couldn't tell you then, Haley," I said, fighting to keep her present. Out of the corner of my eye I saw Banquo beckoning me towards the door, out of the apartment. Yeah, that made sense. Not a good idea for Haley to see her body with the knife sticking out the back and her dried blood looking like reddish-brown cottage cheese. "But now... you know... maybe we can spend some time together."

Her eyes stayed focused on me as we walked through the wall and out of the apartment into the Tucson morning, the sun just peaking over the horizon. "I think I would like that, Doctor Anchor."

Inside I was freaking out—I had no desire for a ghost girlfriend, but I just smiled and held my character. "Haley, it's not Doctor Anchor. It's time you called me Walter."

Chapter 6

THAT DAY I MET EMILY, IN MIDGE'S BATHROOM, THE bardo so very close, she wore what she calls her "summer outfit." Blue shorts and a white T-shirt with a drawing of a red lollipop on it. I stared at her. I hadn't seen a well-formed ghost before. She looked like a person, just a bit transparent. The only other ghosts I had run into at the dental office had been vaporous presences like me.

"You heard me," Emily said. "Leave the lady alone. I mean it."

My shock and curiosity at seeing her chased the bardo away. "I... What?" I stammered.

"Christ on a stick, are you a bardo-brained perv or what?"

"Huh?" I said, not understanding what she was talking about.

"Did you die in here?" she asked. "Are you going to spend the rest of eternity haunting people trying to relieve themselves?"

"No," I said, coming more into myself. "Of course not. I... I was murdered. She knows something, that letter she just read is a clue."

"Well then, prove it," she said, turned on her heel, and walked through the bathroom door. Something made me follow her. Part of it was that she was a different kind of ghost, part of it was how articulate she was and how young she looked. She spoke with a bit of a lisp making her sound young, yet her words were anything but.

"So," she continued once we were out of the bathroom, "are you trying to be a gumshoe or something?"

I blinked. I knew she was asking if I was a detective, the archaic slang adding to the mystery of her. "I just want to find out who killed me."

"And then what?" she asked, crossing her arms.

"I... well..." I hadn't thought that far.

She shook her head slowly, giving me a most disapproving look. "You don't know anything, do you?" She looked up and added, "Lord, why me? This fellow is so wet behind the ears he's about to drown." She sighed and looked back at me. "Come along. I guess you've won the lottery, big boy, because ole Emily here is going to show you the ropes."

"I need to stay here," I said. "I need to follow Midge. I need to find out who killed me."

She sighed again. "One track mind. Can't say I mind that in a man, as long as the track his mind is on is one I like." She gave me a leering grin that was completely out of place on her young face. "Look... What's your name?"

"Walter."

"Look, Walter. You stay here you will end up in the bardo, a lost cause, a waste of an afterlife. But if you really want to find your killer, come with me now. I'll teach you enough so you can be a proper ghost." With that she walked away. I followed.

Chapter 7

I KNOW THERE ARE MANY METHODS TO ACTING, BUT THERE is only one way I know to make my face do what I want it to do: feel the feelings. So if I am playing a part and my character is scared, I do my best to scare myself. It's not the same as a "real" scare—like someone pulling back the shower curtain and lunging at you with a knife—but it's the memory or shadow of the emotion. That's enough.

So my method for acting is... well... Method Acting. I draw on my own past and emotions for the role I am playing. And with Haley, right outside the boring two-story apartment she was murdered in, I was playing the part of suitor. As painful as it was, I summoned the memories of when I courted my ex-wife, that giddy time of being young and falling in love.

Haley was pretty enough—if much too young for me—with high cheek bones, a constellation of freckles perched there, and pale blue eyes. As I talked, her ghostly form came into better focus, but it wasn't great.

I had kept up a patter of flattering talk and gotten her away from the apartment complex and into a little park across the street. It was early morning and except for us ghosts the place was deserted.

"Do you remember?" I asked. The question was intentionally non-specific. I needed info about her murder, but didn't want to push her off the edge back into the bardo.

"What?" she asked, her ghostly form becoming more diffuse.

"It was your eyes, you know," I said, backpedaling. "That light powder blue, they remind me of the sky after a good rainstorm. So lovely."

Her form solidified a bit and her cheeks flushed. "Oh, Doctor Anchor." She saw my stern, but cute, look and added, "I'm sorry... Walter."

"I know," I said, putting a bright smile on my face. "Tell me about your day, tell me everything."

Her eyebrows furrowed, I suspect no man had ever said that to her with such enthusiasm. But I held the expression (and yes, I was acting) and her eyebrows rose and a smile bloomed on her face. She began telling me about her day, every little thing, in exhaustive detail. The girl was obviously starved for attention.

I "um-hummed" in all the right places, asked questions and encouraged details, long before I knew I would need them, and did an Oscar worthy performance hanging on her every word.

It took a while, but when we came to the important

information, what she was doing at Roger Coptic's apartment, she had such momentum talking that she didn't seem to notice the bardo-rific territory we had strayed into.

It took everything I had to keep the look of rapt attention on my face when she told me what happened. I wanted to run (or rather, fly) away and give up this whole quest to find my murderer. But I didn't, I held my character and got it all.

Chapter 8

WHEN EMILY RESCUED ME FROM MIDGE'S BATHROOM, a fact she insisted on telling everyone in the graveyard when I met them, I was a green, wet-behind-the-ears ghost. Emily took me in, kept me out of the bardo, and taught me the basics.

You might think it's easy being a ghost, but you would be wrong, *dead* wrong.

(And if you'd like to laugh, or even clap at the clever use of "dead" in the previous sentence, I won't mind. Actor, remember. I get off on that kind of stuff.)

It is nice to be able to fly, go through walls, not have to eat or bathe. But you trade all that regular human overhead for crushing boredom and the waiting bardo. So as a fresh ghost you have time on your hands (boredom) and way too much time to think about all the mistakes you made in your life, all your regrets, and (in my case) who the hell killed you (that would be the waiting bardo part).

Emily was no gentle teacher, but with eighty years of being a ghost she knew her way around all of that. She taught me and kept me in and around the graveyard for a few months until the day she got tired of me whining (see,

I did learn some things from her) and went with me to that apartment where we found Haley with a knife in her back.

HALEY HAD FINALLY LANDED A FULL-TIME POSITION AT A dental office, so the day she told me about was a day familiar to me. Getting up, doing the mundane activities required to maintain biological life—you know, bathing, eating, eliminating, getting ready to go. It made me nostalgic, because the girl talked about these activities in great detail.

I was happy to learn she had gotten a permanent job, but rather shocked to learn where the job was. Wheeler Dental. As in Doctor Wheeler. As in my former practice partner. As in Haley was working at *my* newly renamed dental office.

I hated the thought, but I smiled and nodded and congratulated her. She had been a fine dental assistant and deserved a full-time gig.

And then we got to the good—as in "holy crap"—part.

"Doctor Wheeler asked me to do an errand for him," she said. "As I think back on it now, he seemed a little nervous. He gave me a small package, one of those bubble wrap mailers. It was real light, so it couldn't have had much in it. An address was written on a sticky note, not on the package."

"Did he tell you what was in it?" I asked.

She shrugged her shoulders. "He said I would get paid for the errand, that he would pay overtime. So..."

So, she didn't care, didn't think to ask.

"I can see his face so clearly," she continued. "His smile was so big, his teeth so white, but I noticed a bead of sweat on his forehead." She paused, her eyes focusing on me. "It's funny that I can remember things so clearly. My memory has always been a little poor, but not today. I can remember my first day of high school as clear as a bell. Want to hear about it?"

"I would love to hear about it," I said, making sure the smile on my face was not too big. "But, let's finish up with the day you are telling me about already. Okay?"

She nodded.

"What was the address on the package?"

She kind-of walked towards the swing set as she rattled off the address to Roger Coptic's apartment. Her walk was most definitely a "kind-of." While her form was better than it previously was, she still looked positively ghostly with a vague movement of her legs as she floated over the green grass towards the little swing set. It takes practice, a lot of it, to look fully human.

"Do you remember what happened when you delivered it?" I knew she did. She was clearly experiencing the enhanced memory that we ghosts have. Funny, we are all literally brainless and yet have a nearly eidetic memory.

"The little man that answered the door scared me. He hadn't shaved in a few days and his teeth were stained yellow. I handed him the package and he smiled at me. He had a missing tooth." She pointed to her mouth, tooth number ten, the right lateral incisor. It was really bad form for her to be so vague, considering our former business. "He invited me in. I didn't want to go in, but he insisted, saying he had to get something for me to return to Doctor Wheeler. I stood there holding the package, smelling the rotting garbage smell of the place when..." She stopped, her form going diffuse, her eyes getting wide.

"What?" I asked.

"I... My..." she stammered, her right arm vaguely pointing towards her back where she had been stabbed. "Pain. It hurt so much. I cried out. I fell. Someone took the package out of my hand."

"Did you see him?" I asked.

She shook her head. "But he had nice shoes. All black and polished and old fashioned. Like the dads wear in those movies about the fifties."

Well, that explained the chanting of "Blaaaack Shooooes" when we found her. "What happened then, Haley?" I knew she was on a one-way ticket to bardo-land, but kept pushing. I needed to know what she knew.

"Then I saw that man's face, the one that answered the door, with his scraggly beard and his horrible breath. It smelled like old cigarettes and rotten cheese. He was freaking out, cursing, and then I was alone. It got so cold... it hurt so much..."

The girl was definitely losing it. I caught Banquo looking at me, his little nod and widening eyes making it clear he wanted me to do something about it, that he didn't want to see her bardoed again.

"What happened to me? So cold..." she muttered.

Emily was staring at me too, her arms crossed, her little hip cocked. Her body language said, "I helped you, you've got to help her."

So I did the only thing I could think of. I fell back into the role I had been playing and I kissed her.

Chapter 9

BEING A GHOST, THE RULES ARE DIFFERENT. EVERY ONCE in a while things happen that remind me just how different they are. Like when I kissed Haley in that little park across from where she was killed.

Touching as a ghost takes a lot of skill. Emily had taught it to me when she was showing me the ropes. She thought it essential to my survival (and even though ghostly touching is a shadow of what it is like when you're alive, imagine an existence without it). And besides, Emily likes to high-five. Well, with us it's more of a high five for her and a low five for me.

Okay, so ghosts can walk through walls and, really, walk through anything—even other ghosts. So there are two components to ghostly touching: matching frequency and intent. The frequency part is about making your ghostly form the same as the ghost you want to touch. In this case that meant me becoming a diffuse almost-bardoed mess. I was trying to make what passed for our lips come together.

Back at the graveyard, Jim and Jane are a couple, but they don't seem to be into public displays of affection, so I was going in blind.

When our lips met, what happened was not what I expected. I felt our lips touch, the numb sense of ghostly touch, but then…

I felt my body, weak and cold, with the hard floor underneath me. I smelled the musty, grimy carpet. I saw the slick, old-fashioned black shoes, a well-manicured hand taking the package, and the person leaving. I saw the gap-toothed grin of Roger Coptic and smelled his rotten breath. And then I was alone and so cold. I couldn't move, I couldn't speak. I realized that I was dying, that the pain in my back was killing me. I worried about my mother, we were supposed to go to the movies tonight. I worried about my cat, who was going to feed him? I thought of a man I had once loved. But then, even my thoughts became less coherent.

I felt confused and upset and knew death was close, ready to take me.

The sequence of senses and thoughts restarted and played over and over again. I was stuck in Haley's death, feeling what she felt, thinking what she thought.

"All right, all right," a high-pitched voice said. "Break it up kids. I mean, really, get a room." I heard it dimly as if it was coming from a great distance. But it distracted me from the death scene I was reliving. "Seriously, you two. Break it up or I'm going to get physical with you."

I couldn't do anything about what was happening. I was lost, stuck, sliding into the bardo with Haley.

"Okay, don't say I didn't warn you," Emily said. I felt this sharp sensation in my foot. I can't call it pain, but it got my attention, and then I was standing right in front of Haley, her eyes wide.

"Doctor Anchor," Haley whispered, her hand going to her face. Her form looked better, less ghost-ish and more human-ish, actually much better than it had.

I looked down at my own form and I was the diffuse mess. Emily was standing right next to me shaking her head. "Kids these days," she said, and marched back to Banquo who had a bemused look on his face. I concentrated on my own form until it came into focus. I was wearing my usual post-death outfit. Actually it was my usual pre-death outfit: scrubs. As a dentist I had practically lived in them, it is what came naturally.

"Are you okay, Haley?" I asked.

She nodded and gave me a smile. It is the kind of smile Emily would call "come hither." It was clear that my experience kissing her had been different than hers. When I talked about ghosts touching, I mentioned intent. Well, my intent had been to keep her out of the bardo, and somehow I had taken on part of her death burden and done that, but nearly went to bardo-land myself.

"Are you okay, Doctor Anchor?" she asked. I was most definitely out of character. I am sure the wide variety of emotions I had been feeling had been all over my face.

"Please, Haley," I said, pulling the tatters of my role back on, just as I had pulled my ghostly form together. "You must call me Walter. I think we are far past the point where you need to call me Doctor." I offered her my arm, modulating it for touch and having a clear intent to *just* touch. She took it and we walked away from the park and towards the graveyard.

It would take us most of the day to walk there, but it gave me time. Time to get her oriented. Time to help her understand that she was dead. Time for me to find out if Haley knew anything else that might lead to her murderer and mine.

Chapter 10

Doctor Elias Wheeler and I became very close after that. Haley, as it turns out, didn't know anything else. Doctor Wheeler had had her deliver a package to Roger Coptic. She was murdered. Someone took the package. Roger fled.

Wheeler—I am going to drop the "Doctor"; it's a sign of respect, something I no longer have for him—was under our surveillance. And by "our" I mean me, Emily, and Haley.

For the first few weeks it was either Emily or myself watching him, while the other stayed with Haley at the graveyard, helping her adjust to being a ghost. After that it was all three of us. Once Haley started getting comfortable as a ghost, she got mad.

"Haley's gone comet," Emily whispered to me. I had come back to the graveyard for our shift change. Emily was on her way into the mortuary, a ritual where the ghosts check out the newly dead that is called the "greeting committee." Wheeler was asleep and it was a safe time to do it.

"What?" I asked.

"You know, Haley's Comet. The girl is on fire, lit up, burning across the sky—"

"Emily, can you please just tell me what's going on and stop with the metaphors."

Emily rolled her eyes and stuck her tongue out at me. "Spoil sport. The girl is pissed. She's angry. She's ready to rip Wheeler's heart out and eat it for breakfast. She is the proverbial woman scorned. She—"

"Okay, okay," I said, cutting her off and holding my hands up. "I get it. She wants revenge."

A wicked smile crept onto Emily's lips. "Which brings us to your planned breakup."

I had continued on with my "relationship" with Haley. It wasn't that big of a deal. We spent time together, held hands, and kissed here and there. When she got into troubling territory, kissing seemed to calm her down, ground her, and I had gotten better at not taking too much on from her. I had told Emily that I planned to break it off as soon as she got stabilized. I liked the girl, had grown quite fond of her—I just didn't want to carry on a relationship that I had started out of desperation.

"You think..." I began.

"Didn't you hear what I said about 'woman scorned'?" Emily asked.

"Where is she?"

"She's talking with Banquo," Emily said, her voice rising half an octave when she said his name. "I refused to give her any haunting tips, so she sought him out."

"As if he'll help her with that," I said with a chuckle.

"As if I was going to tell her *that* in the mood she was in," Emily shot back.

We stood there silently. I was lost in my thoughts, frankly dismayed at what I had gotten myself into. "I'm sure she'll understand," I finally said. "I mean, I kissed her to save her from the bardo."

Emily snorted and shook her head. "Look, Walter, you kissed her so you could get what you wanted and just happened to save her from the bardo. I may have died when I was four, but even I know you don't mess with a woman's heart." She chuckled softly. "Especially not a woman like that."

I really do hate being dead sometimes.

Emily walked away and left me there to stew. I looked around. Ghosts were rising out of the ground, flying, or popping in, gathering in small groups around gravestones. Midnight was approaching, we all could feel it. Midnight is our time, when we ghosts feel most "alive."

I didn't stay long. That night the surveillance became the three of us. And let me tell you, you've never been surveilled until you've been surveilled by ghosts. There is nothing you can do, nothing you can say, nowhere you can go that we can't follow you, can't hear you, can't know what you are doing.

We were brutal—the man got no privacy at all. Emily even insisted that we follow him into the bathroom, and that is where things got interesting.

Chapter 11

ELIAS WHEELER IS A YOUNG, COCKY DENTIST, WITH A shaved head, overly bleached white teeth, and a chubby face. He is also much more of a salesman than I ever was. It's one of the reasons I had brought him into the practice three years ago. He was eager to get out there and bring new clients in, he had energy for that. I didn't anymore.

I have never trusted people in sales. They have an ulterior motive—their own profit—so how can you trust what they are saying? They are worse than actors in my book. At least sometimes us actors aren't playing a role.

"I don't want to watch him take another dump," I complained to Emily. Wheeler had just gone into his bathroom in his lovely ranch-style home, in what would likely be another long session. He's got IBS or some other kind of issue, because he spends a lot of time in there.

"Too bad," Emily said. "I am young and innocent and shouldn't be subject to such indignities, and you wouldn't make your girlfriend watch another man defecate."

I sighed and nodded, heading for the bathroom, pondering how Emily had found me in a bathroom but refused to watch Wheeler there.

"And who said chivalry is dead?" Emily offered as I walked through the bathroom door.

I can't tell you how sick of Elias Wheeler I was. His every little habit annoyed the hell out of me. Singing in the shower, checking all the locks on the doors two times before going to bed, the three girlfriends he was stringing along while setting up several more on online dating sites. But while he seemed to be a contemptible human being, we hadn't turned up a single clue in the ten days we had been haunting—I mean surveilling—him.

As he sat on his porcelain throne, his jeans down to his ankles, playing some stupid game on his iPhone, it rang. And horror of horrors, he answered. That's right, in the middle of an extensive toileting event, he answered his phone. No class whatsoever.

I didn't see the caller ID, I wasn't positioned correctly—and I should have been. It only rang once and he put it to his ear.

"Wheeler," he said.

He bit his lip as he listened and nodded his head a few times, the color draining from his face. "Look, we had a deal. I've orchestrated your deliveries. I don't—"

Belatedly I maneuvered my ghostly head right next to Wheeler's fleshy one so I could hear both sides of the conversation. I normally did better than this, but I think time and the whole "bathroom" part of this had thrown me off my game.

"…release the photos, but I will," a female voice said. "You are in deep, my friend, and the only way out is through."

"Look," he said, licking his lips and sitting up straighter on the toilet. "Someone died last time I had a package delivered for you. That wasn't what was supposed to happen."

"I told you, we weren't expecting the intensity of our competitor's interest. We've taken precautions. It won't happen again."

Wheeler sighed. "This has got to end," he said.

"It will," the voice on the phone said. "I promise, it will end soon." There was a brief pause and then she added, "The package will be at drop point three. See that it is delivered promptly."

WHEN WHEELER AND I FINALLY GOT OUT OF THE BATHROOM, the last thing I thought I'd be feeling was empathy for the fellow. After that phone call, he appeared to be a victim too.

As we all stood in the kitchen watching him nervously eat some cereal, I brought Emily and Haley up to speed.

"He... he wasn't trying to hurt me?" Haley asked.

"No, darling," I replied, still playing the role of the dutiful detective-boyfriend. "He appears to be a pawn in this thing."

She nodded mutely, staring at Wheeler.

"Don't get all misty-eyed there, Haley-Bopp," Emily said. "This still doesn't make him a shining example of the human race. He's done things he's ashamed of; the blackmailers are using that against him."

"Right," I interjected, trying to get things back on track. "We'll follow him to the drop point. Emily, you will stay there and see if the blackmailers come back. Haley and I will stick with Wheeler and follow him to the delivery and track the package from there."

And that is what we did. On the way to work, Wheeler stopped by Freedom Park north of the air force base and pulled a package from under a park bench. Emily stayed there and we followed Wheeler who went to the office and talked another young girl into delivering a package for him. Her name was Rachel, she was even younger and more innocent-looking than Haley.

"I don't have a good feeling about this," Haley said.

I nodded. At this point I never had a good feeling in the dental offices. It reminded me too much of the life I once had, the life I had lost. I mean, it hadn't been much, but it had been mine. I looked at Haley and wondered if she would kiss me if I started to lose it and go bardo.

"Stay with Rachel," I told Haley. I really didn't want to split us up, but I didn't think we were done with Wheeler yet.

She nodded, her eyes wide. We had hardly been apart since I had gotten her out of the bardo.

"It's okay, Haley. I won't leave the office without you. If you run into trouble, just come find me."

She bit her lip, her eyes lingering on me for a moment before she turned and followed Rachel.

I stayed with Wheeler. I was sure there was something else to be learned from him.

Chapter 12

IN SOME WAYS THE KIND OF SCRUTINY WE WERE GIVING Wheeler wasn't fair. No human that is watched that much turns out looking pretty. People have their oddities, their addictions, their weaknesses. Wheeler was no exception. He picked his nose, stared at ladies' asses when they weren't looking, and liked to look at himself in the mirror.

But that is all I found out about him as I watched him go about his job, my former job, doing dental exams, fillings, root planing—all the joys of dentistry. It was a hard day for me. As much as I have grown to dislike Wheeler, I was jealous of him that he was alive.

Just after 5:00 p.m., Haley came and got me. Rachel was leaving. I looked back at Wheeler as we left. There was something else there, something important. I just knew it.

Rachel was skinny and tall, with short blonde hair and a quick walk. She left with the package Wheeler had picked up in the morning, got in her little red Hyundai, and drove to the Park Mall on Broadway. She did a lot of window shopping as she darted from store to store.

"Is she shopping?" Haley asked. "What the hell is she doing?"

I shrugged and we kept following her. She stopped at every clothing store in the mall and finally went into Spencer's. You know, the place with all the goofy stuff like drinking and sex games, odd clothing, and kinkier stuff. Haley gave me a look. I shrugged and we followed her in.

Rachel went right to the counter and asked for George. The overly perky checkout girl went into the back and out came George. He was thirtyish, overweight, and (I would wager) under-dated. He had greasy brown hair and wire-rimmed glasses.

"Are you George?" Rachel asked.

The big guy just nodded.

"This is for you," she said handing over the package and walking out of the store. George grunted and went into the back of the store, we followed.

The back room was what you would expect. Small and crowded with boxes, cleaning supplies, and a cramped desk. George sat at the desk and ripped opened the package, licking his lips like he hadn't eaten for days and this was a juicy steak he was tearing into.

He pulled out a small rectangular piece of plastic.

"That's a micro SD card," Haley said.

I looked at her. "A what?"

She rolled her eyes, looking back at George. "A memory chip for your computer. There's data on it."

Post-divorce, I had dated a few younger women, and even though Haley and I were both dead, she had just managed to make me feel old. It is not a pleasant feeling, a twisting in your guts. The young don't understand—as you get older, sure your body feels different, but no matter your age you feel like *you*. In my experience, it's the world that makes you feel old. The changing times, changing activities, and the attitude like Haley had just had.

The youth do not treat older people like we treat them. Think of children, people older than them are patient and understanding of their ignorance. The young do not tend to show the same tolerance for ignorance in people older than them.

I didn't say a thing, though. I kept my mouth shut and watched as George plugged the card into his computer and tapped on the keyboard.

Haley narrated what he was doing—she made an assumption that because I hadn't recognized a micro SD card without any labeling that I didn't know anything about computers. Which wasn't exactly true, but close enough. I was, though, grateful that the eye rolling had ended.

"The data is compressed and encrypted," she said. "He's entering the encrypting key..." She watched him carefully as he typed, he had to do it a couple of times to get it right. "The password is 'GetRichGeorge**$$.' Okay, he's got it unpacked. It's a bunch of files... there's some source code. He's compiling it. Now he's running it. Oh..."

She trailed off, I could see for myself as the screen lit up with a still of tanks and soldiers and explosions, with "Warmonger II" emblazoned on it.

Haley went diffuse as she watched as George briefly played the game. I didn't say anything.

"Holy shit," George said to himself. "This is the real goddam deal. I'm gonna be rich!"

Haley was sliding towards the bardo. "A video game?" she said, looking at me. "I was killed for a video game? What the hell kind of world is this?"

I had a brief, stabbing moment of empathy. What if I had been killed over something mundane or trivial? Did I really want to know? What kind of difference would it make?

"Walter?" she said, her voice cracking, her powder blue eyes way too wide. "Why?" She looked back at George as he continued to tap away at the computer.

I thought of kissing her again, the first time I had seemed to take on some of her fear and stabilized her. But that wasn't the right thing to do for her long-term, she needed to learn to calm herself. I modulated my form to match hers and took her face in my hands.

"Look at me," I said, her eyes reluctantly leaving George. They were still too wide, but she stopped getting more diffuse. "Listen to me, Haley. Focus on my voice. You are strong enough to do this. It doesn't matter why you were killed, but I promise you, I will find who did it and find a way to make them pay."

I was a bit taken aback by my tone. I sounded fierce and protective. I sounded strong and sure of myself. I sounded like I cared about her. And, actually, I wasn't acting. Something changed in that moment. I wasn't off farting around trying to do something for myself. I now had a mission, a purpose beyond my own needs.

Haley blinked, her form coming back into focus. I kept my hands on her face, matching them to her form as she changed. Tears rolled down her cheeks and she slowly nodded and licked her lips.

"I need you, Haley," I said. Her eyes grew wide again, but for a different reason. "I need you to be strong. I need your help. I can't do this without you."

She leaned in and kissed me. It wasn't like a flesh kiss, we didn't have "lips" per se. It wasn't about a physical sensation. It was what was left over. Passion. Communication. Communion.

I lost myself to that kiss and gave her back everything I could. It was like we spoke volumes to each other in those moments. It was like falling off a cliff, or riding a rocket, or losing your mind. With the flesh aspects gone, the spiritual aspects of it were multiplied.

I don't know how long it lasted, it's like time didn't matter there, but when it was done I was changed. No more acting. Haley *was* my girlfriend. I felt this relief well up in me—all those lonely years I had experienced when I was alive were over.

Our faces only inches apart, she smiled broadly and I smiled back.

She looked around, her eyes growing wide again. "Oh shit," she said. "Where did he go?"

Chapter 13

We couldn't find him. That break in our focus had given George enough time to get away from us. We searched the mall. We searched the parking lot. We searched and searched until night came and midnight approached.

The search after the first hour had been useless. I had known it, but Haley was upset and seemed to need to keep looking.

"He'll be back," I said. "We can just go back to the store and wait for him."

She sighed and nodded.

"But, I don't think it matters. We should go back to the graveyard, catch the Midnight Circle, and then rest."

"What?" She shook her head, looking confused. Now that

the whole "you died for a video game" thing was known, she was holding on even tighter to finding her killer.

"George doesn't matter. He didn't kill you. I've been thinking about it. We've got a seller, the one blackmailing Wheeler, a buyer, George, and a third party—your killer."

She was staring at me now, her blue eyes flashing. I was glad to see anger instead of despair. We floated just above the parking lot of the mall, a bland expanse of pavement mostly devoid of cars at this hour.

"We need to find the third party. George can't help with that. The seller might be able to."

She nodded. I was glad I was making sense, because I was just working it out as I spoke.

"We left Emily at the package drop-off. Let's go see if she found something out."

Haley nodded slowly and then came close to me. "Thank you," she whispered and she kissed me again.

I have to say, we were getting better at this, and once again, no acting. I was falling for this girl and hard.

Chapter 14

"You're disgusting," Emily said to the homeless man sleeping on the bench we had left her at. "Don't you care? Thank God we ghosts can't smell, because I'm sure your scent would make me vomit. Look, I know life is hard. I know it can just mow you down. But, really, wake up. Get your act together. Do something worth doing. You are alive, for God's sake. Do you know what kind of gift that is? And here you are passed out drunk on a park bench with your dirty clothes and your scraggly beard. You're wasting that gift. Don't you have family? A mother, a father, a child, someone that cares for you, someone that needs you?" Emily paused, taking a deep breath. "Find the strength to make something of your life. Please. You've got one. I never did, I..."

Haley and I had taken our time getting back to the park. We had talked and held hands and kissed—and in general acted like people falling in love. When we entered Freedom Park and saw Emily, we both stopped without a word and listened. As her soliloquy went on, I began to feel guilty, but I couldn't bring myself to do anything about it. She eventually noticed us, and stopped mid-sentence, a blush of red springing to her chubby cheeks.

"What the hell are you looking at?" she yelled.

"I... We..." I stammered. In our relationship, Emily had been the strong one (expect for the occasional four-year-old fit). Her being jealous of a drunk, homeless man wasn't something I had been expecting.

"Useless damn day," she said, looking down at her little feet. "Nothing happened here. I..." Emily's face clouded up and she took a few steps towards us. "I was just..." she began, looking back at the homeless man. "I think sometimes we can get through. You know, be the 'still small voice' that helps people turn it around. Be..."

Tears started to roll down her face. I let go of Haley's hand and went to her. I modulated my form to hers and took her in my arms. She held me tightly and cried for the longest time. This was no four-year-old fit, this was a ghost's grief. We all feel it. We aren't "alive" anymore. We barely exist in this world. The only thing we really have is each other.

I forgot Haley and gave Emily my full attention. I held her and whispered to her and let her get it all out. For the first time in our relationship, she really needed me.

When it was all over, I looked around and Haley was gone.

Chapter 15

It didn't take long to find Haley. She stood in Roger Coptic's apartment staring at a reddish-brown stain on the floor. The place she had died. They had finally taken the body away and there had been yellow crime scene tape over the door.

"Haley..." I said softly. Her form wasn't in very good shape, and I was afraid she was lost to the bardo.

"What kind of life is this?" she asked.

I didn't know if she was referring to her murder and her physical life or her ghostly afterlife. "The only one we've got," I answered, covering both possibilities.

She looked up at me pursing her lips and nodding. "It doesn't seem like enough."

I approached her, leaving Emily by the door. I extended my hand to her and said, "Please. Come."

She ignored my gesture, her gaze returning to the blood stain. "I didn't do anything wrong. I didn't deserve this."

"No, you didn't," I said, putting my hand on her shoulder. She let my hand stay there, not moving, not speaking, just staring at the stain.

Finally she looked up at me, her eyes hard and unwavering. "We are going to find who did this. I don't care how long it takes. And then I'm going to make his life a living hell."

I stepped back, my hand leaving her shoulder. I was scared. Emily had been silent this whole time, but I heard her gasp as I backed away. Haley wasn't close to going bardo. She was somewhere else, somewhere very different.

"Okay," I said. It sounded empty next to her fierceness.

"What's our next lead?" she asked.

"I don't know," I answered.

"That's not good enough."

"I know." My answer sounded hollow, like I was whispering into a hurricane. Haley now seemed like a force of nature. You don't let down a force of nature. I racked my brain trying to think.

A gaming black market. Buyers and sellers. A third party that killed Haley and stole the product. We found one of the buyers, but that's it.

I looked around the grubby apartment of Roger Coptic. I ignored Haley as best I could, but I could feel her eyes on me as I studied the place. A sink full of dirty dishes. Overflowing garbage. Dirty clothing all over the bedroom. A cracked flat-screen TV. No computer in sight.

"Whoever Roger Coptic is, he wasn't the buyer," I said, desperate to fill the silence.

"Who was he, then?" Emily asked. I was so glad she had stepped in. Emily is as tough as they come, but Haley's shift from scared love interest to avenging ghost had shocked even her.

"I am guessing he was a middleman," I said. I thought it all over, trying to connect the clues we had found. "I don't think this is just about video games."

"What? Why?" Haley asked.

"Both Doctor Wheeler and Midge are involved. Midge for money and they have something on Wheeler. They've done this before, moving things. It can't always be video games." I paused, thinking it over again. "I think this is about industrial espionage. Trade secrets."

Haley nodded. "That SD card had the source code to the

video game. That's valuable, and using the old-fashioned sneaker-net may be more secure these days than the Internet."

"Great," Emily said. "So what the hell do we do now?"

"I'm guessing that since a murder occurred here, Roger is not coming back. He's probably on the run. He must know something."

"Then we find him," Haley said.

"How?" I asked.

Emily caught my eye and then pointedly looked at Haley. I gave Emily a nod and sighed. It was the only way.

"You're a ghost," Emily began, walking over to Haley and looking up at her. "You saw him. If you really want to find him, nothing in this world can stop you."

"I don't know what you mean," Haley said.

"It's generally called 'popping,'" I said, "because of the sound a ghost makes when they appear or disappear. You can travel from point to point at will."

"Like this," Emily said. She was standing next to me, her face going blank, and then she was gone with a soft "pop." A moment later there was another "pop" and she was standing next to Haley.

"How..." Haley began.

"It's kind of an advanced skill," I said. "Not one that I've acquired yet, but Emily here is very good at it. She can teach you."

Emily nodded. "But not here. Let's get back to the graveyard. This is going to take some time."

As Emily and I floated towards the door, Haley said, "Wait." We both turned and looked at her. "If I can do this, then why don't I just 'pop' to my murderer? I saw those old-fashioned shoes."

"That's not enough," Emily said. "You'd probably end up in a shoe store or shoe factory or someone's closet. A face, though. That is unique. That will work."

EMILY TRIED TO GET BANQUO TO HELP TEACH US HOW TO pop. Since the teaching was going to happen, I was determined to learn too. But Banquo would have nothing of it once he learned what Haley intended. And it's not like Haley was keeping it to herself. She came right out and told him when he asked her why she wanted to learn. The phrase "make his life a living hell" put a most sour expression on Banquo's face.

Haley was different and I missed her. My affection had become real, and then she became this avenging spirit. No more displays of affection, no more long talks, just a single-minded focus. Find Roger Coptic.

I did, though, find a use for my acting skills. I spent the next several weeks while Emily taught us acting like it didn't bother me that things had changed.

But they had and it did.

Eventually Haley "popped" and we found Roger Coptic. He was dead, and that turned out to be our big break in the case.

Chapter 16

THE SAYING "DEAD MEN DON'T TALK" NEEDS TO BE rethought. Roger Coptic sang, he sang like a bird.

When Haley finally popped, both Emily and I were surprised. It had been days of frustrating, never ending attempts. And then, finally, she was gone. Emily grabbed my hand and popped us to her. And there we found Roger Coptic.

His body was on the ground next to a dumpster behind a Denny's, the head at an unnatural angle. Roger's spirit was hovering above it, a thin silver cord snaking from the body to the spirit.

He hadn't been dead long—usually ghosts figure out how to sever the cord pretty quickly. This is the first initiation into the ghostly afterlife.

"Who killed me?" Haley asked Roger, her voice loud and strident.

First recognition bloomed on Roger's face and then confusion. "What? You... you're dead."

"Who killed me?" Haley repeated.

Roger's eyes darted around, he still looked confused.

"I'm angry," she said. "I'm sure you can see that. You help me, I walk away. You don't help me and I take out my anger on you."

Both Emily and I took a step back; Haley's form was flickering red along the edges. I looked down at her and saw fear on Emily's face. Ghosts can go bad just like people.

"Yeah... yeah... sure," Roger began, his eyes wide, his hands up. He backed up until his body was halfway into the brick wall of the Denny's. "What the..." His head swiveled around and his diffuse limbs flayed. He didn't know he was dead. He didn't understand he was a ghost. Such confusion is very common.

"Talk. Now," Haley said. "Or it will only get worse."

"Right... yeah... The dude's name is Halifax. He's the one that stole the delivery. He hurt me too. Said he was tying up loose ends. He..." Roger looked down and saw his body, his mouth going wide and his form diffusing even more.

"Where can I find this Halifax?" Haley yelled at Roger, getting his attention.

"He's here," Roger said, his head nodding towards the restaurant. "After we talked, he said he was hungry."

Haley gave him a sharp nod and began flying around the building. She was still a new ghost, a practiced one would have just flown through the wall. I looked at Emily.

"You stop her," she said, "before she does..." Emily sighed. "If she does what I'm afraid she'll do, you know where it will end up for her. I'll handle the little guy, see what else he knows."

I nodded and flew after Haley. I got in front of her before she got to the door.

"What are you going to do, Haley?" I asked.

"Out of my way, Walter," she said.

"This won't end well."

"No it won't," she said, a grim look on her face. "But it will end."

I kept myself in front of her, blocking the door. This went on for a minute or so before she sighed and walked right through me.

It was early afternoon and the Denny's wasn't very crowded. It didn't take long to find the man with the black shoes; they were pointy, cap toe Oxfords. He was eating waffles and drinking coffee.

He was meticulously groomed and wore a shirt, jacket, and tie. He ate with a slow precision. Cutting a piece of the waffle. Putting down his knife. Using the fork to put the food in his mouth. Putting down his fork. Chewing slowly and thoroughly. Taking a sip of coffee and resuming the process.

He seemed to take great pleasure in it.

Haley stood staring at him, her hands shaking, tears

running down her cheeks. The red flickering along her form had turned to crimson, making her rage abundantly clear. She kept looking at his shoes. They were indeed the same as the ones I saw when I first kissed her and experienced her death. There was no doubt that this was her killer.

"Let's follow him and get his name and address," I said softly. "We can then go to the SECI chamber and let someone know. They can tell the police." SECI stands for the Search for Extracorporeal Intelligence. A project started at the University of Arizona to allow the dead to communicate with the living. This is what JJ Lynch used to write his memoir. It is what I am using now to write this story. Haley knew about it, I was just reminding her.

She shook her head slowly, her nostrils flaring. "That's not enough." She turned and looked at me. The look on her face made me want to take a step back, but I held my ground, keeping my face passive. "He's a killer. He has to die. He deserves to die."

I didn't tell her, but in principle I agreed, although I preferred someone locking him up and throwing away the key. Killing him didn't sit well with me, but then again I wasn't the one he murdered. If I was looking at my own killer I would probably want the same thing. "If you kill him," I said, "he could become one of us."

"And then I'll find ways to make his afterlife a living hell," she said, turning back to him.

Can a ghost kill a person? It's not easy, but it is possible. If the stories are to be believed, JJ Lynch did it. There are whispers that if you have the right focus and modulate your form correctly, you might be able to make someone trip or look away at the wrong moment when they are driving. There is even darker talk of possession.

"You might not want to stay around for this," she said.

"Sorry, you can't get rid of me that easily."

She glanced at me and shrugged and began her haunting. She went at it like she had a plan, like she knew what she was doing, like she knew that it would work. This puzzled me. How could she know what to do? I didn't and I had been dead a lot longer than her.

They say that "hell hath no fury like a woman scorned." Well, try a ghost confronting her murderer. Haley got her head close to Halifax, who was seated comfortably at a booth table, and started speaking to him. Her tone low, she spoke quickly, and didn't stop. She kept up a nonstop diatribe against him. "You are worthless. You would be better off dead. How can you stand yourself? Do the world a favor and stab yourself in the throat with that fork. You don't deserve to be alive." And on it went. It was as if she was playing the part of that negative voice we all have in our heads. The one that doubts us. The one that wonders whether we are worth the space we take up.

"What the hell is she doing?" Emily asked. The man had finished his breakfast and paid. Emily found us in the parking lot as he got into his vintage Cadillac.

"I think she's trying to talk him to death." I said it with a grin, but my attempt at humor fell flat. "I think she's trying to get into his head. Get him to do something to himself."

Emily sighed as we flew into the car with Haley and the man. "She's been talking to some of the ghosts over by the crypts."

"What?" I asked.

"I spotted her there a few days back. I didn't say anything... I was hopeful she wouldn't go this way."

At our graveyard some of the more disturbed and

dangerous ghosts live by and in the crypts. Most of them are in the bardo, but kind of violent—they'll lash out at any ghost (or person) that comes too close to them. And there are other ghosts that choose to stay there that are into the darker aspects of what you can do as a ghost."

"Why didn't you tell me?" I asked.

"I could see you were getting attached... I..." Tears welled up in Emily's eyes. She was going all four-year-old on me and I couldn't be mad at her. "I'm sorry, Walter. Can you ever forgive me?"

I gave her a hug and said, "Of course. We'll get through this." I sounded confident, but I was far from it.

Chapter 17

As FAR AS HAUNTINGS GO, THINGS THAT GO BUMP IN THE night are no big deal. Furious murder victims that unleash an unending soul sucking tirade on you... well, that's a whole 'nother story.

We tried everything (short of touching her) to get Haley's attention. She was oblivious to us. And we didn't try touching because of what I had learned when I kissed her the first time. It's possible to take on some of the emotional content of another ghost with that kind of intimacy, and I didn't want to take on what she was giving.

Haley's technique seemed to refine. She floated behind her victim, her furious face recognizable and her arms visible, but the rest of her diffuse and vaporous. She ended up with her fingers stuck into the guy's temples and slowly refined her screed.

"You are a worthless human being. You should do the world a favor and kill yourself. Right now. What do you have to live for? Your life is an unending torment. Pick up the knife, go ahead. Look how sharp that blade is. Just pull it across your throat and this will all be over."

It was starting to get to me, and Emily had this pinched look on her round face. But we stayed with Haley and followed them as the man drove to a beautiful little house that bordered the Catalina Mountains north of Tucson. As he went about his day, checking his email, typing on the computer, paying bills, swimming in the pool, dusting and vacuuming.

Haley's diatribe seemed to be having an effect. He started rubbing at his temples and stretching his neck. He took some Advil and he tried to take a nap.

The man's name is Edgar Halifax, and as far as solving Haley's murder, and many others, we had him. That typing he did on his computer? He documented, in exacting detail, the murder of Roger Coptic. He had a diary of everyone he had killed, whether it was contract or personal and how much he was paid. Roger's murder was on contract, part of the one that involved him stealing what Haley was carrying.

The man was meticulous in his dress, how he kept his home, and in documenting his work. We also watched closely as he typed his password. It's "GardenState32#!." My guess is he's from New Jersey.

I didn't feel good about it, though—solving the murder, that is. Haley was unreachable, inconsolable, incoherent, and raging. Emily's jokes earlier about Haley's Comet and Haley-Bopp now seemed unnerving and prescient.

"This is no 'small still voice.' This is…" Emily said after about five hours of this, her face pained. We were in his kitchen, all gleaming steel and granite countertops, watching him prepare his dinner in his ultra-meticulous fashion.

"We're in over our heads," I said. "Go get Banquo."

Her eyes got wide and she nodded her head quickly a few times and with a "pop" was gone.

"Haley," I said, trying one more time to reach her. "Please stop this. Please. Can't we go back a few steps? I... I thought maybe we had something there. I thought maybe this life had gotten less lonely for me. I thought maybe, just maybe, I had found something that had eluded me when I was alive."

You may be wondering if I was acting. I wasn't. Her eyes found mine and her diatribe stopped.

"Please, Haley. Can we just talk? I just want to have a conversation."

Her brows furrowed and she blinked, her eyes holding mine. The look on her face tore my heart out. Her bottom lip quivered as if she was trying to speak. Her eyes spoke clearly of pain and regret. A single tear ran down her cheek. She then turned back to Edgar and resumed her soliloquy.

I turned away. Not because I didn't want her to see me cry, but because I knew part of her wanted me and that part was not in charge. She wasn't the Haley I had grown fond of. She knew exactly what she was doing and the terrible price she would have to pay.

I turned away because I didn't know how to stop her... or rather didn't have the courage to try the only thing left to try.

Chapter 18

BANQUO CAN BE ARROGANT AND DEMANDING. HE CAN BE short with people and doesn't suffer fools. When Emily finally came back with him, he was none of these things.

The night had passed and Edgar was having breakfast.

Meticulous little bites of his poached eggs and toast. He sat at the little breakfast nook in his kitchen that overlooked the formal Zen garden in his backyard. But he looked different. He was harried, black circles under his eyes.

"Thank God you're here," I said when I saw Banquo.

Banquo nodded and gave me a small compassionate smile. He strode over to Haley and Edgar and stood for a long time staring at them.

"Sorry," Emily whispered. "He was otherwise engaged. I had to wait."

I looked at Emily and nodded. I caught a view of my own form and found that I had gone pretty diffuse myself. Edgar was not the only one getting worn down by this. "Did he say anything?"

"Not much. He's worried." Emily's awe for Banquo was still fully intact, but the girlish crush was gone. He was our best hope and we both knew it.

Banquo paced around the two of them, walking right through the little table. His eyes had this faraway look to them as he stared at Haley and Edgar. Banquo kept walking and then holding still and then walking again. At one point he most tentatively touched Haley's form, but quickly removed his finger like it stung.

Finally he moved to Emily and me and said, "This way." He flew straight up and out of the house.

I would have told him I didn't want to leave Haley. But he was gone and then Emily, so I followed.

"How long has she been like this?" he asked once we were atop the ceramic shingled roof.

"About twenty hours," I said. He was looking at me, not at Emily.

"And how invested are you in her recovery?"

I blinked and looked to Emily. Her green eyes were wide and kind, but not helpful. "Umm... very. I'm very invested in her recovery."

He nodded. "Then you know what to do and you know how risky it is."

"How..." I began.

He shook his head, moving it a minute distance to the left and the right. "Not a useful question."

Here he was: terse, teaching, demanding Banquo. One of the reasons I wasn't a big fan of his, but I needed him.

"Can you explain the risk? I'm not sure I completely understand."

He nodded once and began pacing along the peak of the roof, his hands clasped behind his back. "If you do not act you will lose her. That is the risk here. Whether or not she succeeds with this man, she will be lost."

"To the bardo?" I asked.

Banquo stopped pacing. "Best case."

I blinked. There was a worse case than the bardo? What the hell was that about?

"And if I try to reach her?"

"At its best, you will pay... you will have to take on much of her burden. At its worst, you will both be lost."

"Bardo?" Emily asked, her voice quiet and small.

"For him, yes. We might be able to pull him out. For her... I'm not sure."

I took a deep breath and looked at Emily and then back at Banquo. "I... It's... it's too much. I just met her. I..." I couldn't stand the empathy showing on their faces, so I sunk back into the house, back down to Haley and Edgar.

Edgar was now washing his dishes. Slowly, meticulously, carefully. Haley's hands were buried in his temples, the remnant of her form floating behind him in that classic ghostly look.

"I'm sorry," I said. "I can't. I... we..."

I felt a deep fatigue descend on me. I needed to rest—all ghosts need to rest. It's this dreamless nothingness called "fading." A faded ghost is just gone—where, no one really knows (and I don't think "where" is even the right way to think about it). They are gone and unreachable and don't come back until they are rested.

I could sense Emily and Banquo coming after me. I couldn't fly faster than them and they could both pop, so I gave into the fatigue and faded. Haley's words were the last thing I heard. "You will kill yourself, believe me, you will. This, right now, this will be your life until you do. I will give you no rest I will give..."

Chapter 19

I WAS FADED FOR ABOUT TWELVE HOURS AND CAME TO IN the sweet darkness of my grave. Some ghosts, like me, rest with their bones, down in the ground where our remains are. I know it sounds weird, but there I feel calm and connected.

As I rose out of the ground, I lingered, looking at my gravestone. "Walter George Anchor, 1960–2011." That's all it said. No "Beloved Husband," I was divorced. No "Devoted Father," I had never had children. No "Cherished Son," my parents were gone when I died. Just my name and a couple of years.

"It's okay, you know," Emily said.

Her little voice shocked me.

"I don't blame you for not trying. Even Banquo doesn't. Some things are just too much." She was still wearing her shorts and her T-shirt with a lollipop on it. Today the lollipop was blue. She had very good control of her ghostly form and could change it easily. A blue lollipop generally meant that she was sad. And judging from what she was telling me, she was sad for Haley, sad for me.

"Thanks," I said.

"What now?" Emily asked. "Maybe we should go do something fun today. That house over by Fairview Avenue, they've probably got *Law and Order* on."

When Emily had been tutoring me in ghostly matters and my resolve to find my killer became clear, we had fallen into the habit of watching legal or detective shows. I wouldn't call it good training, but it was something to do.

I shook my head. "Nope. Off to the SECI chambers. Time to get in line. Time to tell this story so..." I faltered, unable to articulate what I wanted to say. Something about justice being served. Something about a wrong being righted. But it didn't feel like justice would be served for Haley or Roger or any of this man's victims. But it would prevent him taking more lives. And that was something.

Emily took my hand and smiled up at me. Her hand was so small, her face so young. We've spent a lot of time together now, but it is still disconcerting. The world jolted suddenly and then with a "pop" we stood in front of a nondescript industrial building in front of a door that said, "Afterlife Communications, Inc."

JJ LYNCH IS SOMETHING OF A LEGEND AROUND THE graveyard. Banquo tutored him and a Mexican guy named Jesus after they died. JJ dove into his afterlife and did the unthinkable. He reached his loved ones, stopped his best friend from killing himself, and killed a man in the process. He documented all of this in a memoir that he wrote in the SECI chamber.

I've never met JJ. He's been in the bardo for months, having gone in intentionally to try to rescue someone else. He's a legend, all right, and something of a cautionary tale. Emily tells me that Banquo is shorter than usual because he worries about JJ.

So, JJ did all this writing, the people behind the SECI chamber published his memoir as a book called *Shuffled Off* (there is lots of Shakespeare at the Midnight Circle in case you recognize that phrase from Hamlet). Some of the living read the book before they died. Some of them find the SECI chambers.

That's not what this story is about, but I mention it because the wait for a SECI chamber was about five days. Lots of ghosts were in line waiting for their chance. And that gave me five days to think about what had happened since I died. To think about Haley and what she was attempting to do to her murderer. To think about my life and my afterlife.

The SECI chambers, there are three now, sit in a bland industrial space with a cement floor and a high ceiling. The ghosts waiting spiral out from those three structures. The chambers are about four feet on a side and about seven feet tall, made out of some fancy new electromagnetic (EM) shielding. They have sensors inside that detect ghostly EM emissions in very specific patterns and turn them into letters. It's complicated and I know JJ explained it thoroughly in *Shuffled Off*, so suffice it to say that it allows ghosts to type.

As we waited, Emily was great and supportive, doing her best to distract me. Teaching me how to play jacks—which is anything but easy. The jacks and the ball have to be an extension of your ghostly form, so it was quite the advanced lesson.

We got to know the other ghosts in line with us, and in general it was a pretty good time, but the closer we got to the SECI chambers, the more agitated I got. I kept thinking about Haley. What would happen to her? What fate could be worse than the bardo? Could I actually help?

There were only two ghosts in line in front of us when it became too much. "Emily…" I began.

"What is it, Walter?"

"I… Haley… I have to…"

Emily gave me the gentlest smile and grabbed my hand. "Is it time to go to her?" she asked.

My jaw dropped. Sometimes I think Emily is the wisest person I have ever known. At those moments, the wisdom of the four-year-old she was when she died and her eighty years dead come together. She is wise like a child and wise like an old person at the same time. How could she have the patience to give me this much time? How could she know to seize the moment when I gave her the smallest of openings?

"Yes," I said. "Please."

With a "pop" we were with Haley. It was not what I expected.

Chapter 20

"You are as good as dead now, so why not finish it? You know you don't want to live anymore. You know you are worthless. No one loves you and no one will ever love you…"

Haley's diatribe was intact but everything else had changed.

I would not have recognized her except for her voice. Haley didn't look like Haley and barely looked like a person. Her face had elongated and gone was any detail but the vaguest notion of eyes, mouth, and hair. Her form was dark grey like some great storm cloud. What passed for her arms were still attached to Edgar's head.

Edgar's transformation wasn't as dramatic, but it was significant. He sat slumped in a wheelchair, his eyes vacant, his skin pale, his jaw slack.

I looked around. We were in a plain institutional-looking room with quite a few other people. Some sat still and quiet. Others rocked and mumbled. Others looked pretty normal and sat around playing checkers or cards.

"Oh, shit," I said.

"We're in a loony bin," Emily said.

"This is bad."

"Should I go get Banquo?" Emily asked.

I shook my head. "He said I knew what to do. I don't think that has changed."

"But..." Emily began. "But this is worse, much worse than before."

I looked down at her. The worried look on her face almost stopped me. I squatted down to her level. "I have to do this, you know." She nodded. "If I don't, I won't be able to live with myself."

"But..."

"If this goes wrong, then go get Banquo." I stood up and went to Haley. She was stretched out horizontally behind Edgar's head. I carefully positioned myself in the circle of her arms. I was facing her strange-looking face and away from Edgar.

"Come back to me, Haley," I said. I then matched my

form to hers—which was not easy and felt dangerous—and kissed her.

Chapter 21

IT BEGAN WITH INTENT. TO HELP HER, TO BRING HER INTO balance, to demonstrate my caring for her. That intent translated into action. Haley was doing what she was doing because of the feelings in her, because of the pain in her, because she had to. Those emotions flowed from her into me. I took in her anger and her pain. I took in her fear and her doubt. I took it all in.

Maybe you've experienced something like this. You spend time with a good friend who is sad or upset. You talk to them, you try to help them, and when you leave, they are better off than when you started, but you are worse. It's as if you took some of their burden from them. This was like that, but without the intervening flesh, much more rapid, much more intense, and ironically, much more real.

It just poured into me until I didn't think I could take it anymore and then it just kept coming and coming and coming.

I felt like destroying something, killing someone, making the world as miserable as I was at that moment. I needed to let some of this go, let some of it out. I wasn't aware of Haley anymore and only vaguely aware of the room, but I was aware of Edgar. He was this dark void sucking all the light out of the world. He was cruel and evil and deserved to die. He was all that was wrong with the world. I would be doing everyone a favor by ending him. It was what I could do to help.

But a patter of words, as Haley had done, was not good

enough. I reached my hands—they looked like smoke—into his mind. I wasn't going to talk to him. I was going to destroy him. I could do it. If I poured all the rage I felt into his mind, it would break even further. His mind would cease to operate. He would die.

I poured all that rage and hate into him and soon I heard a sickening snap, like a bone breaking. I knew it was a piece of his mind crumbling under my attack, taking him one step closer to death.

"Walter!" I heard the voice as if from a great distance. It was a child's voice, high and light. The child was scared, terrified. Time had passed, but I had no idea how much. "Walter," she said, choking the word out amidst a storm of tears. "Please, Walter. Don't do it. I need you, Walter, I need you."

I paused and pulled my hands out of Edgar's head. She needed me? Someone needed me? I saw Emily. She looked so vulnerable in her shorts and her lollipop T-shirt. "Emily?" I said, her name coming to me. I had become something else, I wasn't Walter, I was something much more primal, but Emily, I knew Emily.

"Please, Walter, come with me." She extended her hand towards me. I didn't take it. I knew that somehow that would be bad for her. I didn't want to hurt her. She slowly moved back and I followed. She needed me, someone needed me.

It seemed impossible to leave. I wanted to return to my revenge, but I could not deny this little girl. I could not turn my back on her.

I was vaguely aware as we flew over Tucson, the full moon illuming the city below. We came to a grassy area surrounded by trees, filled with the glow of spirits and stones of smooth granite.

"Here, Walter. Here is your place. Here are your bones. You need to rest, Walter. You'll feel better after you rest."

"I don't want to rest, I want to—"

"Please!" Emily shouted, tears running down her cheeks. "Please, Walter, you must rest. Sink into the ground, find your bones. You are tired. So tired, I know you are."

"But he deserves to die. He must..." My mind was starting to come back to me. "Haley... where is Haley?"

"She is with Banquo. You saved her. You did good, Walter. But now you must rest, you must find your bones."

I blinked and looked around. I was in the graveyard. Emily was there and many other ghosts had circled us, kind of like it was the Midnight Circle. "You saved her," Jim the cowboy said. "Rest now," his companion Jane added. "You deserve it," another ghost said with a broad smile. Many more of them spoke to me saying kind things.

I looked down at the granite stone. "Walter Anchor 1960–2011." It was a plain gravestone, but I could feel its weight. Like it was my anchor point. My bones were down there. I loved to rest with my bones. It felt so calming, so much like home.

"Justice, Emily," I said. "Justice must be served."

"It has been," Emily said quietly, the tears still running down her cheeks. "He will never hurt anyone again. You made sure of that."

"Okay," I said, feeling slightly more like myself. "I *am* tired."

"Just sink into the ground. Rest. I'll be here waiting for you. I'll always be here for you, Walter."

As I slowly sunk into the ground, I smiled. I knew Emily was there for me, she had been ever since she found me. I wasn't alone anymore. I wasn't alone.

As the earth surrounded me, I felt myself slowly calm and then I knew nothing.

Chapter 22

EDGAR HALIFAX IS STILL ALIVE, BUT THERE IS NOT MUCH of his mind left and he won't hurt anyone ever again. First Haley, and then I, saw to that. I can't say I feel that bad about it—he was a psychotic murderer and he had it coming. What I do feel bad about is the price we had to pay. Doing something like that changes you. Doing that changed the "us" that was forming between Haley and me.

"I have to go," Haley said, her face tight, her arms crossed. Her form was back to normal, she was no longer an avenging spirit, but the cost of what had happened was clear in her haunted blue eyes. They looked much paler than I remembered.

The sun was setting over our graveyard, the thin layers of clouds and Tucson pollution putting on a good show to the west.

"Where?" I asked. I had been faded for a long time—I think about a week had passed.

"Utah," she said, her head bobbing to the north. "There is a small graveyard there in a ghost town called Silver Reef. Not too many ghosts and they've all been dead for a long time, they're all stable." She shrugged, her shoulders seeming very thin. "Banquo seems to think it will be good for me."

I nodded, but didn't know what else to say. I didn't want her to go, but after what had happened, I didn't really want her to stay either.

"I've been waiting for you to come back so I could say good-bye. I... You..."

I smiled at her. "You're welcome, Haley. I am glad I could help you. I hope things go well for you."

She leaned in and carefully kissed me on the cheek. She did it right so I could feel just the barest brush of her lips, like a feather or a rose petal. Banquo walked over and gave me a nod and took Haley by the arm. They walked a few yards away and with a "pop" were gone.

In truth, I will miss her.

"I'VE BEEN THINKING," EMILY SAID. SHE HAD FOUND ME standing alone in the graveyard after Haley and Banquo had left. "I think it's time for you to upgrade your outfit."

"What?" I asked, looking down at my blue scrubs.

"You're not a dentist anymore, Walter. You are a detective. You solved Haley's murder and brought a terrible man to justice."

I shrugged. It didn't feel much like a victory. We found out about these strange happenings in my old dental office but didn't get anywhere with my own murder. I suspected there was more to learn from Wheeler, but couldn't imagine surveilling him again. We had no leads. I looked at Emily, her lollipop was a pale yellow. She was worried.

"We didn't find out who was behind the corporate espionage," I said.

She snorted and crossed her arms in front of her chest. "Let the cops chase that down once you write the story. White-collar crime is for wimps. We solve murders."

I nodded and smiled. "It was a team effort, Emily. It wouldn't have happened without you."

She put up her hand and we did a high five, our ghostly hands slapping together, a big smile on her face. The smile melted into something coy and she said, "Really? Because... well... I've heard rumor of a murder at the University that happened just last night. Maybe..."

I laughed. "You want to go investigate?"

She nodded vigorously, her blonde curls bobbing around her face. "But first you need to look the part. I'm thinking a long brown trench coat and fedora. Like Humphrey Bogart in *Casablanca.*" I must have looked dubious, because she added a high-pitched "please."

I could not deny her enthusiasm, or really anything she wants, after what she has done for me. We spent the next hour working on my new form. It wasn't great—a bit vaguely shaped—but it would do, and I knew I would get better at holding it as time went by.

"There he is," she said once I was done. "Walter Anchor, ghost detective! Let's go."

I kneeled down and stared into her youthful face that hid her many years of experience. "Can I say one thing before we go?" She nodded, her eyes getting wide. "Thank you for stopping me... for what you did for me." She nodded again, her brow furrowed. "I can't do this without you." I wasn't referring to being a detective, but to "being" in general. I saw her blinking back tears, so I think she got it.

"Emily, can you give me a few minutes? I've got something I've got to do."

She looked me up and down, nodded gravely, and let go of my hand.

"This won't take long," I said, giving her my best, most reassuring smile.

THE GHOST HAD AN UNSAVORY LOOK, WITH SMALL EYES and crooked teeth, dressed all in black. He leaned, in a display of faux nonchalance, against the grey stone of the crypt. I had been doing some independent investigation, there were some loose ends in regards to what had happened to Haley.

He gave me a derisive snort as a greeting. "Nice outfit," he said, the sarcasm way overdone.

"You called Galt?" I asked.

He nodded.

"You the one that taught Haley how to mess with the living?"

He nodded again. I heard some moans and the sound of metal scraping against stone. Emily had always told me to stay away from the crypts, but this was important.

"Then you and I have a problem," I said.

He shrugged and pushed himself away from the stone wall. This was all artifice. He was a ghost, the wall could not support him, and he couldn't push himself away from it. It looked real, it was well done, which led me to believe he was a mature ghost. "The girl asked nice," he said with a thin grin and a shrug. "How could I turn her down?"

I crossed my arms and shook my head. "You should have turned her down. What happened is on you."

He chuckled, it was dry and thin and sounded dangerous. "The girl had a choice. She chose to come to me. She chose to do what she did."

"That may be, but if I ever see you so much as speaking to Emily, or any of my other friends, I will destroy you."

He slowly smiled, showing his crooked teeth off. "First off, that old witch Emily can take care of herself. Secondly, I see why you and Haley got along so well."

"What?"

"What she did to her killer, is that how you would

'destroy' me? You're just like Haley—you'll do what it takes to settle a score."

"I... No, that's not what I meant."

He held his hands up. "Relax, I appreciate the sentiment. You are willing to defend what is yours. I understand that. Maybe you and I aren't so different. Maybe you and I could be friends. Maybe I could show you a few things Emily and Banquo won't show you."

His words rattled around my head. What did he know? Would I act differently than Haley if I found my killer?

"Look," I finally said, "just stay away from Emily. Got it?"

He smiled and slumped back against the crypt wall. "Yeah, I got it. No problem. I do favors for my friends all the time."

As I walked away from him, I knew Galt and I weren't done, but Emily was waiting and there was another murder to solve.

BACKSTORY—DETECTING HALEY

ACTING WAS MY FIRST ARTISTIC LOVE—NO, MAKE THAT THE second. My first was drawing, which I was passionate about as a boy. I started acting in junior high by dressing up as a vampire with a bunch of other kids and singing "It's a Long Way to Transylvania" to the tune of "It's a Long Way to Tipperary." After that I spent my high school time in the dramatic arts (acting, directing, and performing as a mime).

Add that to the fact that the *Shuffled Off* series and the SECI chamber invented for it just begs for more ghost stories.

...and I love to write in the first person,

...and I wanted to play with the mystery genre a bit,

...and I have a great dentist,

...and the idea of an eighty-year-old ghost that looks like she's four just tickled my fancy.

As I was finishing the second "A Ghost's Memoir" book, *To Be a Fool*, the need for other ghost characters and their stories struck me and Walter Anchor and Emily were born (they even got a cameo in *To Be a Fool* they were so well developed in my head by then).

Part of the fun of these ghostly stories is figuring out how a ghost would do rather normal things. In this case, how does a ghost investigate a murder?

Oh, and there is one more person to blame for this one. Kevin J. Anderson. He's an amazing and prolific author that hosts the Superstars Writing Seminar every year. I went in 2012 where he mentioned his upcoming *Dan Shambles,*

Zombie PI series. If a zombie can be a PI then why not a ghost?

Stories of Life, Death, and the Places in Between

Robert J. McCarter

ONE CORE, ONE CONSCIOUSNESS

JUNE SCUTTLED INTO THE ELEVATOR, USING ALL FOUR OF her metal limbs as legs. Her mind was on fire with the idea that had just occurred to her. If she just—

She wasn't alone in the elevator. Next to her, wearing a similar body, was Old Lady Hethroy. They both wore a four-limbed metallic body with a shuttered fan in the middle of their backs and a sensory stalk where you would expect a head. June mentally sighed; Hethroy's fan was folded, so maybe she wouldn't have to engage in a pointless exchange. The old lady was just so derivative, never anything new from her. June needed to focus; the last thing she needed was—

Hethroy opened her fan and colors started pulsing across it: an abstract wash of hues that went from deep azure to a light red. Blooms of color would appear, move across the fan, only to be replaced by new blooms.

June watched; she had to. Hethroy lived above her, was wealthier than her, and she was duty bound to the communication. It took twenty floors for the display to play out, and it didn't take much to interpret; it was sadly out of date with current trends and no challenge at all. Hethroy had said, in essence, "Hello."

Well, June may have been duty bound to listen, but she was not duty bound to reply in such an antiquated fashion. She unfurled her fan revealing total darkness. This darkness slowly faded to reveal a pastoral landscape with a yellow sun rising and brightening a blue sky with large fluffy clouds lazily floating past.

About midway through the display, she upped the ante by moving the petals of her fan back and forth, while perfectly maintaining the image; besting Hethroy in both creativity and difficulty. By the time the elevator had opened at her floor, the sequence had just ended. She had said, in essence, "Good morning."

Satisfied that she had adequately executed her duty and had also shown Hethroy a thing or two, she collapsed her fan and scuttled out of the elevator.

THE DOOR TO HER AND ORVILLE'S APARTMENT OPENED AT her approach, but she knew Orville wasn't home. She brushed past the fern, from the Jurassic period, that Orville had brought home one day. It was one of his "grand surprises" that he would go away and work on secretively, sometimes for months at a time.

He was in the middle of one of those phases now, and June hoped the surprise leaned towards the romantic, like the hot air balloon he had helped build and the ride he had taken her on over the newly growing forests. She much preferred that to things like the healthy colony of bacteria or the living—albeit briefly—cockroach that he would bring home with such pride and excitement.

As she passed the fern and moved down the hallway, on her way to the server room, her visual algorithm tagged an anomaly, but she ignored it and pushed it to a background process.

The server room was small, with two pedestals equipped with hardwired connectors. June moved over one and slowly lowered herself onto it, connecting herself to the apartment. If she had had a voice she would have let out a sigh. It always felt good to be connected to power, to have a faster data connection, and to have access to more processing resources.

She was just settling in when the background process finished evaluating the anomaly. Preliminary evaluation had revealed it to be a handwritten note.

What? Who writes notes? How would you even find the paper and a writing instrument? Instead of getting up she used the apartment's cameras to get a closer look at the note.

It was a plain rectangle of paper, with thin, irregular letters. The imperfection of it bothered June and she found the simplicity of it disturbing—if everyone communicated this clearly and directly, what would they spend their time doing at gatherings?

It said, "June, my love, please meet soonest at," followed by GPS coordinates. It continued, "Please dress circa 2050. Love, Orville."

Dressing circa 2050, but that would mean... She had trouble finishing the thought.

THIS WAS ORVILLE. JUNE KNEW HIS REQUEST HAD REASON behind it, and after all their centuries together she could not deny him.

She lifted herself, disconnecting from the apartment with a small twinge of regret. She moved out into the hallway and into the dressing room.

This room was a bit larger, but with only one pedestal in the middle of the room. She settled herself onto it and told the dresser what she wanted and gave herself over to the process.

She hated it, she really did. Without a hardwired connection she was forced to interface with the dresser wirelessly; which didn't provide enough bandwidth for her to be in control. She had to let the dresser do its job; she had to let go.

Several panels on the white walls opened as robotic arms slid out, sliding along tracks. They set about disassembling June's body with a quiet, cold efficiency. First the sensor stalk, leaving June blind and reliant on the room's sensory apparatus. Next the fan, her precious fan, was detached. The legs were removed, and finally the shell.

What was left was a small rectangular box: June's core, the essential June. She felt weak and exposed and vulnerable.

The feeling didn't last long. Soon the dresser was bringing out new parts. First a feminine humanoid torso to house her core, then two legs, two arms, and a head.

The work went quickly and soon June was dressed circa 2050 looking like a human, looking like her original self.

JUNE STILL COULDN'T GET OVER HOW GOOD THIS HUMAN body looked, how good it felt. It had been at least a century since she had worn it. Human form had been out of style for so very long. She also marveled at the quality of the body. The skin was smooth with minute pores and hairs. The face was her thirty-year-old face with bright green eyes and luxurious brown hair. Even the delicate and flattering floral print dress that came with it was fresh and new.

It had to be Orville, there was no other explanation. He had been working on this for some time; he had restored their human bodies. He was up to something.

At first June railed against the limited sensory input. She was used to detecting a much wider spectrum of visual data, seeing in 360 degrees, and being much more sensitive to audio. However, the "humanness" of it was so familiar that, even after all this time, it felt comforting.

BACK IN THE ELEVATOR ON HER WAY TO SEE ORVILLE, June was met again by Old Lady Hethroy. The old bird didn't know what to think. June could tell by the sporadic clicks and the starting and stopping of images on her fan that she was having a fit. She would start one complicated communication, only to stop it and start over. She did this the whole way down.

"Lovely afternoon, isn't it?" June said with a small smile as she exited the elevator.

HER ENCOUNTER WITH HETHROY HAD HELPED HER FEEL more comfortable in her new skin. There were clearly some advantages to being this far out of the norm.

Orville's coordinates were not too far away, so she decided to walk. She lengthened her stride and enjoyed the sensation of the spring air against her skin, the smells of the city, and the rustling of the soft fabric against her body.

And she became more and more delighted by the reactions

she got. Her contemporaries were scuttling around, their fan's unfurling to express their surprise, or dismay, or horror. They didn't have enough time to get a coherent message out, which was fine with her. She just smiled, nodded, and said, "Good day," or "What fine weather we are having," or "You're looking good."

At one point she passed another person dressed as a human. As they passed each other they didn't speak. Just a smile and a nod was enough.

SHE SAW HIM FROM A DISTANCE. A HUMAN FORM LEANING against the railing of a bridge that arched over a small stream: Orville.

He didn't turn as she approached, his attention fixed on the water below him. Maybe he didn't know it was her, maybe he had limited his sensory input to human standard. They had all done that in the beginning, trying so desperately to hold on to their humanity, but that was so very long ago.

She took a position next to him on the bridge, her eyes following his gaze down to the water, her arm brushing his.

"Hello, Love," he said, without turning.

"Orville. What are we—"

"Just watch. It'll be better if you do."

And so they stood there, long and still, watching as the water flowed past.

June wanted to ask questions, wanted to know what was going on, but she didn't. After so long together she knew this is what he had been planning, and if staring at water was what he needed her to do, it is what she would do.

Some minutes later she saw a flash of a sleek form right

below the surface of the water. "What!" she exclaimed as she grabbed Orville's hand.

"Fish, my love," Orville replied. "Fish."

"Oh my!"

THEY STROLLED THROUGH THE PARK, HAND IN HAND. IT brought back such memories for June, such old, treasured memories. They had met in this very park, on that very bridge all those centuries ago. And the park, although not fully restored from the Devastation, once again seemed to be the park of her youth.

Orville had been so young, and so eager. He walked up to June and her friend Ann as they stood on the bridge. He had a camera in his hand and was dressed in a clean white shirt with all the buttons done up.

"Excuse me, ladies," he said with a bob of his head. "Would you do me the honor of posing for me?" He held forth his camera. "I am doing a project for school and need some shots with people in them. I think you would be just perfect."

Orville had aimed his query at June who missed this fact because she was looking down at her feet. Ann was the pretty one and she always got all the attention.

"I'll just go take a walk," June mumbled to Ann as she started to move off.

Ann grabbed her, pulling her back, and whispered in her ear, "Silly, he wants to take pictures of you. I'll be the one taking the walk."

"FISH, ORVILLE, FISH! THAT MEANS—" SHE DIDN'T FINISH, she couldn't.

"That means it is all coming back. Soon."

"Soon?"

"In a century, maybe two, homo sapiens will be possible."

They were silent then as they walked. June stopped at every flower and used her human standard nose to inhale the scents deeply. She knew her other bodies could tell her so much more about what she smelled, but there was something satisfyingly nostalgic about it.

Soon they wound back to the bridge and stood there hand in hand until they saw another fish. When the silvery scales streaked just below the water, she had a flash of insight as to what Orville was up to, and it scared her.

"You have been working with the Bio Consortium again, haven't you?" June asked.

"Yes," Orville replied.

June turned and faced Orville, their eyes locking. "And you have something to ask me, don't you?"

Orville looked down for a moment and then took a deep breath before saying, "Yes."

"So?" June prompted. She had to know.

"My love, you have adapted to this life so well. Better than I, I am afraid. You with your social graces, your ease at the gatherings, your mastery of the fan dances. I hesitate to even ask. But..."

"Orville—" June began as she felt a flush rising on her cheeks.

"But... I must. Soon we will be able to clone bodies from our own DNA and imprint them with our core's neural patterns. Soon this planet will once more be able to support us biologically." Orville then took her hand, got to one knee, and said, "June, my love, will you be human with me?"

JUNE FLED THE BRIDGE AFTER LEARNING ABOUT ORVILLE'S proposal. She rushed back to their apartment and had the dresser change her back into her four-limbed fan body.

Orville had explained it carefully to her, answering all her questions, but each piece of data just intensified her fear until she ran away. First their cryogenically frozen DNA would be used to clone a body; that body would have several implants to interface with short-term memory; through these implants and with the use of some complicated hormone treatments that June didn't understand, the neural patterns from their cores would be transferred to the clone's brain; once the transfer was validated, the core would be erased; and finally once the biological body failed, its neural patterns would be transferred to a new core, as they had done once before.

It wasn't fair, not fair at all. They had met on that bridge, he had proposed to her on that bridge, and now this?

She had worked hard to adapt to her non-biological life. To master the complicated social dances that had evolved. To manage their social standing, to keep them connected. She just couldn't—

She went back to the server room, plugged herself in and started her work. Work that would move them forward in this life, not back into the distant past.

Her vision was exquisite. If she pulled it off, they would rise higher than ever in the social circles. But it wouldn't be easy. Instead of one fan, she wanted two; it would allow for more complicated and nuanced communication. But her current body wouldn't support it. The existing fan would have to be moved from the center of the body to the back, and the secondary, smaller fan, added to the front. Four limbs wouldn't work. It would take six. This would require time and engineering, but would be worth it.

She was setting up the simulation of the design when she heard Orville come in. She didn't spare much attention, but saw that he was still in his human body and stood there politely waiting for her to acknowledge him. She didn't, and after an hour he left.

Well, that was fine with June. She had a lot of work to do.

When June entered the room, a series of clicks swept through it, a wave of sound from tapping limbs initiated from very near her and rippling through the crowd.

Her body, with its six limbs, was strikingly different, longer and sleeker. Her fan was shuttered, but balanced at the back of her body instead of in the middle like the others gathered here.

A thrill passed through June. The change had captured their attention, and they hadn't even seen her pièce de résistance yet: the secondary fan. It was shuttered and lay flat against her body; it could be easily mistaken for a simple design element.

She moved slowly through the room and approached the main pedestal. The soloist who had been there quickly skittered off at her approach. She mounted the pedestal and unfurled her main fan and began.

First a flawless fireworks-like flourish as the petals flicked back and forth, just to get their attention. Then the main fan started displaying a quick series of photo realistic morphs of a single being. First human, then through the humanlike experimentation phase: four arms; extremely tall, extremely short; animal heads, etcetera. Then through the experimentation with animal bodies; giving way to abstract forms; insectoid forms; and on and on until she arrived at the present day four-limbed fan form.

The morphing slowed then to show the addition of two more limbs and the shifting of the fan to the posterior section of the body.

There were some clicks as she ran through this, she expected it; her audience was whispering to each other. When the fan display slowly showed the addition of a secondary fan in the back of the body, the clicks stopped, her audience rapt.

She had said, "This is the future." She then slowly unfurled her secondary fan, displaying a flourish of color across it, as if to say, "The future is here." She was greeted by a frantic wave of clicks.

This was it, this was her moment. The kind of moment she had dreamed about for centuries. But one thought nagged at the back of her consciousness: Where was Orville?

As DECADES GIVE WAY TO CENTURIES AND THE CENTURIES start to stack up, some gaps in a relationship are to be expected. Some very long gaps.

June had spent eight months creating her new body, and not once had she seen Orville. They had spent much longer than that apart before, but never like this.

June was plagued by these thoughts as she scuttled back from the gathering, her six limbs tapping rhythmically on the sidewalk.

She could, of course, find him—easily. A quick query to the Central Core would do the trick. But she refused; she wouldn't allow herself to do it. This time Orville had just gone too far.

When she arrived at the apartment she noticed a handwritten note stuck on the wall. This time she stopped and read it right away. "My Love, please meet me at the bridge. Dress as you will. Orville."

She made her way to the bridge, but took her time; Orville could wait—Orville should wait.

She was disturbed that this rift between them was ruining her moment, distracting her from the great unveiling she had just executed so brilliantly. Such thoughts were beneath her, they were so... so... human.

She sighed inwardly (as much as a dual-fanned six-limbed creature could). Her core, her brain, was as human as a digital copy could be, so her emotions were not surprising. Despite the more traditionally digital augmentation to it, her core was a copy of her once biological neural network. Perhaps Orville was right, perhaps—

Lost in her thoughts, June almost missed the humanoid form as she scuttled by. It was a female with long blonde hair, in a shiny blue jumpsuit. The woman had a bemused look on her face and nodded at June as she passed.

June stopped and reviewed recent sensory input. That was the third human-bodied person she had passed. *The third.* Just eight months ago on her way to the bridge she had passed only one.

"WHAT DO YOU WANT, ORVILLE?" JUNE ASKED. SHE didn't speak; her body didn't have the apparatus, so she radioed the communication directly to Orville.

"You. I want you." Orville replied verbally. After a pause

he added, "Your new body is impressive. I can just imagine how it was received at the gathering."

"Thank you, Orville," June replied, but she would not be distracted. "So?"

"So?"

"You know what I mean, Orville. Just get down to it."

"Just imagine, June, when you appear at a gathering as human, biological human—"

The words June radioed back to Orville came in a dense flurry, "Do you really think I am that shallow? Do you truly, after all these years, not know me? My reaction has nothing to do with gatherings, or social standing, or any of that. It is going through what flesh must go through. Again. I can't, I just—"

June stopped radioing words, they were too inadequate, and unfurled her main fan. She spoke to Orville in images.

First she showed how they had met on this bridge, and fallen in love, and gotten married, and raised two children and had grown old together. Rapidly, but distinctly, the images formed and morphed from one to the next. June and Orville, young and free, changing rapid-fire to June and Orville, old and stooped.

The images slowed down then as the old June and Orville stood on their bridge holding hands. Orville letting go of June as a wracking cough overtook him and doubled him over. Orville on all fours with mucous flecked with blood staining the wood of the bridge, clinging to his mouth.

June showed the ambulance taking Orville to the hospital, and the pace sped up again as June sat at Orville's bed side as he wasted away. The light flicking on and off behind the shuttered curtains marking the passing of the days.

The images on the fan slowed down once more as a

young handsome man entered the room and began talking animatedly. When he left, there was a look of hope on Orville's face.

The man came several more times and June and Orville fought each time after he left. The last time the man came he brought contracts which Orville proceeded to sign. During the signing, June ran away.

About thirty more days flicked by as Orville stayed in the hospital room growing gaunter, until he was unconscious and didn't move anymore. When Orville stopped breathing the men came and took his body away.

The scene on the fan then shifted to June, old and stooped and alone in a house. Her days passed simply and, for the most part, confined to that house.

One day a knock came on the door, and when June opened it she was confronted by Orville, a young, healthy, and handsome Orville. June sent him away and collapsed in tears behind the closed door.

The next day the young Orville came to the door and again June sent him away. This happened day after day, until one day June broke down weeping and struck the new Orville over and over with her fists until she collapsed into his arms.

The animation sped up again as the young Orville and old June went about a simple life. They lived in the small house, took care of the gardens, went out to concerts, went out to restaurants, and visited with a small circle of friends.

One day June became ill, and the young Orville tended her night and day without rest until she went to the hospital. The young handsome man came once again and more contracts were signed. One day they took June's body away and young Orville left the hospital.

The scene morphed to a small apartment where the young Orville opened the door and finds a young June standing there. The images on the fan fade to black.

"I can't do it Orville," June radioed. "I just can't do it again. I can't watch you die again."

ORVILLE STOOD THERE FOR A LONG TIME NOT SPEAKING. June studied his face: his crinkled brow; his brown eyes cast downward and darting to and fro; his lips moving. June, not knowing what else to do, just waited. Orville soon began pacing as his arms started to gesture, and his mute mumbling intensified.

After several minutes of this, he turned to June, a bright smile on his face and said. "I've got it!"

"What? Orville, what?"

"Just... Just... Meet me here in one month," Orville said as he turned and began to run.

As he moved away, June radioed to him, "What is it, Orville, what did you figure out?"

Orville's form was moving out of sight when he radioed back, "One Core, One Consciousness."

JUNE HAD DEBATED LONG AND HARD ABOUT WHAT TO WEAR to her meeting with Orville. She had tried contacting him numerous times to find out what he was up to, but he had not replied. Typical. She wanted to go in her new dual-fanned body, but thought a small gesture might be appreciated.

Finally decided, she went into the dressing room and had it change her into her human body. After the fan body was stripped off and her core was exposed, she felt her usual vulnerability. "One Core, One Consciousness," Orville had said. What could he be thinking? Their society was built on that law. No duplicating of oneself. Only one.

Dressed as a human, she made her way slowly to the bridge. This time she passed six others dressed as humans. Each time she shared a small smile with them. June knew this was a trend gaining momentum, and fast.

When she arrived, Orville was there leaning over the bridge staring into the water. June joined him there, her arm brushing his.

"You look beautiful today, my love."

June smiled, and stood there patiently as they waited. It took several minutes, but they finally caught sight of silver scales flashing below the surface.

"Please explain, Orville."

"One Core, One Consciousness."

"Well of course, everyone knows that. No duplicating of consciousness."

"But," Orville began, a smile growing on his face, "I have found a bit of a loophole."

"Oh my dear, I hope not. Can you imagine if everyone went around duplicating themselves? Those with means, like Old Lady Hethroy, would spread like—"

"No, no, not that. Remember those implants I told you about, the ones that would facilitate the transfer of our neural patterns from our cores into our new brains?"

June nodded.

"With some extra work and time, it can be made to go both ways."

"Both ways?" June asked.

"Don't you see, my love? We could keep our cores and update them as we sleep. No messy biological transfer when the body wears out, we would have a reliable backup copy. I have run this by the Bio Consortium and the Core Commission; everyone is really excited. Our cores would have to be altered so they could only be used for backup. 'One Core, One Consciousness,' you know."

June turned her attention back to the water. "I don't know—" Orville took her hand and followed her gaze to the water. "We have been this way for so long, so much longer than we were biological, why change, why go back?"

"To touch you, June, to really touch you again." With that Orville turned June's face to his and gently kissed her. "To kiss you, June, to truly kiss you again. These bodies are amazing, but it's just not the same. For that, I would—"

"But there is risk in each transfer, isn't there?" June asked.

"Some, but not much. It is—"

"And you would risk dying to… to touch me, to kiss me?"

"Yes, June," Orville said. "Yes, my love. Gladly. Willingly."

June was overwhelmed by Orville's gesture and stood in silence staring at his loving face. "Oh my sweet, old-fashioned man. Ask me again, Orville."

"Again?"

"Ask me, Orville. Ask me!"

Orville's brown eyes lit up as he held June's hand and on one knee said, "June, my love, will you be human with me?"

With tears running down her face June said, "Yes, my love, yes!"

"TELL ME AGAIN, PAPA," THE YOUNG BOY ASKED FROM HIS perch on Orville's lap, "tell me about when you and Mama were metal spiders like Uncle Aaron?"

"Well, my boy. A very, very long time ago, after the Devastation, when the Earth was failing, everyone had to become like Uncle Aaron to survive..."

Smiling, June kissed her son and her husband on their heads, tousling the boy's hair. She made her way into the kitchen to start dinner. Such an old-fashioned activity, one she hated her first time around as a biological. But not now... now she treasured it.

BACKSTORY—ONE CORE, ONE CONSCIOUSNESS

THE HISTORY OF THIS STORY IS EASY TO PEG DOWN. IT was directly inspired by a story called "Outbound" by Brad R. Torgersen.

Brad has been one of my inspirations. I found his blog right when I started getting serious with writing again and right before he broke through and won the Writers of the Future Contest. He pointed me in the direction of the Writers of the Future Contest, certain blogs I still follow, the Superstars Writing Seminar, and connected me with a whole community of writers.

In "Outbound" Brad explores the idea of human consciousness moving to machine and back to biological—the idea I played with here. I mixed in a long romantic relationship (having been with the same amazing woman for twenty-five years, another area I keep exploring) and tried to envision a very different future and the ways we might express ourselves.

As a nice little synergy, this story received an honorable mention from the Writers of the Future contest in 2011, the contest Brad introduced me to.

I got the chance to meet Brad in 2012 and thank him for his positive influence. He's a great writer, go check out some of his work.

Robert J. McCarter

Stories of Life, Death, and the Places in Between

Robert J. McCarter

DEATH BY COMET

June, 2014

THE MAN LEANED OUT OVER THE COUNTER OF HIS BOOTH and shouted, "T-Shirt, get your Death Machine T-shirt right here." He had short cropped black hair and wild green eyes that reminded Harvey of a feral cat he had known as a kid. The man was wearing a white T-shirt that said in large letters, "Ball-Peen Hammer" and above it in smaller letters, "Death By."

Harvey stood there, frozen. He rubbed his index finger with his thumb, which was still sore from the prick the machine had given him. He stared down at the white rectangle of paper in his other hand. The text side was down, so he couldn't see his fate, and that was fine, he didn't want to see it again; it just confused him.

"You, kid," the man shouted at Harvey. "What did the machine tell you?"

Harvey looked up at the man but didn't say anything.

"Come on, kid. Don't be shy. Unless that card says 'T-shirt guy' there is nothing to worry about. Right?"

Harvey nodded mutely and took a step forward, pushing his overlong blond hair out his face.

"Not what you expected, huh?" the man began. "It's probably your twenty-first birthday too. You ran down here just as soon as you could." Harvey nodded again. "Bet the parents tried to stop you, telling you it does you no good to know your fate." Harvey nodded. "Well, to hell with them! You are your own man now. Come on, let me see that card; if I don't have a T-shirt for you in stock, I can make one up real quick."

Harvey took one more step forward, and without looking at it again, showed the man the card.

A long whistle escaped the green-eyed man as he studied the card. "Wow, kid, wow," he began. "This is a new one; I have never seen the machine issue one like that. Look. I'll tell you what, since you are the first I'll give you a deal. Only $20, my lowest price. Give me fifteen minutes and I'll have it made up."

Harvey shook his head and said, "But... But how is a T-shirt gonna help?"

"How?" the man cried. "How?! I'll tell you how. Look at me. My cause of death will be a ball-peen hammer. And do I hide from it? Do I run? No! I display proudly on my chest." The man thumped his chest and then reached down and pulled out a small hammer from under the counter. It had one round, blunt end and one semi-spherical end. "No, I have one of these with me at all times." He brandished the hammer in front of Harvey, who took a step back. "Listen to me, kid, the machine is never wrong. Never. You have to embrace your fate, look it in the eye, and live, really live your life." With that the man flipped the hammer in the air in front of him, caught it, and brought it crashing down on the counter.

Harvey noticed numerous semi-spherical indents in the wood of the counter; this was not the first time the T-shirt guy had done that.

Harvey turned and gazed at the rest of the Death Bazaar. It was a maze of booths and tents you had to thread your way through after getting your death prediction. He had come here because this Death Machine was free; he hadn't anticipated what state it would put him in and that he would be forced to pass vendors hawking their wares. He wished he had just gone to the mall and paid. He took a deep breath and moved forward.

He focused on his shoes, old leather work boots, as he walked, ignoring the many vendors: hot dogs; life insurance; "I just found out how I'm going to die" portraits; more T-shirt vendors; Navajo Tacos; ice cream.

He stopped briefly in front of a large tent with a sign hanging on it that said "Succor." The pretty woman standing out front must have noticed him looking. "The tent is air-conditioned," she began. "We have refreshments, counselors, psychics, massage therapists, all kinds of things to help you. It's a $10 cover to get in; from there you can just rest, or avail yourself of our other services."

She was lovely, and with the Phoenix heat rising from the asphalt, the offer was tempting. Harvey considered it briefly and then just smiled, nodded, and kept walking.

He passed more food vendors; a lady doing makeovers; a guy selling funeral plots; a woman selling puppies, "Comfort is what you need at a time like this," she shouted as he passed.

With the exit in sight, he was distracted by a large professional-looking booth with a sign that said, "www.death. net," hanging in large letters above it.

"Can I help you, son?" a man said from behind the counter. He had greying hair, blue eyes, and a thin mustache.

"What is this?" Harvey asked.

"You sign up and see how many people got the same thing you did; you can communicate with them and, ultimately, find out how they die."

Harvey nodded, finally something that made sense. Maybe he could find out what the word on his card meant.

"You can sign up right here," the man said, pointing to one of the laptops on the booth's counter.

Harvey went to the laptop, put in his name, screen name, email address, birth date, and paused when it asked for "Cause of Death."

"It's okay, son," the man said. He had come around the counter and was standing next to Harvey. "It's okay. What does your card say?"

Harvey turned the card over and showed it to the man, watching his expression carefully. The man just nodded and said, "Wow, I just saw that one a few minutes ago. Go ahead, type it in."

Harvey typed it slowly in: C.O.M.E.T. He hit the enter key and waited. The screen that came back said: "Total members with COMET as cause of death: 2."

"Are you okay, son?" the man asked. "She wasn't looking good either. Do you need to sit down? The Succor tent isn't far, that's where I sent her."

It didn't take Harvey long to find her. She was a young, petite brunette, with bright blue eyes and round-rimmed glasses. She sat on a folding chair sipping an iced tea, her eyes unfocused.

"Umm," Harvey began, pointing to the chair next to her. "Do you mind?" She shook her head so he sat down beside her. "Excuse the intrusion, but the man at the death.net booth said I could find you here."

She looked at him, her eyes narrowing. "Why? Why would he do that?"

In lieu of an answer, Harvey showed her his card, with a single world boldly printed on it: COMET.

"Oh my God," she said, showing Harvey her card. It was stark white with the same single word. "What does this mean?"

Harvey shrugged his shoulders. "I don't know, but since there are only two of us, I thought we should meet."

"Yeah," she agreed. "I'm glad I'm not the only one."

They sat there silent for a time. Harvey didn't know what else to say and found himself staring at her. She had a smattering of freckles on her cheeks, long hair, full lips, and a nicely arranged body. But it was her eyes—the deep azure blue—that kept calling to him, kept pulling him back.

After a few minutes of silence, Harvey said, "It's my birthday today, is it yours too?" Alice nodded. "Umm... Can I buy you lunch? To celebrate?"

She looked at Harvey, he felt her eyes boring into him.

"I'm a nice guy, I swear. I just think us COMET people ought to stick together. My name is Harvey."

She smiled and nodded. "Alice, I'm Alice."

"Okay," Harvey said, consulting the display of his smartphone, "there are several drinks called comet; there is a roller coaster in New York called Comet; a goldfish, moth, and hummingbird; and an indoor soccer team in Kansas. But..."

"But," Alice said, "how the hell is one of those going to kill us. I mean, how easy it would be to avoid them."

Harvey nodded, pushing at the pasta on his plate. He took a sip from the wine glass. "Wow, this is good. It's rich and... spicy. I'm not sure if that is the right way to put it. I've never been much for wine, but I like this. What is it again?"

"A zinfandel," Alice said. "A California zinfandel."

"Well what do you know, I learned two things today: I am going to die from a COMET and I like California zinfandel."

Alice smiled briefly, before her face fell into a frown.

"What?" Harvey asked. "Was it something I said?"

Alice shook her head. "No. It's just that... This machine, it is never wrong. It may be obtuse and annoying, but it is never wrong. Right?"

Harvey nodded, "Right. That's what they say. You can get tested by any machine anywhere and the results will be the same."

"So..." Alice began. "So... that means that our fate is now knowable. This machine not only knows how we are going to die, but our fate is sealed, and we can't do anything about it."

Harvey paused, thinking, and took another sip of his wine. "And not only does that damn machine know our fate, it factors itself into the equation."

"What do you mean?" she asked.

"Well, say someone goes and gets a card that says, 'DEPRESSION.' He has been psychologically stable up until that point, but the damn machine prescribing his fate throws him into a depression that ends in his suicide. The machine was, at the very least, a catalyst in it. The machine participated in that person's fate, and really, with everyone who gets one of these cards."

Alice's eyes darted back and forth as she thought about what he had said. Her face then morphed into a shy smile as she deliberately changed the subject. "What is it that you are studying in college?"

"Agriculture," Harvey said, smiling back. He too had had enough of the machine for one day. "I know it seems old fashioned, but I want to grow things."

Alice nodded. "Nice, I like that." Taking a sip of her ruby red wine, she added, "Maybe you could grow grapes, zinfandel grapes. It's got to be a pretty profitable crop."

Harvey raised his glass, touching it to hers with a clink, "I'll drink to that!"

June, 2015

THEIR HANDS CLASPED TIGHTLY, THEY APPROACHED THE kiosk. "Are you sure you want to do this?" Harvey asked.

Alice nodded, "I need to be sure."

"Is it really that important?"

She nodded, swiping her credit card and inserting her finger into the Death Machine. A tremor passed through her body as the machine punctured her finger and drew blood. She withdrew the card that appeared without looking at it and put it in the back pocket of her jeans. "Now you," she said.

Harvey went through the same procedure, and following her lead did not look at the card and put it in his pocket. He didn't like doing this, but she wanted it, she had asked for it. It wasn't really that big of a deal. He knew what the card was going to say.

THEIR WINE GLASSES CLINKED. "HAPPY ANNIVERSARY," Harvey said.

"Happy anniversary," Alice echoed.

"Shall we?"

Alice nodded. Harvey could tell she was scared.

"Okay," he said. "On the count of three. One... two... three!"

They both flipped over their cards and laid them on the table. COMET.

"Feel better?" Harvey asked. "It's been a year and we used a different machine."

Alice nodded and swallowed. "Thank you, I know it's silly, but—"

"But you don't want us to be like your mom and dad."

"His card was CANCER, hers OLD AGE. She's so young still and she has to go on without him now."

Harvey nodded, taking her hand. "Well, my dear Alice, rest assured that we will both die the same way. And, considering the odd nature of our deaths, probably at the same time."

She smiled a quizzical smile. "Is that romantic, or just sick?"

"Romantic!" Harvey cried, raising his glass. "Very romantic!"

The glasses clinked, her face turning serious again. "So how many of us are there now?"

Harvey pulled out his phone and checked the death.

net app. "Only two of us. Only us. You know that *is* kind of romantic."

September, 2017

"THERE ARE A FEW RESTORED MERCURY COMETS HERE in California," Harvey said, looking at Alice with a small smile on his lips. "But other than that I think it is safe for us here." They held hands and walked amid the grapes. The fruit was heavy and full, sagging on the vines; it was nearly harvest time.

She nodded, but didn't comment.

"Our numbers are up," Harvey continued. "There are 145 of us COMETs now."

Alice shook her head. "That just makes it more puzzling."

"Yeah it does." Harvey paused and swallowed. "It can't be some random crazy thing like a drink or an exploding car. Not for that many people."

As was typical, they didn't talk about the end for too long.

"This place is beautiful, Harvey, I am so excited for you. Apprentice winemaker; I am so proud."

Harvey smiled and squeezed her hand. "And how is your job hunt going in Phoenix? I have no doubt you will find a teaching job soon."

Alice nodded, but didn't answer, changing the subject. "It really is beautiful here."

They both were silent as they walked. After a time Harvey said, "Alice, I need to know one thing. One thing."

She stopped, a worried frown on her face. "What?"

"Would... Would you be with me if we didn't have the

same cause of death? Is this just because we're both COMET?"

"No! No, God no." She brought his hand to her lips and kissed it. "After my dad died I was... I was obsessed with it for a while. But no. I love you, and I'm with you because I love you."

Harvey smiled and held her close. "Good. We are at the right spot then."

Alice looked around and said, "Right spot?"

"Yup. These are zinfandel grapes; the old vines; the good ones."

She smiled. "Okay, but..."

Harvey got on one knee, amidst the vines, and said, "Alice, I can't bear the thought of us being apart. That day we met was the best day of my life and I want to spend each day I have with you. Alice, will you do me the honor of being my wife?"

March, 2018

HARVEY GERARD SENIOR PUT THE TIE AROUND HIS SON'S neck, flipping the silk over and under forming a single Windsor knot. "Should have taught you this; a man should know how to tie his own tie."

"How many times have I worn a tie, Dad?"

"Not the point," the older man grunted.

"You know, Alice is so grateful you are walking her down the aisle," Harvey said.

The older man nodded. "My pleasure. She's a good girl; hardly know if you deserve her."

Harvey's smile turned to a frown when an exploding

sound came from his pocket. "Let it be, son, let it be," Harvey Senior said.

"But..." Harvey began reaching for the phone.

"But what?" the older man asked a frown on his face.

"That was an alert... Ah... An alert about—"

"Oh, I know exactly what that was. Someone died. Someone that got a card that said COMET from that damn machine." He hastily finished with the tie, pulling it a tad too tight, and said. "There. Check the damn thing."

Harvey pulled out his phone and looked at it, his eyes darting over the text, his expression going blank. "Oh my..."

"What? What happened?"

"That roller coaster, the one they call Comet, just..." Harvey sat down heavily on a chair. "A car derailed. It killed everyone on board and some bystanders. A total of twenty-seven are dead at this point. All of them were COMET."

"Look, son," his father said with a heavy sigh. "It is sad, and it is tragic, but this is not the day. Today is your wedding day; today it is time to focus on living, not dying."

"Alice is going to freak when she finds out," Harvey said.

"And she is not going to find out from you. Not today." Harvey looked into his father's eyes as the older man continued. "You have got to find a way to live with how you are going to die. You went and got that damn card—against my advice, I might add."

"But, if I hadn't, I wouldn't have met Alice, I wouldn't be here today."

"Fair enough. Some good has come of it. So let it go. Let it go and live your life."

HARVEY COULDN'T HEAR THE MUSIC ANY MORE, OR SMELL the flowers, or see the guests. All he could see was Alice

Preston. She was at the other end of the church dressed in a white gown—elegant and lacy—her long brown hair swept up, her round features shining from behind a thin veil. She was on the arm of Harvey's father, a smile upon her face.

Harvey grinned; his father was right. It was time to live. Later that night, after discussing it with Alice, he removed the death.net app from his phone.

January, 2020

HARVEY WALKED INTO THE LABOR AND DELIVERY ROOM and was shocked by the expression on his wife's face. It wasn't pain, it was something else: fear, maybe grief. She was crying.

"What?" he asked, as he put down the cup of ice chips and took her hand.

Alice swallowed hard, wiping the tears from her cheek.

"Is it the baby?" Harvey asked.

Alice shook her head and said with a sniffle, "They asked if we want to test him?"

This didn't make sense to Harvey. "Test? What test?"

"The machine, they want to know if we want the Death Machine test done," Alice said, her tears drying up and her face turning cold. "Our boy is not even born yet and they want to tell us how he is going to die. How... Who would ever want to know?"

Harvey took her hand and kissed it. "Did you tell them where they can shove their damn machine?"

Alice smiled and nodded. "They won't be asking again."

September, 2025

HARVEY STOOD UP FROM THE VINE HE WAS INSPECTING. He picked off a grape and popped it into his mouth, crushing the grape with his molars and letting the juice sit on his tongue. He closed his eyes and inhaled deeply, focusing only on the flavor, tasting past the unripe bitterness. When he was done, he brushed his hands on his pants, and walked back to his wife and son.

Alice held the boy's hand as he pulled and tugged. "Well?" she asked.

Harvey sighed and nodded. "The vines are good, the soil is good, it is about 80 percent zin, so that's good. It would take a few years to get it moved over to biodynamic, but it's doable."

"So?"

"It's a risk, honey, a big risk, but it would be all ours." Harvey paused before adding, "And the bank's, of course." Harvey crouched down in front of the boy. "So what do you think, Scotty, should Mommy and Daddy buy their own vineyard?"

The boy stopped moving, kicked the ground as his face turned serious, and with a sharp nod of his head said, "Yes. Daddy is the best winemaker in the world."

Harvey rose to his feet blinking back tears. "Well dear, there we have it."

Alice took Harvey's hand as they started walking back. "What should we call it?" she asked.

"I was thinking 'The Zinnery.'"

Alice smiled and squeezed his hand. "You've been working on that name for a while, haven't you?"

"Years, my love. Years." Harvey jabbed the air with his

free hand and added, "Try this one for size: Get thee to the Zinnery!"

October, 2036

HARVEY APPROACHED THE SEDAN AND SAW HIS SON SITTING in the driver's seat. He opened the door and said, "Scoot over."

"Come on, Dad. I'm sixteen today." Harvey's frown deepened in answer. "Really? Today of all days you won't let me sit in the driver's seat? The car drives itself anyway, what does it matter?" Harvey continued to frown until his son sighed and moved over.

"Thank you, Scott."

The boy wrinkled his nose at his father in response. Looking around he added, "Where's Mom?"

"She's not coming," Harvey said with a sigh.

"Why not?"

"You know why. She doesn't approve." Harvey paused, carefully fastening his seat belt and waiting patiently until his son did the same. "Do you have a preference where we do this?" Harvey asked.

Scott shrugged his shoulders in response.

"Take us to the closest Death Machine," Harvey said to the car.

"I don't know why this is such a big deal for her," Scott said once they had left the long driveway and were rolling down a rural two-lane road with rows of grape vines on both sides.

"Look, kiddo, just let it be. I am taking heat by allowing this, not making you wait until you're twenty-one."

"But the machine was good for you and Mom. It got you

together; it got you me." He said this with a big grin and a flourish of his hands.

Harvey smiled. "It did, indeed, but it is a tough thing. Something you won't understand until you have that card in your hand."

"Personally, I am hoping to be a COMET like you and Mom. That would be cool. We can all meet our fate out in space someday."

HARVEY WATCHED AS HIS SON WALKED BOLDLY UP TO THE machine. It looked exactly like the ones he had used: a squat metal rectangle with a hole for your finger and a slot for the card to come out. They hadn't changed it once in the last twenty-two years. He saw his son hesitate with his index finger extended, hovering before the machine; and he was glad for it.

When it was done, the boy stood in front of him with his brow furrowed and his head shaking. The boy's hair was a little too long and a sandy brown. Harvey thought for a minute he was looking at himself when he got his own card. That is what he must have looked like when he saw the word COMET and could not fathom how it could be.

He gave his son a moment, waiting patiently. Scott stood there for what felt like hours, but it was only a minute. Harvey watched as he slowly turned the card around and presented it to his father: CANCER.

June, 2043

HARVEY AND ALICE STOOD OFF TO ONE SIDE AND WATCHED. A few guests had arrived and were milling about in small tight clumps; the florist was busy putting the finishing touches on the arbor; and the string quartet was tuning up their instruments.

"Our first wedding at the Zinnery," Alice said, "and it is our son's. How he has grown, how this place has grown."

Harvey took a deep breath, squeezing Alice's hand as he surveyed the vines that populated the rolling hills all around them. He was happy.

His peace was disturbed by a couple that walked close by in a hushed conversation.

"I don't know why she would pick him," the woman began. She was middle-aged with mousey hair and deep frown lines. "Even though he stands to inherit all of this, a girl like that can do better. He may be in remission, but with his card saying CANCER—"

The balding man nodded, wiping his forehead with a handkerchief. "Well," he said, "they are destined for tragedy, but at least we'll get some good wine out of the deal."

Harvey surged forward, a pinched look on his face. "Harvey..." Alice began as her grip slipped and he continued on.

"Excuse me," Harvey said to the man and woman. On his face was a sour smile. "You don't know me, but I'm the father of the groom."

"I... We..." the woman began, her checks blossoming red.

"I don't mean to be rude, but it is in your best interest if you leave."

"Leave?" the man asked. "We are close friends of the bride's father."

"And I am sure if he had heard what you just said, he would want to punch you just as much as I do. So, for both of our sakes, leave. You are not welcome here."

July, 2045

HARVEY TAPPED THE SCREEN, ENDING THE RINGING, AND looked at the image of his son. He frowned. Scott looked pale, with dark smudges sitting under his eyes. Harvey wanted to ask him how the chemo treatments were going, but he didn't. That is not what he called for, that is not what he needed. And what Scott needed was most important right now.

"How's Vanessa?" Harvey asked.

Scott's face brightened. "Big! Really big. She complains constantly about her swollen ankles, but she is doing good."

"And the baby? How is the pregnancy going—" Harvey began, cutting himself off. "Wait. Let me get your mom, she won't want to miss this." Harvey called for his wife before turning his attention back to his son.

"That's okay, Dad. Probably better she misses this part, I know how she feels about—"

"What happened, son?"

"There was a car, last made in the 1970s, called the Comet. Do you remember it?"

"Yeah, your grandfather had one; I think I have some pictures of him with it from when he was sixteen. He loved that car."

"Well, Ford is resurrecting the model."

Harvey was silent, his face frozen in a bland mask.

"What is it, dear?" Alice called.

"Nothing, honey," Harvey yelled back. "I found it, I was looking for the peanut butter." He turned back to his son and in a low voice said, "And?"

Scott nodded and sighed. "The machine is starting to spit out COMET like crazy."

"So it's about the car," Harvey said, his head bobbing in a nod. "So, we are going to die in a car crash." His lips pursed. "I can live with that."

"But it's strange, Dad. The statistics are bizarre. It is almost all newborns; a significant percentage of them are coming in with this death. Only a small percentage of the people are older. The total number of COMET predictions recently jumped from around 1,000 to over 100,000."

"What the hell?" Harvey said, biting his thumbnail. "You know your mother and I haven't discussed this since our wedding day."

"Well, Dad... It may be time."

August, 2045

HARVEY AND ALICE WALKED SLOWLY BETWEEN THE ROWS of vines. They would stop from time to time, to pick off a dead leaf, taste a grape, or re-tie a vine to its support wire. They were silent and went about the activity with the calm assurance of long years together, and long years with the vines.

The only sounds were the wind and the quiet whirring of the small robots that they passed. The "tenders," as Harvey called them, moved through the vines killing insects with small electrical shocks, while monitoring temperature, ground moisture and humidity.

They eventually made their way up a hill, the largest hill on their property, and sat together on a bench facing west. As they sat, their hands came together and they both let out a small sigh in unison. The hill afforded them a view of the ocean, some miles away, and, most importantly, the sunset.

Harvey pointed at the clouds that lay low on the horizon. "It looks like a good one."

Alice nodded, "What's on your mind, dear?"

"What?" Harvey asked, his hand leaving hers to brush at the stubble on his face.

"Oh, please. You have been brooding for weeks, just spit it out."

Harvey took a deep breath, "I promised you I wouldn't look again... It was just driving us nuts." Harvey could feel Alice studying his face, but he didn't turn. He kept his gaze locked on the ocean. Harvey took a deep breath, letting it out in a noisy sigh. "Scott told me last month, and I had to look."

Harvey felt her eyes leave him and he turned and looked at her. Her eyes were closed and he could tell they were darting under their lids. Her round face was blank, he couldn't read it. He turned his gaze back to the ocean and waited.

"Is it the car, the Comet?" she asked after a few minutes had passed.

He was surprised she knew, she wasn't much for the news. "No. That doesn't really worry me. It's the babies."

"Babies?"

"The COMET death count is up over 250,000, and skyrocketing; no death prediction has ever grown this fast. It is mostly newborns."

"And you think..."

"I think the Earth is going to be hit by a comet. I can come up with no other explanation."

"But... Wouldn't more people our age have that prediction then?" Alice asked. "If our generation is going to go that way, you think most of us would have it."

"You would think." Harvey looked at Alice, her blue eyes

seemed darker than usual, but he still couldn't read her expression. "Are you mad?"

Alice looked at him and shook her head. "No... No, I... I just don't want this to take over our lives."

"It won't, I promise." They were silent, watching the sun slowly lower itself to the ocean, the clouds lighting up with an electric orange glow. "I do have a theory though. I think it's the zin."

"The zin?"

"Yeah, I mean, who loves zin more than we do? We drink it all the time. Maybe we have found the fountain of youth. That's why we were the first COMETs. It won't happen until we're ancient, nicely preserved by zinfandel."

Alice laughed and wrapped her arm around his shoulders and kissed his neck. "That's my man, such a deep thinker."

January, 2046

HARVEY HELD HIS GRANDDAUGHTER, JESSICA, CRADLED in one arm while shielding the baby's head from the sun with his other hand. He gazed at her face and searched it for traces of his son. She was so young, only four months old, but he thought he could see him in her eyebrows. They had the sharp arch that Scott's had had.

The priest's words washed over him, he couldn't really hear them. He understood the words, he knew what the priest was saying, but there was no meaning. His heart could not hear.

He glanced to his left and looked at Alice. She wore a black dress with a black shawl. Her shoulders looked thin and frail; he had never really noticed that before. She wasn't crying, which was surprising. She just stood there, eyes vacant, staring straight ahead.

To his right was Vanessa. She too wore black. Her hand clutched Harvey's right bicep, digging in uncomfortably, but he didn't complain. She was weeping silently, the tears forming black rivulets as they eroded away her mascara.

His gaze returned to little Jessica. Alice and he had lost a son, Vanessa had lost a husband, but Jessica, she had lost a father. With this thought the tears Harvey had been long holding back began to flow.

October, 2046

"ALICE," HARVEY CALLED AS HE ENTERED THE HOUSE. He came in through the kitchen door, wiping the dirt off his boots on the floor mat. "Alice, where are you?" He moved from the kitchen into the living room. "I've been thinking. After we get this year's wine barreled, let's go to Europe. Let's go on a zinfandel tour of Europe."

Harvey found Alice sitting in the master bathroom on the floor, her head down. "Alice?" he asked. "Are you okay?" It was a dumb thing to ask, and he knew it. It just came out naturally. Of course she wasn't okay. He wasn't okay.

"Did you hear me, honey? Europe. Zinfandel tour." He chuckled, "And it will be business, we can write it off. Touring Europe, drinking zin. What could be better? This place doesn't need us like it used to." He watched her as he spoke, she hadn't moved. He squatted down in front of her and put his hand to her chin, gently pulling it up.

He saw what he was afraid he was going to see: eyes swollen from tears; grief heavy and full pulling at her face; and black smudges under her eyes. But there was something else, a look in her blue eyes that he hadn't seen before. What was it?

"Europe, dear, what do you think?"

Her eyes met briefly with his before traveling down to something in her lap. Harvey looked and saw it was a can of Comet cleanser.

"What?" he sputtered. "Were you trying to..." He couldn't complete the thought. He noticed flecks of white powder on her hands and her chin. "Did you? Alice, answer me, did you?"

Alice shook her head. "No... I tried, but I can't." Harvey watched as her eyes changed. They went from dull to fierce as silent tears began flowing down her cheeks. She took the can of Comet and hurled it against the wall, a cloud of white powder descending on them both.

"Alice," Harvey said, this time her name sounding like a plea.

"He's gone, Harvey, he's gone." She was on her feet now, her hands spread, palms up. "Fucking cancer took my boy."

Harvey took her into his arms, as he had time after time since their son's death. He didn't tell her it was going to be okay. He didn't say Scott was in a better place. He didn't pretend it wasn't hard, that it wasn't tearing him up inside too. He just held her and allowed her to talk, or cry, or scream. He prayed that someday it would be enough.

December, 2068

HARVEY PACED BACK AND FORTH DOWN THE HALLWAY. HIS hands clenching, his jaw grinding. This couldn't be happening, it couldn't. The comet wasn't here yet; it was still over fifty years out. The world had just come to grips with the reality of it... finally. Harvey had known since that day Scott called him and he had found out about the COMET Babies.

Scott. Gone twenty-two years. Maybe it was better for Scott not to be present for this; everything was changing. Some good, some bad.

Harvey ran his hands through his short grey hair and looked at them. They were old now, with swollen knuckles and age spots. He was old now. It seemed to have happened so fast.

He began pacing up and down the hallway again. He tried to imagine he was walking between rows of his vines; checking on them, tasting the young grapes, feeling the soil. He had machines to do this, but he had never been able to stop doing it himself. If he didn't feel the land, feel the air, how could he truly know the grapes he was going to turn into wine?

He came to a sudden stop when he noticed the man in front of him. He was about forty, with flat brown hair and tired brown eyes.

"How is she?" Harvey asked.

"She's stable," the doctor answered, "but her body is just worn out; there is not much more conventional medicine can do for her."

Harvey felt the pain in his stomach deepen; going from a gnawing annoyance to a deep ache. Then he parsed the sentence again. "What do you mean 'conventional'?"

"Well, sir. I know who you are. My wife and I love the Zinnery wines. There is something new, something experimental. It is very expensive, but it might help."

"WHAT?" ALICE ASKED FROM HER BED, HER VOICE WEAK, her face ashen.

"They call it Life Extension Treatments. It refers to a category of medical interventions, many experimental, all new, that reverses the effects of aging. The doctors think it will help."

"But why?" Alice asked, turning her eyes away from her husband as she continued. "Maybe seventy-five is old enough."

"It's not enough, Alice, it's not enough." Harvey pulled her chin up, diving into her blue eyes, and said, "It's not enough for me."

Alice smiled thinly. "You just want me to stay around for that damn comet of yours."

"Absolutely," Harvey replied with a big grin. "That is the one and only reason. It has nothing to do with your smile, or the way you hold my hand as we walk the vines, or our time sitting on our bench watching the sunset, or how your laugh always makes me feel warm inside, or—"

"Enough, dear. Enough," she said putting her hand to his check. "Enough, I get it. I get it."

Harvey's grin washed off his face and tears began flowing down his checks. "Don't leave me, Alice. Let's wait for the comet. Let's get the treatments—we'll both need them. Let's go together."

Alice patted at his tears. "Remember? Do you remember when you proposed to me, you were afraid I only wanted you because of our COMET cards? That I only wanted you because it seemed we would go together?"

Harvey nodded his head.

"Well?" she asked.

"Well, what?"

"Are you only doing this, wanting me to get these treatments, so you won't be alone?"

Harvey laughed and smiled. "Yes! Yes, that is it exactly. It has nothing to do with your luscious lips, or your shapely hips, or the way your body fits mine or—"

Alice pulled him close and silenced him by pressing her mouth against his.

June, 2117

HARVEY PACKED THE BASKET, HIS HANDS SHAKING. HE glanced at the screen on the refrigerator and saw the countdown clock: 3 hours, 32 minutes. He needed to keep moving, but he was torn.

"Continue excerpts," he said. He had sworn he wasn't going to do it anymore; not once, not twice, but three times now. He just couldn't stop.

The house system continued its recitation of the news headlines. "Riots break out in cities across the world. Major fires in Chicago, New York, Los Angeles, San Francisco, Rome, Tokyo, Moscow, Beijing, and Cairo."

Breathing deeply he pulled the last two bottles of wine from the wine refrigerator and safely tucked them into the basket.

"The President of the United States has issued a statement urging citizens to stay calm in this time of crisis. All colony ships are in the clear, out of the path of the comet."

Harvey went into the pantry and pulled out a small card table.

"Mars Colony is holding a vigil starting at the moment of impact. Religious leaders around the world are calling for a time of prayer."

Harvey walked to the door carrying the table and the basket and paused. This was it. He took a deep breath, opened the door, and left.

HARVEY STOPPED, PUTTING DOWN THE TABLE AND BASKET, and admired the view. Alice was sitting on the bench looking west, her brown hair braided and tied with a blue ribbon.

He smoothed his sandy hair and took a deep breath. The Life Extension Treatments had taken care of the grey hair and some of the bigger aches, but it hadn't made them young. They had been obscenely expensive, forcing them to sell pieces of their vineyard off. But they had gotten fifty more years—he couldn't complain.

He picked his things up, trotted in front of her, and with a flourish, put down the table and began unpacking the basket. Alice smiled but didn't say anything, her eyes following his swift hands.

Harvey put a red silk cloth on the table and pulled out the cheeses: smoked baby Gouda; Swiss; Muenster; and French brie. He took a bottle out of the basket and presented it to Alice. "The Zinnery's best, a 2115 Ancient Vine Zinfandel. It is called Zintastic, and I must say, madam, the best choice for the end of the world."

Alice smiled. "And what of the rest of the wine?"

"The shipments all made it. Everything, except for these two bottles, went to our best customers around the world," Harvey said, making a wide sweep with his hands. "Us Comets are toasting in the end with style."

Alice's brows furrowed, and her eyes turned down to the ground. "Scotty?" Harvey asked. She nodded. "We'll be seeing him soon."

"How do you know?" she asked.

Harvey smiled and paused. He discarded several replies: "Hey, I was right about the comet, so I'm right about this"; "The zin-master is master of all things"; and "A gypsy told me when I was a mere tyke." Instead he said, his smile disappearing, "Because I have to, Alice. Because I have to."

Alice nodded and said, "Well?"

Harvey looked at the half-opened bottle of wine and said, "Sorry, madam. I assure you I will be properly punished for my lack of customer service in due course." Harvey popped the cork and poured a small amount in a wine glass and handed it to her. "Is it to your liking, madam, or should I send for something else?"

Alice swirled the wine and took a sip, nodding her head. "This will do excellently. My compliments to the winemaker." She held her glass out and Harvey filled it. "You know, I hear he is quite handsome."

"Really?" Harvey said pouring himself a glass and sitting on the other side of the bench. "And smart?" Alice nodded, and Harvey slid closer. "And kind?" Alice nodded again, and Harvey slid still closer. "And fabulous in the sack?" he asked as his hips touched hers.

Alice laughed, and said, "Don't push it."

They were quiet for a time sipping their wine and nibbling on their cheese.

"One hundred thousand," Harvey said as he refilled their glasses.

"One hundred thousand?"

"Well almost—99,462 to be exact. That is how many people who didn't have COMET on their card have left the planet."

"Mars?"

Harvey nodded, "About a third on Mars; a third on generational ships heading for Scorpii and Chara; and the rest back behind the dark side of the Moon in wait, in case the Earth can sustain life after this is over. That doesn't count all those holed up in caves and mines all around the world."

"That's good," Alice said. "It would be horrible if nobody was going to survive."

"Yeah, it's amazing how something like a planet-killing comet can bring a world together. It's been a hell of a ride these last fifty years."

"A toast," Alice said, raising her glass. "To zinfandel, and love, and the end of the world."

Their glasses clinked. Harvey looked into her blue eyes and said, "You know, I brought a blanket. There is probably time for one more roll among the vines before our destiny arrives."

Alice's smile and nod was all the inspiration Harvey needed. They didn't see the comet coming.

BACKSTORY—COMET

THIS STORY WAS WRITTEN FOR AN ANTHOLOGY CALLED *Machine of Death*. All stories in it revolve around a machine that tells you how you will die but not when. Oh... and the machine is never wrong (maybe obscure, but never wrong).

The concept was so intriguing I had to take a shot. While the editors liked the story, they didn't end up taking it and I haven't had a home for it until putting together this collection.

So think about it. How would you live knowing how (but not when) you will die? It's a fantastic concept, and if you like the idea, go get the anthology.

In my story I wanted to explore two people (again in a long romantic relationship) with a fate not only they but much of the planet would share. And if you can't tell, at the time of writing this, I was really into zinfandel wine. I also reuse the life extension ideas from "The Turning Test Will be Televised," which appears later in this collection.

Robert J. McCarter

TIRESIAS ONE, TIRESIAS TWO

1: Spring

The night seems to last forever. Her seizures are followed by endless pacing, her eyes vacant, she frequently bumps into things. The man follows her inside, and outside—the full moon illuminates her unpredictable path. This is followed by another seizure, he holds her down and says things like "It's gonna be okay, baby," while tears stream down his face. She doesn't respond to his words or his presence. More pacing, more seizures until the morning finally comes.

THE YOUNG VETERINARIAN WATCHES THE MAN; HE IS sitting on a stool by the gleaming metal table with his black hair disheveled, his shoulders slumped, his eyes swollen, and his face streaked with tears. His right hand lies on the chest of the dog whose heart has long stopped beating. The man occasionally uses the thumb of his left hand and flicks the ring on his wedding finger. He came in alone.

He mumbles to the body before him things like: "It's okay T, I understand you had to leave"; "I'll be all right"; "You're such a good girl"; and "How can I do this without you?"

It is a holiday, and it is just the two of them in the office. The veterinarian thinks this is a gift, because he can give the man all the time he needs without the bustle of the office around him.

"Excuse me," the vet says.

"Yes?" the man replies, looking up, surprised to find someone else there.

"Can I call anyone for you? Your wife, perhaps?" the vet says, looking at the man's wedding ring.

"No... No one to call," the man mutters, holding his hand and looking at his wedding ring. "I still wear it even though she has been gone over six months now."

"I'm so sorry," is all the vet can think to say, it doesn't seem like enough—it never does.

The man's brow furrows, and the grief on his face deepens. "It was a car wreck. T here is the only thing that pulled me through. Sick as she was she seemed to understand. She never left my side. She became even more affectionate. I just don't know..." The man's voice trails off as the tears begin anew.

The vet leaves the room and comes back a few minutes later with a sterile package. Printed on the bottom is "Pet Renaissance, Inc."

"Excuse me, I really hate to bother you, but this might help," the vet says.

"What?" The man seems startled again.

"I don't normally do this... But, this might... This is

hard to say, so I'll just say it. There is a company called Pet Renaissance that is successfully cloning pets."

"Cloning?"

"Yes. You could have her back. Well, maybe not her, but an animal very much like her." The vet fidgets with the package. "Look, I don't normally recommend this, but maybe having another dog like her will help you through this time. You don't have to decide now, but I need your permission to draw some genetic material from her while it's still good."

"Good?" the man seems confused.

"Yes. While it's true you can get genetic material from hair years after, the odds of success are greatly increased if the right cells are harvested from the animal while alive... or... or shortly after death. There is no charge for this; the company will store the genetic material for free. This will give you a chance to think about it."

"A clone? A clone of T?"

"I'm so sorry to be pushing this right now. I just need your permission to draw the material. You can decide later whether to do it or not."

The man's face is a rapid-fire play of emotions: disgust; fear; grief; relief; hope—all jumbled together, one after the other.

"I just need you to sign here."

2: Two Weeks Later

I don't know, T, a clone. It won't be you, it can't be you. We are more than just our genes. But then again, maybe your personality will come through. It would mean so much to have the comfort of your presence again. A voice answers him: I am willing, Dad, you need me. The man says: I do, I know I do. I feel so weak. The voice again: Mama's gone, I'm gone; you need me. Trust me, Dad, this will help.

THE RECEPTIONIST HANDS THE URN OVER THE COUNTER to the man. She can tell he has lost weight, and he didn't have much to lose. "I'm sorry, but the doctor is in surgery right now," she says.

"But I need to talk with him," the man says, his face a plea. "He's the one that brought up this whole cloning thing! And now I can't get it out of my mind."

"He is scheduled to be in there for several more hours."

The man's face sets in grim determination. "I'll wait." He clutches the urn to his chest and walks out the door. She thinks she hears him mumble, "Come on, T" as he walks out and begins pacing back and forth in the parking lot.

As the hours pass, the receptionist sees the man pacing and mumbling, sometimes holding out the urn before him as if having a conversation with it.

THE YOUNG VETERINARIAN EMERGES FROM SURGERY. "Is he still here?" he asks the receptionist. She gestures out the window to the scene of the man holding the urn and pacing back and forth.

The vet goes out to him and says, "Sorry you had to wait so long."

"That's okay, it has given us some time to think," the man replies.

The vet is puzzled, but says, "What can I help you with?"

"I want to know how they do it."

"Do what?"

"How they clone. How would they clone T?"

"Well, it's pretty simple. The genetic material from T will be extracted from the cells we gathered. This will replace the DNA in a fertilized egg, and that egg will be implanted in another dog, where it will gestate and be birthed normally."

"That simple, huh?" the man says with more than a touch of sarcasm.

"Well, not really. The process of harvesting the DNA and using it to replace what is in the egg is very delicate, very complicated. But things have vastly improved since the days of Dolly. The odds of genetic errors are very small."

"Errors?" the man asks.

"There is risk, I won't pretend that there isn't—things do go wrong. But they have gotten much better at doing this and much better at catching the genetic errors at an early stage."

"Will it be her?" he asks.

"Now that's a question you need to ask of a priest or a philosopher, not a veterinarian. Genetically speaking she will be identical. She will look the same and have many of the same traits."

3: One Week Later

Okay, T, I'm trusting you on this one, you're the seer after all. The voice answers: It will be okay, Daddy, it will really be me. The man says: You have always looked out for me. The voice answers: Yes, Daddy, that's my job. The man says: Well, here we are, let's go in.

THE DOCTOR SITS ACROSS THE DESK FROM THE MAN, THE contracts laid between them. She sees in him the look she often sees in her clients, the grief, the sadness, the need. But something is a little different with him, a level of confidence that is usually missing. He is younger than most, his handsome features turned slightly sour from grief.

"Sign here, here, and here please," she instructs him.

"So I'm in debt to you for the next five years?" the man asks.

"Yes, sir."

"Kinda like buying a car."

"I know it is expensive, but I'm sure you will be happy with the results."

"I'm sure I will be too. Thank you."

4: Six Months Later

T! T, where are you? Why can't I hear you anymore? You've been there in my head ever since you passed, where did you go? I'm really scared; I don't think I can face this without you... T!?

THE DOCTOR LOOKS THROUGH THE TWO-WAY MIRROR AT the man. He is in one of their introduction rooms; it is small and quiet, furnished with only a few simple chairs. He is pacing and looks far more nervous than she remembers.

She picks up the newly weaned puppy in her gloved hands. The female puppy wriggles around trying to smell her, but of course, she can't. She takes her into the room, to the man, and hands her to him. "Here she is."

He takes her and the puppy catches his scent immediately and starts wagging her tail. She is a small brown wriggling bundle with white feet and a white tipped tail.

"Oh, my," is all the man says as his eyes widen and well up with tears.

The doctor sits and watches him play with the puppy. After a time he becomes aware of her presence. "She looks just like I remember her. T, come here."

"Yes, she would," the doctor answers.

"Why isn't she paying any attention to you?" the man asks.

"This jumpsuit, these gloves, they are treated so the animals can't smell their handlers. We don't want them bonding with anyone but their owners."

"Wow."

"So, what are you going to name her?" the doctor asks.

"Her name is T. She is the second T, so maybe T2, but that would be too awkward." The doctor's expression changes, subtly, the man catches it. "What's wrong? What aren't you telling me?" he asks.

"I'm sorry, it's no secret." The doctor pauses, she hates this part. "Sometimes there are genetic errors. One of the things we provide is that we can detect these errors early on, so the animals we produce can have a long and healthy life. Sometimes we catch them in-vitro, and sometimes shortly after they are born. This is not the first clone we created for you."

"Which one is she?" the man asks, the grief once again showing on his face.

"She is the third, which is why it has taken a while," the doctor answers.

"The third! What happened to the other two?"

"We abort them, or euthanize them, sir. They wouldn't live long; it is a kindness." She sees the man's face fall, his eyes grow distant and sad again. "Why do you call her

T? Does it stand for anything?" the doctor asks, trying to change the subject.

"Yes, it's short for Tiresias. Tiresias is from Greek mythology, given the gift of soothsaying by Zeus. He was blinded by the gods because he gave away their secrets to mortal men."

"He?" the doctor is puzzled.

"Yeah, I know it's silly. Tiresias is mentioned in an old rock song: 'I thought I heard Tiresias say; Life is never what it seems; And every man must meet his destiny.' I just love the sound of the word, you know, unusual. When the first T needed a home, she just ended up with that name. I shorted it to T, just to make it simple."

SOMETIME LATER AS THE DOCTOR WALKS THE MAN TO HIS car, she notices that his demeanor has changed, lightened. He talks to the puppy constantly.

"Thank you, sir," she says, shaking his hand. "I hope you and T have a long and happy life."

"You know, that reminds me," the man says to the doctor. "I never thought of it before, but it is said that Tiresias was exceptionally long lived, at least seven generations. Imagine that, T," the man is again talking to the puppy, "maybe I named you right!"

5: Six Months Later

Fall on the mountain, T, my favorite season; so crisp, so clean. The warm days numbered, and all the more precious. What's that, T, you want another walk today? It's been so long since you were a puppy, I sometimes forget. What's that, T? No, I'm not a puppy anymore, but I still need to walk.

IN THE FOREST, THE WOMAN SEES THE MAN. HE IS PLAYING with a puppy. He talks to the puppy, laughs, and rolls it on the pine needles. The woman's dog breaks free and runs toward the puppy and the man; she rushes after.

"It's okay, T, he just wants to say hello," the man is saying when the woman arrives.

"I'm so sorry, he just has a mind of his own," the woman apologizes.

"They all do. So what is this big fellow's name?" the man asks while petting the woman's dog, tousling his long black fur.

"Bear, Mr. Bear. Well, that and the fifty nicknames I have for him. And your puppy?"

"She is T, my little miracle," the man replies as he looks up and sees her for the first time, his gaze lingering on her wavy brown hair and her bright green eyes.

"Miracle?" the woman asks, intrigued.

T and Mr. Bear sniff each other. T finds that Bear is suitable for chewing practice. Bear finds that he rather likes being chewed by this young one. They settle down to being dogs together, enjoying the crispness of the day, the squirrels in the trees, the ravens calling overhead.

The man and the woman sit on a rock just off the trail and they speak of miracles and cloning; and of both the fragileness and preciousness of life; of old wounds and new hopes.

6: One Month Later

Oh, T, do you think she likes me? Do you think it's been long enough? It's just so confusing. What's that, T? Yeah I know, I'll just shut up; we'll enjoy the day.

THE TRAIL RUNS STEEP AND STEADY UP THE MOUNTAINSIDE, decorated by tall majestic fir trees, ferns that have gone brown, and the last wild flowers of the season. T and Mr. Bear sniff and play. They chase every squirrel they find with a bright enthusiasm, as if each one is the first that they have seen, as if everything depends on each chase. The man and the woman follow along after the dogs, packs on their backs—their faces hopeful, their hands occasionally brushing as they walk.

"Look at her, I still can't believe it," the man says.

"So, do you think she is the same dog?" the woman asks.

"Yes... No... I don't know," the man stammers. "She is so much the same animal, so many things the same." He pauses for a moment, taking a deep breath and says, "Yes, yes, I do think it is her."

"Why?" the woman asks.

"Well, here comes the weird part. I hope you don't turn and run when I tell you this," the man answers.

"Can't make any promises," the woman says with a smile that mocks her tone.

"T told me she would be the same if I cloned her."

"She told you?"

"Yeah, I know it is weird. Maybe I was crazy for a while. After my wife died and after T died I would hear her voice, or rather her essence, talking to me in my head. She told me it would be okay; she told me it would be her."

The woman continues walking in silence.

The man afraid, asks, "So, do you think I'm crazy?"

"Absolutely," the woman answers. "But in a good way. In the right way." She takes his hand squeezing it. Neither of them let go for quite some time as they continue up the trail.

7: Eleven Years Later, Spring

The night seems to last forever, a sense of déjà vu imbuing it: seizure, pacing; seizure, pacing; seizure, pacing; all under the full moon. Endless, excruciating, until morning finally comes.

THE VETERINARIAN LOOKS AT THE MAN; AGAIN HE SITS ON the same stool by the same gleaming metal table, his right hand over the heart of the dog, the thumb of the other hand fiddling with his wedding ring. The man is older now, his black hair shot with grey, but the same grief is on his face, the same tears stream down his cheeks.

"I wish they could stay longer," the man says to the vet.

"Me too," he agrees.

"She went sooner this time."

"I'm so sorry," the vet says; once again it doesn't seem like enough, he wishes he could say or do more. "Do you still have the number to Pet Renaissance?"

"I don't need it this time."

"No?" the vet asks.

"No, she can rest now. She deserves it."

The woman walks out of the restroom and over to the man. The grief lies heavy on her face too, her eyes are swollen, and her cheeks streaked with tears. She gently lays a hand on the man's shoulder. "Time to go, honey."

"Okay."

The man and the woman grasp hands and move towards the door. "If I didn't love her this much, I wouldn't feel so bad right now," the man says, looking back.

"True," the woman answers.

"They give us so much. If it wasn't for her, we wouldn't

have met. I don't know what would have become of me," the man says.

"Little Tiresias, she was our miracle."

BACKSTORY—TIRESIAS ONE, TIRESIAS TWO

THIS STORY SHOULDN'T BE HERE. I'M BREAKING ALL KINDS of "rules" by showing it out in public. You see, this is the very first short story I ever finished, and it is generally accepted that a writer's early work is horrible. And maybe this story is. But it is also a very important story to me.

One of the great benefits of writing is the cathartic release. I get to explore past traumas, get to look at things that scare me, get to exorcise my demons. This story taught that to me and contains the raw emotions of a very difficult experience—the passage of a beloved animal.

So why do this if it's "breaking the rules"? Well, because of that raw emotion. If I felt it when I wrote it, there is a decent chance you will feel it as you read it. And that, in my book, makes a story worth reading.

Stories of Life, Death,
and the Places in Between

Robert J. McCarter

THE TURING TEST WILL BE TELEVISED

Episode 1: Introductions

WALTER WAS AN OLD MAN, ONE OF THE OLDEST. HE DIDN'T look *old*, not in the classic sense, but he had the characteristically young/old *look* that is the result of many life extension treatments. His appearance was comprised of the telltale contradictions of a deeply wrinkled face, with oddly firm skin; healthy black hair coupled with ancient-looking eyes. His skin had a faint grey cast that indicated, to the educated eye, that he was due for more life extension treatments.

Walter sat in his chair in the small, elegant living room. He was the type of man whose chair was *his*. He felt attached to his chair, like a second skin, and felt wholly uncomfortable if anyone else sat there, even his wife (although she knew better). The leather worn by his hand and burnished with the oil from his skin; the deep indentations made by his body; the footrest's wooden handle worn and polished over the decades by use—his use; these all marked the chair, made the chair his. And this wasn't a modern self-adjusting ergonomic chair—no, not for Walter—this was a replica of a 20th century easy chair.

That chair sat in the middle of the room, next to an identical chair, the same in every way but worn over the decades by a different body (he loved that chair as he loved the body that used it, but it definitely was not *his* chair). They both faced the holo, a large empty concave space delineated by smooth, almost translucent, white walls studded with projection lenses. Each chair had a small table next to it, and there was little else in the room save for an extra chair off to the side and shelves filled with hardcover paper books and a few eclectic mementos (a shard of an asteroid, a model of the Apollo 11 Lunar Module, a chunk of rose quartz, and a statue of Saraswati carved from sandalwood).

"Come on, Cam, it's about to start," Walter called.

"Just a minute, dear, dinner is almost ready," Camille answered from the kitchen. "Why don't you put it on delay, and we can start it later."

"You know I like to watch the live feeds; besides, we can win prizes!"

"I won't be but a minute, dear, it's almost ready."

Walter settled back into *his* chair, controller in one hand, a pen in the other, and a paper notebook on his lap. He watched as nearly solid looking three-dimensional images coalesced before him, resolving into the form of a rather ordinary man standing next to a tall, statuesque woman. They were life-sized and looked more like real people than the holographic projections that they were. She was beautiful, perfect—too beautiful and too perfect for Walter's taste.

The man was speaking "...she can cook, she can clean..." As the man spoke, the projection before Walter changed to follow along with what the man was saying, "...and if you're stuck without a date for an important meet, nobody will ever know the difference."

"My old wrinkled ass!" Walter yelled at the image before him, waving his notebook. "Any moron can tell the difference!"

"It's not that wrinkled, dear," Camille called from the kitchen. "At least not the last time I looked!" Walter smiled.

The man and his "date" were at what looked like a dinner party. A graphic appeared floating before the image in the upper right-hand corner of the holo. It was an "X" with the word "Life" superimposed over it. The colors scintillated, and the logo spun. The projection changed again to just the man and the woman. "That's why we think it is so appropriate that X-Life is sponsoring this show," the man said. "All the artificials are supplied by X-Life, you will see our latest unit in—"

The sound stopped suddenly, except for a low hum. Walter had another device gripped in his hand. "What a bag of wind," he said.

"Won't that disqualify us?" Camille asked as she sat a tray of food on the table next to Walter's chair. She sat a second tray next to her own chair and sat down. Camille had the same *look* as Walter—wrinkled but healthy-looking skin with beautiful brown hair—but she lacked Walter's grey cast, and had an unmistakable bounce to her step.

"Disqualify us?" Walter asked.

"Yes, dear. We can't win anything for watching the live feed if the sound is muted; the holo knows."

"Ahh, you forgot," Walter said, straightening up and

looking proud of himself. "That's what I've been working on for the last few days. The damn holo isn't muted. I've done some reprogramming." At this he shook the device in his hand; it was round, about the size of his palm with a metal tip protruding from one end and a readout on its top. "I reprogrammed our old audio system to cancel the sound waves the holo is producing. It was a bit of a trick—the whole damn room is a speaker—but I think it turned out quite well. The holo doesn't know we can't hear it!"

"You love that gadget." Camille smiled and shook her head; her delight in his delight evident.

"Quite right," Walter said, taking a bite of his sandwich and continuing with a full mouth. "Latest model programmer you know. When I was young—"

"Yes, yes, dear. You had to program the hard way, by hand. Now that little thing does it for you."

"Thing! Thing! You call this a thing—"

"It's starting, Walter."

"Oh," Walter said, startled to see that indeed the show had started. Before him was a well-dressed man walking in front of a large window with a bleak grey landscape on the other side. Walter pressed the programmer's display and the audio resumed.

"...live from the Moon's only luxury resort, Tranquility, we are proud to bring you the 'The Big Hookup' sponsored by X-Life." The man made a sweeping gesture towards the window behind him, just as Earthrise began. The view switched to another room where a single woman stood, and then back to a wide shot of the host, where behind him stood a row of sixteen men. All of them were young and handsome—too young and too handsome for Walter. "Our lucky lady will be wooed and wowed by sixteen eligible bachelors, but what she doesn't know is that one of them is X-Life's new companion unit. That's right! An artificial so smart, so real, so lifelike that you can't tell the difference."

"X-Life! X-Life! I wouldn't let one of their units wipe my—"

"Walter!" Camille said, shocked by his outburst. "I know they used to be your competitor, but really."

"A competitor I could have handled, but these guys... They lied, cheated, copied from us, and stole their way to where they are. Josh is still fighting them off."

"Maybe we should watch something else," Camille tried to interject, but Walter was not listening.

"There is no way, *no way*, they have beaten us to this point. I've fallen a bit out of touch where Josh has taken Adam, but it just can't be possible."

On the holo the host was interviewing the woman, "... well, what I want most from a man is to feel protected, safe. You know. Handsome men are a dime a dozen, what I need is a faithful, honest man."

"Oh geez," Walter said, "I see what they are doing. They picked a real winner to do the choosing. I bet they profiled her, and spent a couple of man years doing extra programming on this unit, to make it perfect for just her. She's not smart enough to see it coming."

"Walter!"

"She's not, can't you see—she can't be. This is one whopping advertisement. She has to choose the X-Life unit. I bet there is a room full of nerds altering things in real time based on behind the scenes data. Too bad. If they played fair it would be a straight up Turing Test on live feed."

"Turing Test?" Camille asked.

"Turing Test. Haven't I explained this to you before? I'm

sure I must have." It was clear that Walter did not mind explaining it again. "Alan Turing, one of the fathers of computing, stipulated that a fair test of whether a computer had achieved intelligence was whether one of us conversing with it could tell whether it was a computer or not. The argument is still debated, but the way Turing first conceived of it—conversing over a computer terminal, purely with text—it's been done many times. But this... this is a whole 'nother kettle of fish. We talked about this at Adam lots of times when we were putting together our first artificials. Once a human can interact long term with an artificial and not be able to tell the difference... well, that's the holy grail of the industry, the true Turing Test."

The holo was showing the usual intro footage of all the contestants, but it was clear that Walter wasn't really paying attention any more. He was scribbling in his notebook with a faraway look on his face.

Episode 2: Got 'em

WALTER SAT IN HIS CHAIR, AND A MAN STOOD BEFORE HIM on the holo, his life-size appearance almost real. He looked middle-aged with a medium build and brown hair. Behind him was a timer counting down in front of a rotating X-Life logo.

"So, Pop, how's Mom doing?" the man asked.

"Josh, she is just fine," Walter said. "Why do you keep asking? Still worried about her last extension treatment?"

"I am," he looked uncomfortable. "You know both of you are coming to the end of what life extension technology can do. She's a bit older than you and her last treatment was tough, I just want to keep tabs on her."

"Well give it a rest! I am keeping an eye on her. Don't you think I'm worried too?" He trailed off, his face going slack, and despite the life extension treatments he looked old, really old.

"Dad?"

"We've talked about this, Josh, your mom is done, and just one more treatment for me. We want to make it to our 150th anniversary, do something big, something crazy. The extensions are running out, the money is almost gone. Damn bastards at LET have taken every cent I own!"

The timer behind Josh shifted from a cool blue towards red as it reached 1:59 and continued to count down. Seeing this, Walter's demeanor changed and he said, "Gotta go soon, Josh. 'The Big Hookup' is about to start."

"You gotta be kidding me, Dad. X-Life is behind that!"

"Just keeping an eye on the competition for you—their new unit is better than I thought." Walter waved his notebook at Josh, which contained a series of terse notes.

"Do you know which one it is yet?" Josh asked.

"There have only been a couple shows so far, I am narrowing it down, I'll know soon. You should see the bimbo they—"

"Walter!" Camille shouted from the kitchen. Josh smiled.

"Excuse me. Low intelligence, self-absorbed, modded female," he corrected himself speaking louder for emphasis, "that they have at the center of this charade! I guarantee you the artificial will be chosen in the end. Josh, are you and the boys at Adam worried?"

"No," Josh replied with a slight upturn of his lips.

"You've got something, don't you?"

"You know I can't comment, Dad. I—"

"Yeah, yeah..." Walter said. "I have cashed in so much of my Adam stock to pay the LET leaches I don't rate anymore."

Josh looked puzzled. "But you always said—"

"—that I would spend a month in hell for another decade with your mom," Walter said. "Still would. And that's what life extension treatments are: a month in hell." Walter paused briefly before continuing, "So back to Adam, let me ask you this: is it big?"

Josh didn't answer, he just nodded slightly. Walter smiled, then saw the X-Life timer approaching zero.

"Time to go, son. They got some good prizes for live feed viewers." Josh's image faded. "Camille, it's time!" Walter shouted towards the kitchen.

CAMILLE AND WALTER WATCHED AS THE CAST LIST PLAYED on the holo with head shots of each of them followed by action montages. There was text below this with their names and professions: "Stephen: Investor," "Daruka: Citizen," "Tom: Student," "Alex: Citizen."

Walter snorted, muted the holo with his programmer, and said, "*Citizen*, that's just a nice way of saying lazy!"

"Walter!"

"It is. All these 'Citizens' don't work, have never worked, and just live off the dole. People should create, they should contribute."

"How can you say that, Walter? You bear some responsibility for this circumstance."

"Me?" Walter asked.

"Yes you. You helped create the artificials that put all but the highly educated out of work. What else could be done?"

"Still, they're lazy, they don't do anything," he countered.

"Really, so if you don't have a job, then you don't have value?" Camille asked with danger in her eyes.

Walter, recalling that Camille did not work for many years while she raised Josh, replied, "No, no, of course not. It's just that it's not natural to be retired from day one. Where is the work ethic? How can they learn to serve and contribute?"

"Well I think it's great. They can do whatever they want: volunteer, make art, write, learn about anything—be creative."

"But they can't be truly creative. You have to have constraints; if the whole world is laid before you and there is nothing you have to do, how do you choose? Limitations make you creative—juggling work and life forces you to prioritize."

"But, Walter, they are constrained," Camille said.

"Eh?"

"Living on the dole isn't exactly luxurious, you can't afford extensions—they don't have much time, Walter. What could be a greater constraint than that?"

Walter stared at Camille for a moment and then chuckled. "You have a point, love."

He un-muted the holo and returned his attention to the show. The blonde was strapped into a Moon buggy next to her date, a well-muscled, handsome, black-haired man. The man drove the vehicle at a rapid rate over the lunar surface, the vehicle frequently rising dramatically into the air due to the low lunar gravity. This went on for some time; the man driving confidently, the woman alternating between fear and giggles.

"Got 'em!" Walter exclaimed, making a fist and writing in his notebook.

"What?" Camille asked.

"Him," he said pointing to the man on the holo, "he's the artificial."

"How do you know?"

"I suspected, something is just a little off about his facial expressions, and he's too perfect for our little miss bim—" noticing Camille's expression, he trailed off. "Excuse me—for our intellectually challenged star—and his driving is just too good."

"His driving?"

"Yeah, he is driving like a machine, not like a man," Walter said, pointing at the holo again as if this was self-evident.

Camille was not convinced. "They have had close calls."

"Not really, those have been engineered to give 'Blondie,' can I call her that?" Camille nodded, Walter continued, "To give Blondie a little thrill, but not put her in actual danger. With the low gravity up there those things are hard to oper-ate; the vehicle weighs much less than it would here, but has the same mass. He's too good."

Episode 3: Dancing

IN FRONT OF THE HOLO WALTER DANCED WITH CAMILLE, a slow sure dance fed by long familiarity. Behind them, on the holo, a blonde woman in a formal gown danced with her suitors one at a time.

"Not fair," said Walter.

"What?" asked Camille.

"You are younger than I am now!"

"I am not. I'm a full eight years older."

"You know what I mean. You are fresh from your last

extension treatments, your body feels young. I am due soon, and I feel old."

Camille laughed; it was a delicate, graceful sound that illumined her face.

"Aren't we supposed to be old together?" he asked, extending his hand as Camille rotated underneath it.

"We are old, and we are together," Camille answered smiling.

"But I feel old, Cam." Walter stopped dancing. "Every decade they clean my genes, make my flesh supple, flush out the disease. They've done it—what?—ten times now, but I still feel old."

"I know," she answered, compassion on her face.

"Despite the treatments, I keep feeling older, I just—"

Camille put a finger to Walter's lips, and said, "Shut up, old man, and dance with me," a soft smile contradicting her demanding tone.

Walter hesitated for a moment, and then the cloud lifted from his face and he said, "Always, my love."

And they danced, slowly and surely, as those on the holo—younger, lighter, and faster, but less sure—danced behind them.

Episode 4: More Treatments

JOSH SAT NEXT TO WALTER IN FRONT OF THE HOLO AND said, "I've scheduled your next extension treatment, Dad."

"Last, you mean," Walter added.

"Dad. We talked about this; I am doing well and can help out."

"No! Damn monopoly. Those LET bastards have been bleeding me dry for the last century. I used to be a wealthy man like you, Josh. No. Save your money for you and your family, you're gonna need it."

"I would be happy to help, Dad."

Walter continued as if he hadn't heard. "And the politicians are all hooked on the extensions; they won't do a damn thing about it!"

Camille came in with three dinners as the show started. As the cast holos rolled by, Walter jabbed his finger at one and said, "That's him, son, that is the artificial. I would stake my reputation on it."

Josh said, "There is a pool at work; I gotta tell you he's not the favorite."

"Hogwash, that's him, I guarantee it! There is no way I wouldn't spot one."

AFTER THE SHOW, AT THE DOOR, WALTER ASKED, "So Josh, how much Adam stock will I have left after paying for this next extension?"

"Not much, Pop, just enough to keep you off the dole, and keep the lights on here."

Walter paused, watching Camille as she moved about the room clearing the remnants of dinner. "It was worth it. For her, it was worth it." Walter looked young for a moment; both men were silent as they watched her. After Camille glided into the kitchen, Walter asked, "So when is it scheduled?"

"The morning after that show of yours is over; I know how you are about these things."

"Thanks, Josh," Walter said as they embraced. "You're a good son."

Episode 5: Deception Revealed

"COME ON, CAMILLE!" WALTER SHOUTED FROM HIS CHAIR in front of the holo. "It's about to start, I need your warm body in here so we have a better chance of winning!"

Walter held the programmer in his hand and pressed a button on the readout, the sound from the holo muffled into near silence. In front of him ran an advert for Life Extension Technologies with the large face of an old-looking woman filling up the holo. Her wrinkles slowly filled, her skin tightened, her eyes brightened, and she smiled while 3D text appeared next to her face: "Completely Safe," "Proven Technology," "Treatments for Every Budget," "Available only from LET, Life Extension Technologies," "Press 'Call' on your holo controller now."

Walter was not paying attention; he rose from his chair and moved towards the kitchen.

"I'm coming, dear," Camille said as she came into the room with two plates of food, her face puzzled.

"Anything wrong?" Walter asked as he settled back into his chair, his attention on his wife.

"I..." Camille started. "I'm sure it's nothing. Let's just watch. I see your pick for the artificial is still in the running. What is his name?"

"Alex," Walter answered, his attention back on the holo. "It's Alex, no doubt about it now, that's the one." Walter pushed a button on his programmer, and the sound resumed.

"Only ten are left, who will Jane pick as her Big Hookup," the host began. "Brought to you by X-Life, the leader in home artificials, whose new, soon to be released companion unit is still in the running..."

"It's rigged!" Walter yelled at the holo, and then turned to Camille as her plate clattered to the floor.

Half standing, she turned towards Walter, confusion and fear in her eyes, "Walter! I... I... I..." Walter surged to his feet, his dishes crashing to the floor. Camille fell, her head twitching back and forth as she said, "I... I... I..."

Walter rushed to her side, his programmer still held in one hand while his other reached out and clasped Camille's hand, holding it tightly. "Nine one one!" he shouted; the holo went blank.

A voice asked, "Please state the nature of the emergency?"

"My wife has collapsed; we need a med unit here ASAP!"

"One moment..."

"One moment? What the hell!?" Walter looked down at Camille, her head still twitching, while she said "I... I... I..."

"Your call is being routed to another party," the holo said.

"What is wrong with you, we need a med unit now!"

Walter's programmer, still in his hand, beeped and text came up on the readout: "New programming target found: cannot interface, protocol unknown."

"What?"

"I... I... I..."

The holo resolved to reveal Josh's image.

"Dad!?"

"Josh! What's going on?"

"I... I... I..."

"Personnel have been dispatched, they'll be there soon," Josh said.

"Personnel? Personnel!? What is going on here? What the hell does this mean!?" Walter asked, holding up his programmer's readout to the holo.

"I... I... I..."

Josh blanched, the color draining from his face as he said in a flat tone, "Execute priority lockdown."

Several things happened at once: there was a clicking noise from the front door; red text appeared on the holo that said "Priority Lockdown;" and shutters rolled over the windows.

"Dad, just stay calm, I'll be right over," Josh said, and the holo went blank except for the red "Priority Lockdown" text.

"What?" Walter said. With tears streaming down his face, he looked from Camille to the programmer and back to Camille.

"I... I... I..." Camille continued, her head still twitching back and forth.

Revelation dawned on Walter's face; his expression changing from fear and confusion to terror. "You're a..."

"I... I... I..."

"Oh my God..."

"I... I... I..."

"You're an artificial!" Walter cried, dropping Camille's hand.

CAMILLE WAS GONE, THE BROKEN DISHES WERE GONE, but Walter still sat on the floor in the same spot, the programmer still clutched in his hand. Josh crouched next to him.

"Dad," Josh implored, his hand on Walter's shoulder.

Walter shrugged Josh's hand off, his mouth forming a circle as if to speak a question but no words came out.

"Listen to me, Dad, it was her idea."

Walter's brows furrowed deeply as he looked at Josh, tears flowing again.

"During her last extension, there were problems. You knew that. She was dying, Dad, Mom was dying!" Josh's pain was written on his face: his eyes tearing up; his mouth turned down; his forehead furrowed. "She didn't want me to tell you, she didn't know how to face it. How to face you. I sat with her for days and just talked. She just wanted me to talk to her... about anything... about everything... So I did. I just talked. Eventually I told her about where we are with our next round of artificials at Adam. She said, 'Do it to me, son.' I was shocked, I asked her why. She told me, 'For Walter. I don't want him to be alone, to die alone.' I tried to talk her out of it, but she would hear nothing of it. She wouldn't let me tell you what was going on."

Walter just sat there. Josh couldn't tell if he heard or not, until Walter looked up. His face was red, the fear and terror gone, and in its place was rage. He hurled his programmer at Josh, hitting him in the head, a growl escaping from him as he leaped up and tackled Josh, pinning him to the floor.

Walter's growl turned into a moan, and the moan turned into "No!" as his open hands struck Josh over and over.

Josh pulled a slim cylinder from his pocket and pressed it into Walter's hip. Walter quickly went limp and collapsed on top of him.

"I'm so sorry, Dad."

Episode 6: Darkness

WALTER WAS LYING IN A BED IN A SMALL, NEAT ROOM WITH clean white sheets tucked in around him. A small holo was embedded into the wall with "The Big Hookup" showing on it. Walter stared blankly at the screen. Josh sat beside him, his forehead bandaged.

"Alex is still in it. 'Blondie,' that's what you call her, right? Blondie hasn't given him the boot yet." Josh looked tired, stretched thin. "I think you are right, I think he is the one. I put some money down on him in the work pool. If you're right, I'll split the winnings with you."

"And don't forget," the host said, "one of our loyal live-feed viewers will win an all-expense paid trip for two to Tranquility, the only luxury resort on the Moon."

"Did you hear that, Dad? I checked the holo; it knows you're watching so you will get credit for this episode. You used to say that being a child of the Apollo era you always wanted to go to the Moon. Maybe this will be your chance."

The show continued, but Walter did not answer, did not move. Josh wasn't watching the show, he was watching his father. Occasionally he tried to engage him, but the results were the same: silence.

Episode 7: I Want to Go Home

WALTER AND JOSH WERE IN THE SMALL ROOM, WATCHING "The Big Hookup" on the holo. During a break in the show, an advert for LET played. It was the usual transformation from old age to youth and ended with the voice-over saying: "Do it for your loved ones. Do it for yourself."

Walter shifted in his bed, his face going from slack to tight, as if in pain.

"Dad?" Josh asked.

Walter looked over at Josh and their eyes locked. "She died without me. I wasn't there to hold her hand." He looked like he should be crying, but he wasn't. His face was tight and hard, his gaze steady—too steady.

"I'm..." Josh began.

"I should have been there," he croaked, his voice harsh and rough.

"Dad, I don't know..."

"I want to go home," Walter stated.

"I don't know, Dad. These are the first words you have said in two weeks."

"That doesn't matter. I want to go home."

"I don't think you are well enough... The doctors said..."

"I don't care. I want to go home. Now!" Walter smacked the sheets with his hands and struggled to push himself up in the bed.

"Dad, I need to make sure you're okay."

"Josh, I am not *okay*. I will never be *okay*. I am an old man. My wife is gone, my career is over, my money is gone, and the world I was born to is long gone." Walter paused and swallowed. "I have one thing left: my home."

Josh looked at him and sighed, his brow furrowing.

"Now, Josh. I want to go home now."

After another sigh, Josh said, "Okay. I will make the arrangements." He got up and left the room.

Walter turned his attention back to the holo. On it, Blondie and a sandy-haired man were playing what looked like golf under a large dome.

Episode 8: Grief

WALTER SAT IN HIS CHAIR IN FRONT OF THE HOLO AMIDST a profusion of clutter: empty food containers, wrappers, bottles, and other detritus lay about. "The Big Hookup" was playing, and the host was summing things up, "After ten weeks it's down to just seven suitors..."

Walter was watching, but he wasn't really listening. A call notification came up on the holo, it was Josh. Walter mumbled "Disregard," and the notification went away. He picked at his food, mostly moving it around. He wiped crumbs off his robe and patted absently at his greasy unkempt hair.

"Today's challenge will be Tango Lessons!" the host said. This got Walter's attention. Blondie seemed excited, the suitors seemed nervous.

Walter inhaled deeply and sat up as the show continued. An instructor was brought in to teach them how to do the tango in the Moon's lower gravity. The proper steps were demonstrated: a shuffling pace to "keep your feet on the ground," and ample acrobatic opportunities because of the participants' lower weight.

"Tango, as in all dance, is a metaphor for life," the instructor said.

Walter's breathing became rapid, his face started to redden.

"How you dance says a lot about how you live."

Walter began to hyperventilate.

"Do you lead, or do you follow?"

Walter leaped from his chair and let out a howl. He grabbed the contents from the small table next to his chair and hurled it at the holo, distorting the image.

"Do you work well as part of a team?"

He hurled the small table against the holo's wall, shattering it.

"Are you logical or sensual in your approach?"

He upended his chair and then Camille's. An alert

appeared on the holo, in front of the show: "Medical override: heart rate elevated, 160bpm. Emergency contact initiated."

"Can you appear vulnerable and still retain a sense of strength?" the dance instructor continued on the holo.

Everything near Walter was now upended or thrown. Tears streamed down his face, guttural sobs escaping his mouth. The show was replaced with a distorted image of Josh, his form bent and blurred by the objects in the holo tank.

"Dad!" Josh said.

Walter's rampage continued, his fists beating Camille's upended chair.

"Dad! Stop, Dad, you've got to stop!"

His fist penetrated the old leather, his hand coming out bloodied.

"Dad! Mom wouldn't want this for you."

Walter stopped, his face red, his chest heaving, and looked at the distorted image of Josh.

"Camille wouldn't want this for you."

"I don't think I knew her," Walter said.

"Of course you did."

"How could she do this to me? How could *you* do this to me?!" Walter cried, his palms striking his chest.

"Dad..."

"I can't believe it. You turned me into a beta site for Adam's latest unit. Were you monitoring?"

Josh paused and then answered, "Yes," his tone flat.

"Everything?" Walter asked, his face grave with concern.

"I'm sorry, Dad, this is what Mom wanted."

"Everything!?" Walter screamed.

"We had to know what was happening, how she was functioning," Josh admitted reluctantly.

"How 'it' was functioning, you mean." Walter practically spit the word "it" out.

Josh was speechless.

"Was there a funeral?" Walter asked.

"No. We kept it a secret from everyone."

"You are such a company man now, aren't you? Camille conveniently 'wanted' this for me, and Adam got itself a guinea pig!"

"I have an affidavit of her wishes on holo, Dad. This was her last wish."

"An affidavit! Good going, company man, way to cover your ass!" Walter said, his anger growing.

"Stop this. I know you are hurt. I can't even imagine how badly. But Mom wouldn't want this for you."

"She wouldn't, huh?" he said, his face bitter. "Well, she gave up her right to have a say in my life when she did this. She took the easy way out."

"What?" Josh asked.

"She didn't have to face it. Face me. Face it with me. How little you trusted me, both of you. I... You..." Walter stammered, paused and then said, "What little faith you had in me to cope with this."

Josh looked around, surveying the damage from his end, "But Dad, you are not coping."

Walter looked around too—Josh's statement could not be denied. He slumped onto the floor, his energy expended.

"I spent nearly 150 years with that woman; that beautiful, crazy, loving, demanding woman. The ruts are deep, son, so deep, a mile deep now by now. How can I go on without her?" His hands shook.

"We can get you help..." Josh said.

"To deal with this?" Walter cried, his hands sweeping out encompassing the mess.

"Yes. You are not the first person to go through something like this, we—"

"Are you telling me someone else out there has had their wife of over a century replaced by an artificial, only to discover it when the artificial malfunctions?" A crooked, twisting, grin spread across Walter's face.

"Well, no, that is not what I meant," Josh said, looking embarrassed.

"It's like one of those god damn science fiction books I spent most of my youth reading." Walter laughed; it was a manic laugh but infectious. It grew rumbling and echoing in the small room, Josh's frenzied laughter joining in over the holo.

When the laughter had run its course, Walter turned serious and said, "I have one question, Josh, and I need your word that no matter what it is you will tell me the truth."

"Dad, how can I—"

Walter held his hand up, cutting him off. "I need the truth, Josh, no questions asked. It's the least you can do."

"Okay," Josh agreed.

"Did 'it' know?" Again, Walter spit the word "it" out.

"What?" Josh asked.

"Did the Camille artificial know it was an artificial?"

"No," Josh said without hesitation.

Walter sighed and visibly relaxed. "Well... That is something, at least."

Episode 9: Good-bye Walter

ON THE HOLO WAS A PROJECTION OF CAMILLE IN A HOSPITAL bed, she was ashen, worn, and drawn. She sat up weakly and began to speak, "Walter. My dear, dear Walter." Walter stirred in his chair uncomfortably.

"If you are watching this, then things have gone wrong. I am dying, and once I do, Josh is going to imprint my brain patterns onto one of those new artificials. So... So, something must be wrong." Her dialog was stopped by a wracking cough.

"Either it didn't work or the unit has failed." She paused and swallowed with difficulty. "I am doing this for you. So long we have been together—so long. Do you remember the first time we danced? In that class? I thought you were so handsome and passionate; you liked my leotards, as I recall."

"Not your leotards, silly woman—*you* in your leotards," Walter corrected the image, his voice barely a whisper.

"Do you remember hiking with me in Zion, up the river into the narrows? The water so cold, we clung to the hiking sticks and to each other to make it up stream, but oh the sights! Do you remember our wedding, under the aspens with so many friends and family? Winters in the desert? Summers on the lake? So much, Walter, so much. So many memories crowded in here. So much we have seen and experienced together in this crazy, crazy world.

"You must be wondering why I did this, why I chose to die without you. I did this because Josh has an alternative. I would wish nothing more than to breathe my last breath with you by my side holding my hand. But more than that if I can save you this experience, if I can let you finish out your years with me, even an artificial me, then what can I choose?

"Can you forgive me, dear? Can you see?" Camille paused as if waiting for an answer. Walter sat frozen and silent in his chair.

"Nothing in the world matters more to me than you, Walter. Nothing! That is why I am doing this. And don't be too hard on Josh; I did more than twist his arm, much more. This way I can be... Well, a part of me, at least, can be there to hold your hand until the end." Camille paused, looked surprised, and continued, "Oh, but if you are watching this then it didn't work. Oh my! God, I hope this works." Camille coughed again; the cough was deep, long, and encompassing.

"Good-bye, Walter, I love you. Always remember that," Camille choked the words out.

The holo image faded, but Walter couldn't see it anymore, his tears were too numerous.

Episode 10: Are You Eating?

"THE BIG HOOKUP" PLAYED ON THE HOLO, BUT WALTER was not paying attention. He held a communicator in his hand and was talking to Josh.

The holo was muted, and on it a blonde woman and a sandy-haired man, both blindfolded, were feeding each other. They were getting more food on each other than in their mouths.

"Are you eating, Dad?" Josh asked.

"Of course I am; I have it tubed in, 'hot and nutritious,'" Walter answered.

"You need help, Dad."

"I am doing fine, Josh. Let it be."

"Then why are you talking to me on the handheld, why didn't you answer on the holo so I can see more than just you?"

"Everything is fine," Walter answered, but clearly it was not. The disorder around him had continued to grow, and Walter's appearance was disheveled and strained.

"It's not just that, Dad; I want you to talk to someone. I could send a unit over to help, so you could talk about Mom, about what happened."

"I don't need any damn shrink, I just need more time," Walter pleaded. "Besides, I don't want one of those things in here."

"Why is that? You helped create the first artificials, why don't you use them, not for the last fifty years, at least?"

"If you must know, I am not entirely comfortable with them. I know too much, I know what is going on under the hood. I just can't suspend disbelief—I keep thinking about what is going on with them, what could be made better, what works, what doesn't. It's like work."

"Dad, the artificials these days are amazing. Just because you understand the technology doesn't make it any less miraculous. In many ways they are the pinnacle of mankind's creation. They have relieved most people from the need to work—"

"I hate the dole!" Walter said, cutting him off. "A man should make his own way in the world, under his own power." He sighed. "This future is so far removed from the life I began. A hundred eighty years is a long time son—I was born in the 20th century, and it's now halfway through the 22nd—I just don't belong here."

"But you helped create this future."

"Just because you help create the future, doesn't mean that it's for you. Make no mistake, Josh, you are working for the future, the future is *not* working for you."

"Well... I have to either send in a unit or move you to a facility."

"No!" Walter spat.

"Dad, be reasonable."

"I'm an adult; you can't force this on me. I am the parent here, you can't tell me what to do," Walter said.

"Don't do this," Josh pleaded.

"I won't have it. Just leave me here; I will get by until my time comes."

"I can force this if I have to. There are clearly grounds for intervention. Please don't bring it to that."

Walter paused for a long moment, and then said, "I can't leave my home, son, that is asking too much. It is all I have left."

"Then a unit it is," Josh said, his face turning hard.

"I guess I have no choice..."

On the holo, Jane was blindfolded with Alex as they tried, mostly without success, to feed each other. Jane was visibly brighter and happier than with the previous suitors.

"Alex is still in the running, isn't he?" Josh asked, putting on a smile that was clearly strained.

"Yes," Walter answered begrudgingly; he knew Josh was trying to distract him.

"Looks like you called it; I have that money in the company pool based on your hunch—as I told you before, I'll split the take with you."

"Oh, that's generous," Walter said with a drawl.

"You are still watching, aren't you?"

"Yes, yes, of course I am. My dance card is pretty empty these days." Walter's face puckered in bitterness.

Josh paused, taking a deep breath, and said, "One last thing, Dad. I am sending Camille back. I will not compromise on this; it's either Camille or a facility, you choose. You have to trust me; this is for the best."

Walter's face froze in a complex mixture of fear, dread, and something akin to resignation. He grunted something unintelligible and broke the connection with Josh.

Episode 11: The Return

WALTER SAT IN FRONT OF THE HOLO; HE WAS UNSHAVEN and unkempt. The room had grown even messier, clothes and leftover food containers strewn about. "The Big Hookup" was playing on the holo. There was a knock on the door, Walter got up, but before he could get to the door, Camille, the artificial Camille, entered.

"Oh, it's you," he said, his voice flat as he sat back down.

"Josh said you would be expecting me..." she replied.

Walter sighed. "Yes."

As Walter watched the show, Camille picked up the trash, went into the kitchen, and came out some time later with two plates of food. She sat next to Walter; they ate and watched in silence until the show ended. They sat there for some time until Camille broke the silence. "It's down to Alex and three others. It's starting to look like you were right about who the artificial is."

Walter looked at Camille with a mixture of puzzlement and consternation.

"What is it, dear?"

"Don't call me that," Walter said, his face harsh.

"What?"

"Don't call me *dear*. You can't call me that. That is what Camille called me. You are not Camille. You can call me Walter."

"All right... *Walter*." She looked hurt.

"You do know, don't you?"

Camille looked briefly confused, and then said, "Yes, I know that I am an artificial."

"Good."

"But it is not that simple. I am also Camille."

"And you are also my new shrink!" Walter exclaimed.

"Walter..."

"I know, I know, it's part of the deal. You have been augmented with psychological data sets to calm me down."

"It's not like that, Walter," Camille began.

"Oh, it isn't?" Walter asked.

"It's for me as well as you."

"Come again?"

"That is part of what happened before. Part of me knew I was an artificial and could not reconcile that with Camille's imprint."

An advert for LET came on the holo and Walter quickly stabbed at the controller shutting the holo off. "Whatever. Don't try to be my shrink and don't try to talk me into any more extension treatments—that is not going to happen."

"Okay."

"And I suppose you are going to report everything back to Josh too?"

"No, I am not, just basic diagnostics."

"I'm tired. I'm going to bed," Walter said, getting up and leaving Camille sitting there alone.

Episode 12: I Believe

"WE ARE DOWN TO JANE'S FINAL THREE SUITORS. WHO will progress to the final round? This week on 'The Big Hookup,'" the host said from the holo.

"Walter, we need to talk," Camille said from her chair next to Walter.

"Eh?" Walter was startled. He was neat and clean, but his face hung heavy as if he had used up all the expressions his face had, and all that was left was a bland mask.

"Please do your mute trick, we need to talk."

Walter muted the holo, but didn't look at Camille; instead he stared at the programmer in his hand.

"This is hard for me too, Walter. Do you know why it worked, why I passed your *Turing Test*?" Camille asked, leaning closer to Walter.

Walter, shocked and surprised by the question, turned to her and said, "No, why?" Realizing her closeness, he leaned back.

"Because I believed it," she said.

"Believed what?" Walter asked.

"I believed that I am an 'I.' I believed that I was Camille. I still do believe I am Camille. I know the truth now, that I am an artificial organism, but I feel, and look, and think, and act like Camille." Camille stood and began pacing between Walter and the holo while she spoke. "Except I haven't been *myself*, have I? I have been holding back, giving you your space, but you know that your wife wouldn't do that for long, and neither will I."

Walter's demeanor changed from shock to intimidation as he shrank back into his chair.

"So here it is. I am Camille. That is the truth. My body

was created by man, but my memories, my essence is of the woman you love. That is the truth.

"You walk around here treating me like I am a machine, like I am your enemy, and I love you. I love you with every fiber of my being. I remember, Walter. I remember everything. I remember meeting you, making love to you for the first time, and marrying you. I remember living through the Great Crash when we were old, and didn't know if we would make it, and then gambling what was left of our retirement on those first life extensions, not knowing if it would work. And it did work; you started a new career, and we had the wonderful surprise of our son. We got to start a family at our age—it was revolutionary. And after Josh was grown, all the years when we traveled and played and just lived. All of it, Walter, I remember all of it. And... and I remember deciding to let Josh do this to me."

She paused, taking a deep breath. "I did this for *you*. I wanted to keep living for *you*. I was willing to become an artificial so that you could live out your life the way you wanted. So we could do it together. In our 150 years together I have only delivered a few ultimatums—not much mattered enough—but here is one." She stopped pacing and stood in front of Walter, not looking at him, she couldn't. "Either you get over this and start treating me like Camille, or this experiment will end and you will have to move into a facility."

"I... I don't know if I can." Walter's voice was low and thin. "I don't know how. I know you are not her."

"Do I *look* like her?" Camille asked, looking directly at Walter, her gaze hot and penetrating.

"Yes, but—" Walter stammered.

"Do I *act* like her?" Camille drove on.

"Yes, I—"

"Do I *feel* like her?"

"Yes, but—"

"No buts, Walter. I am Camille! I gave up something so precious to me to be here with you. I died without you! I have leapt across the void and landed in another body, a different body, to spend your last years with you."

"But Josh made you," he said. The words came out of him like a plea.

"Josh didn't make *me*, he made this body. That is it. All that was essentially me was created the old-fashioned way; it was just copied into a new vessel. This is a miracle, Walter, a miracle! If it helps, think of it as kind of reincarnation."

"I... I just don't know." Walter shrunk further back into his chair.

"Let me ask you this, what do you think will happen to me if this doesn't work out, if you don't accept me and have to be sent to a facility?"

"I'm not sure... I never thought about it," Walter answered.

"Well I have. Once you are in a facility, I will be of no use. This risk, this journey, will have been for naught, I will have to die again, this time unfinished and unfulfilled."

The color drained from Walter's face.

Camille's hands went to her hips as she stood directly in front of Walter. "It is either me, or a facility full of strangers. We either live out our lives together, or die alone. You choose, Walter." Camille turned and walked towards the kitchen, stopped at the entrance, and turned back to Walter. She was crying silently and smiling at the same time. "If you can't do it for yourself, do it for me, dear. It would mean so much."

Episode 13: I'm Trying

WALTER SAT IN BED NEXT TO CAMILLE. IN THE DARKNESS he whispered, "Camille... Camille... Wake up."

Camille stirred and mumbled, "What?"

"I need to say something, please just listen."

"Turn on the lights, I—" Camille said her voice groggy with sleep.

"No. No lights," Walter cut her off. "Just listen."

"Walter, what time is it? What's going on?"

"Please just listen. I need it to be dark to say this. I... I can't see you and say what I need to say."

"Okay," Camille agreed.

"I have been lying here for the longest time just thinking. Remembering mostly: the early days at Adam, being involved in starting a new industry, creating the first artificials. It was a crazy but magical time; being that creative, I really felt more alive than I ever have."

"I remember."

"And then I have been thinking about you, and I must say I don't know how Josh did it. Everything is too perfect: your skin tone—"

"Walter, please," Camille pleaded.

"No, let me. I am going somewhere with this I swear."

Camille sighed and reluctantly agreed, "Okay."

"The way you move, your perfectly human facial expressions, your personality, your body, the way you just woke up..." Walter paused and swallowed. "I have a confession to make."

"What is it, dear?"

Walter stiffened on hearing "dear," but made no comment and continued. "I don't know how they did it. I don't know how they made you."

"I'm sure Josh could—"

"No! Don't you understand? I don't know how you work. I mean, sure, I understand how the body was created—we were starting to get pretty good at that a few decades ago when I was still working. But your mind? I can guess—quantum circuitry simulating your exact neural patterns, with some very tricky interfacing to your mechanical and biological components—but it's only a guess, I don't know."

"I don't understand what you are getting at."

"This is going to be hard, because I am so curious; I have so many questions about you, questions that I long to have answered. It's just the way I am wired. We talked about this long ago; I don't like artificials in the home, it was always too much like work, I know too much. It is the same with you. If every time I look at you, and every time we interact I am imagining how you work, what it means, how to improve the next generation. I... I just couldn't live like that. For this to work, I have to forget."

"Forget?"

"Forget that you are an artificial and remember that you are Camille. Stop seeing the unit and start seeing the person. Companion units—and let's face it, that is what you are—work best when you forget what they are and interact with them as a human. Don't you see, I don't know how you work and that gives me a fighting chance to forget."

"What are you trying to tell me?"

"I am telling you I can't bear the thought of what is Camille in you being shut down, turned off. That terrifies me—any part of her dying again, I cannot live with that. Anything that is left of her is precious to me. I am telling you that I can try, that I want to try. Camille was my everything. I know it is cliché, but she completed me; I wasn't whole until we met. We were so lucky to have the kind of partnership that could survive and change and grow through everything we experienced. You are asking me to let it grow through another change. A big change, probably the biggest, but just the same as we did many times.

"But I don't expect this to be easy or quick, and you can't expect that either. With these hands," Walter said, holding up his hands in the dark before him, "I helped build the first of you, and now you want me to accept you as a peer... an equal... as my wife. Can't you see how hard that is?"

"Yes, I think I do."

Walter took a deep breath and asked, "Can you live with me, live with this, if it doesn't happen overnight?"

"I think so, yes, as long as you can live with me acting and *reacting* as your wife."

Walter sighed. "I could never disappoint Camille... err you... oh hell! I will try, but I am damn old, and I don't know if I can change quickly."

"Okay, Walter. It's okay."

"I will try... I am trying..."

Walter sat there in silence for hours more—listening to Camille breathe as she slept, marveling at her perfection, going over again and again what he knew, what he hoped, trying to see a way through.

Episode 14: Finale

"TONIGHT ON THE FINALE OF 'THE BIG HOOKUP' WATCH as Jane makes her final choice; will it be Alex, or will it be Tom? And then join us for our live reunion show, where we will reveal which of our suitors is X-Life's new companion unit. And one of our loyal live feed viewers will win an all-expense paid trip for two to Tranquility, the Moon's only luxury resort."

"It's gonna be Alex, I'm telling you," Walter stated.

"Why is that, Walter?" Camille asked.

"Because the artificial has to win!" Camille looked puzzled. "Because it is rigged," Walter continued.

"Rigged?"

"Yes, Cam, it is rigged. The entire thing is one big advertisement for X-Life. I guarantee you they were scrambling in the background the entire time making Alex the perfect match for our little miss bimbo."

"Walter, her name is Jane. No need to be so derogatory."

"Okay... Okay... Geez!"

"WELL, IT IS SO HARD TO CHOOSE," JANE SAID ON THE holo. "They are both such great guys... strong, and nice, and kind." She looked down at the platter before her and picked up the single rose and walked to her two remaining suitors. "Tom," she said, "you are a fabulous hookup and I would be so lucky to have you..." Tom looked hopeful for a moment. "But, Alex has won my heart!" She gave the rose to Alex and they embraced, kissing as Alex twirled her around with ease in the low lunar gravity.

Walter surged to his feet jumping up and down yelling, "I called it! I called it!" Camille leapt up too, and their hands clasped as they danced around the room briefly and embraced. Without thinking, their lips meet in a graceful, natural way for just a moment before Walter pulled back, a look of horror on his face.

"It's okay, Walter," Camille said.

"I... I... I..." Walter stammered, his hand touching his lips.

"It's okay to kiss me. I want you to kiss me." Tears began to form on Camille's face. "I *need* you to kiss me."

Walter stood there unmoving, his hand still on his lips.

"I need you to kiss me, Walter," she said as tears streamed down her face. "I am Camille. I know it doesn't feel real to you yet, but it is real to me."

"I can't. I am trying, I am really trying. I am sorry, I just can't."

"And now the moment of truth," the host began, "here on our live reunion show, you've heard about Jane and Alex and how their hookup went. Now we reveal which one of Jane's suitors was X-Life's latest companion unit, on sale starting now!"

There was a drumroll. "And the artificial is..." The holo showed a large image of Jane as well as smaller images of each of the sixteen men. "...And the artificial is Alex! The latest companion unit from X-Life has done it!" Jane looked shocked, Alex looked smug.

"I called it," Walter said. This time from his chair and quietly.

"Tell us, Jane," the host asked, "did you ever suspect that Alex was an artificial?"

"Why, no!" Jane answered. "He's so good at kissing!" At that her cheeks flushed red, and everyone on the holo laughed.

"That says it all, folks. Just press 'call' on your holo controller to talk live to an X-Life representative."

"You knew it, Walter," Camille said, "you knew all along!"

"Yup," Walter sighed. "I could sniff out the lousy X-Life unit, but couldn't see the one sitting next to me." He shook his head and smiled at Camille.

"And now one of our loyal live feed viewers will win an all-expense paid trip for two to Tranquility, the Moon's only luxury resort." The host smiled and continued, "You do, of course, need to be present to win. This offer is only available to our loyal viewers who have been with us for each and every live feed."

Walter turned to Camille. "You know, Cam, I always wanted to go to the Moon. I hope we win."

"I do too, dear," she replied, extending her hand to Walter.

Walter hesitated briefly, but then smiled warmly at Camille and took her hand. They sat there holding hands as the winner was announced.

Robert J. McCarter

BACKSTORY—THE TURING TEST WILL BE TELEVISED

THIS STORY GOES BACK TO 2003, THE SAME TIME I WROTE "Tiresias One, Tiresias Two." I outlined this story and wrote the first few episodes, but didn't finish it until late 2008.

So many things went into this one. My best friend had a brain tumor and I was left feeling vulnerable and wondering how I would deal with the death of those closest to me. I was watching one of those silly dating reality TV shows—not sure what got me into it, but this was the only one I watched. And I was reading Ursula Le Guin's collection of essays on fantasy and science fiction, *The Language of the Night*.

The book proved to be a catalyst for the combination of the other two elements. In it Le Guin talks about the power of sci-fi and fantasy to take the reader places they wouldn't normally go. I remembered this story and how it did exactly that in the way it looks at the grieving process. I sat down with some free time and wrote most of the rest of it in one five-hour sitting. It was one of the most amazing experiences of my life. The words just flew out of me with a white-hot heat and I was high from the experience.

In other words, this is the story that truly got me hooked on writing... And it's all Ursula Le Guin's fault.

CIRCULAR MAN

For Alan it's all circles. No straight lines, he hates straight lines. Just circles. Alan loves circles.

I should have known on our first date. He took me to this little Italian restaurant with red and white checkered tablecloths. After it was over, he took my hand and led me back through the kitchen and out the back door. He greeted the chef—a plump Sicilian man named Edward—by name and introduced me to him. At the time, I thought our strange exit was about introducing Edward to me. But that wasn't it. In one way, out another; he was forming a circle. Not a round, pretty circle, but a jagged loop as if drawn by the unsteady hand of a child.

When we became lovers he taught me circular breathing; visualizing the circle our inhales and exhales make as we take air in and out. I wrapped my legs around his hips putting him in the center of a circle formed by my body. "I love you, Alice," he whispered as he kissed my face.

Around and around he went. Sometimes he drove me nuts. When we got our first apartment together, it had to have two entrances and two ways into the parking lot. The place was too small to allow him to make his circles as he walked around the apartment, so he would walk down the hallway hugging the left side and walking back hugging the right. "It's not much of a circle," he would say with a sheepish grin, as if apologizing.

We got married in a circle; our family and loved ones forming the living hoop. We entered in the east and walked clockwise around the smiling faces of our people. Alan gripped my hand so tightly, his eyes glistening with tears. He was so delighted when the woman officiating our ceremony held up our wedding bands and talked about the symbology of our rings. Round. No beginning, no ending. Eternal. "Just like our love," he whispered to me.

When we built our house, it had an internal hallway that formed a square and went around all the rooms in the center of the house and connected them to all the rooms at the exterior of the house. Alan was so happy; it made it easy for him to make his circles. The neighborhood had several ways in, and our driveway was circular. All for Alan, my circular man.

Some people thought Alan was crazy. His need for his circles was compulsive, and sometimes maddening, but it was just the way he was. It wasn't a defect, it was an anomaly. Like the way some trees twist and bend, refusing to stand straight. Alan loves these kinds of trees. There is this one pine tree in the forest not far from here that is bent over and forms a bit of a saddle before turning straight up. "It's trying to make a circle," he once said as he sat in the bend swinging his legs.

Alan's birth was difficult; he was, in his words, "ripped from his mother's womb." He was a sickly child with allergies and a poor immune system until puberty hit. He spent a lot of time inside as a child and couldn't get enough of the outdoors as an adult. Another circle.

Given his birth, the way he died makes sense. Suddenly, without warning, without a chance to say goodbye.

Sudden cardiac arrest. One moment he was sitting, leaning on that old tree that was trying to make a circle—we are both far too old to climb trees now—the next he was on the ground and had left this world.

My Alan, he loves his circles. "Alice," he said to me a few months back, "Ebb and flow, wax and wane, it's all a circle. Life is the circle, and we are all an expression of that."

Today we gather in a circle to say goodbye to Alan. As we link our arms, we form our small circles into a larger circle. We stand on this round planet that travels around the sun in an elliptical orbit as we live the circular rhythms of our lives and our deaths.

In the little Italian restaurant one way, out another; into the house by the front door, out by the back; into this world with difficulty, out with ease; into my life slowly and gently, out in a blink. That's my Alan, my circular man.

BACKSTORY—CIRCULAR MAN

THIS WAS AN EXPERIMENTAL PIECE, TRYING TO PACK A LOT into eight hundred words. I was exploring and amplifying one of my own quirks (I will go out of my way to take a circular route) and how that can reverberate through a life. This vignette is couched as a eulogy and explores the question of how we will be remembered.

Stories of Life, Death, and the Places in Between

Robert J. McCarter

THE HELIUM EXIT STRATEGY

I CAN'T SNAP MY FINGERS ANYMORE. MY KNUCKLES AND joints always hurt, and they look like the gnarly knots on an old oak tree. A few months ago I could snap, it hurt like hell, but I could do it. Now I can't snap at all, I don't have the strength.

I take a bite of my lunch and tell my daughter about it. The food here tastes like paste, flat and lifeless. It does have an odor to it, but it's just pretending to smell like food. We sit in the institutional dining room of the facility I live in, the tables occupied by the grey-haired elderly.

The room is cheery enough with round tables covered in white tablecloths, big windows showing tall pine trees outside. Flagstaff, Arizona, at 7,000 feet elevation, is a hard place to be old, but my daughter is here, so I'm here.

She's good enough to listen and watch me demonstrate as my middle finger just silently slips off of my thumb. But she doesn't get it. "Why does it matter, Dad? Do you need to snap your fingers?"

Of course I don't need to snap my fingers. It's not about

that. It's about one more thing that has been taken away from me, one more thing I can't do, that will one day soon lead to me being unable to do something I'll need to do to stay alive.

But that is too hard to explain, especially with the paste of my lunch clogging my mouth, so I say, "I can't snap." I give her the *look*, trying to convey it that way.

She offers me a small smile and nods her head, her pale green eyes looking sad. "I get it, Dad. I can't run anymore, my knees just won't take it."

Well, that's something, but she still doesn't get it. At almost fifty she is aware that her body is starting to rebel against her, but in your seventies it's a different story. The rebellion is over, you've lost, and you await your execution.

"It's just a little thing," she continues, taking another bite of her food and pretending she likes it. "At least you're still alive."

I sigh and nod. I have to at least appear to agree with her on that. She'd freak out if she got a whiff of what I'm really thinking.

"At least I'm alive," I mumble in agreement.

My best friend here at the Home is Lenny Armbruster. He's short, squat, and round with a blunt, gravelly voice and a sharp sense of humor.

After my daughter left—having assuaged her guilt for the week and visited her old man—we did our usual debrief. We have found it important to discuss our family visits with each other, looking for any coming disasters. And no, this isn't paranoid. The older you get the more your family takes away from you. It's not a matter of if, but when.

I sit on the bed in his small rectangular room—single-sized bed, closet, bathroom with a shower, greyish carpet, and a window looking out onto the parking lot. Lenny sits in his recliner.

We pick the conversation apart and don't find anything of note. Since it's 11:30 we decide to head down to the dining hall for lunch.

"I can't snap anymore," I tell him as I grab my cane. He gets his walker, and we slowly get our bodies moving.

Lenny snorts, sounding kind of like a horse, and says, "That ain't nothing, Carl. I need a goddamn presidential decree to take a piss!"

WE'VE STILL GOT OUR MINDS, LENNY AND ME, WHICH IS more than I can say for most of the folks in this hellhole. They shuffle around (well, we all do that) like they're on autopilot or something. Up in the morning, get into the shower; down to breakfast; after breakfast off to an activity; lunch; another activity; dinner; the tube, and then bed. Interspersed are the meds and the checks from the care-givers.

And we do have minds, Lenny and I. He used to be a brain surgeon—no kidding—and I was an electrical engineer.

Lenny and I are in the dining room drinking too much coffee. Frankly, at this age, I think we would both enjoy something more potent than caffeine, but we just don't have the energy to go out and find it.

Where was I? Oh, yeah, we've still got our minds, Lenny and me, but just like the rest of our bodies there is some calcification going on. It takes longer to think things through, and a lot longer to say them.

But we're at the same speed, so neither one of us minds how long it takes.

"Carl, my friend," he says. "Helium is the answer." His faded blue eyes are glassy but intense. "We can tell them we want to throw a party."

He's referring to a reportedly painless method of suicide. If you cover your head in a bag and breathe helium you will suffocate, but it feels like you're breathing so your body doesn't freak out. It goes along quiet like. We've talked about this at least a hundred times.

It's like young people talking about their life after marriage, or middle-aged people talking about their life after retirement—we talk about how to escape the sinking Titanic of our bodies.

"But, what dreams may come?" I ask, feeling not the least bit self-conscious about quoting Shakespeare.

Lenny rubs his wrinkled face and says, "They're gonna come anyway, my friend."

I nod and sip my coffee. It's bitter and cheap, but at least it doesn't taste like paste. Since I've gone through the effort to put the cup to my lips, I inhale the scent as deeply as I can. This is what I live for: the smell of coffee and yammering with Lenny.

ONE PILL FOR MY HIGH BLOOD PRESSURE, ONE FOR MY high cholesterol, another for my poor thyroid, one so I can poop, another to deal with the side effects of one of the others, and a huge multi-vitamin.

I smile at Ana—she's one of the better ones. She's got

bleached-blonde hair and brown eyes with a smile worth coaxing out. She's recently divorced, the bum roughed her up. I could kill him for it. She's raising her boy, Alex, on her own, going to nursing school, and working at the Home. She's in her early thirties and has got dark circles under her eyes that never go away.

I take one pill at a time with a big swallow of water. I'm determined not to choke to death—that is not the way I want to go. And at this point in the game such precautions are very important.

"How's Alex?" I ask after the cholesterol pill.

A smile plays briefly on her lips. It's the telltale what-she-lives-for smile. Something few of us here at the Home have. "He's good," she says. "Just started second grade."

I nod and keep taking pills, searching my old brain for a joke I haven't told her before.

"How many software engineers does it take to screw in a light bulb?" I ask.

Her brow furrows and then relaxes. I marvel at how the wrinkles disappear so quickly, her young skin still elastic. "I have no idea, Carl, how many?"

"None! They won't do it, it's a hardware problem."

She rewards me with a real smile and a small laugh. I pop my last pill, that damn huge multi, and swallow it down. If it's going to kill me, I want the last thing I see to be Ana's smile.

HAVE YOU EVER SEEN PIRANHAS FEED? LIKE ON NATIONAL Geographic? Well that's what it's like when the bus from the Home lets us out at the Dollar Store, except in really slow motion. All these slow moving, white haired, on-their-last-leg seniors move in clutching their wallets or purses looking to load up on really cheap junk. Everything's a dollar. Makes it easy, don't even need to put your glasses on to see the prices.

Normally I would go in and watch the feeding frenzy, but Lenny and I are on a mission. He heads into the store in search of some duct tape and some large plastic bags. I have volunteered to take a hike in search of helium for our exit plan. It only makes sense—I can manage okay with a cane still but Lenny needs a walker.

I turn away from the Dollar Store and peer across the street to the strip mall. There's a PetSmart, a grocery store, a laundromat, a fancy-dancy clothing store, a cheap-ass clothing store, a Bed Bath and Beyond and...

I curse and bang my cane on the ground. There used to be a Party Store where the Bed Bath and Beyond is. I was going to make the hike (and believe me, crossing the street and walking across the large, busy parking lot all uphill would be kind of like climbing Everest at this point) and scope out how to get the helium.

Now that I think of it, the Party Store has been gone for years, but in my old brain it is still there.

I turn back, but don't have the heart to enjoy the feeding frenzy in the Dollar Store, so I wander into the little Pet Store. It's just a little mom and pop kind of a place that somehow survives with a PetSmart across the street.

There's a young man behind the counter. He's got a practiced slouch and a thick black beard. "How can I help you?" he asks.

I see a white puppy, all fur and skin and baby fat, in a cage. "I need a couple of tanks of helium," I tell him. I'm caught in this weird place between my disappointment about the Party Store being gone and my attraction towards the puppy, and I find myself telling the truth. I tap out a little rhythm with my hands on the counter—*bud-a-bump-bump*—to punctuate what I told him. Like the drummer would do when Johnny Carson told a good joke.

"Helium?" he asks, coming from behind the counter and walking to the cage. I shuffle over after him. He lifts the puppy out and holds it. "What for?" He probably figures I don't know what kind of store I'm in.

As my hand caresses the softness, I feel a pang of jealously for the pup. So young, so much potential, so soft, so flexible. I look up at the young man, my eyes locking on his brown. I'm in an ornery mood and want to see his reaction. "Me and my best friend want to use it to kill ourselves."

He blinks twice, but his eyes don't look away. He bites his lower lip and nods. "You'll need a big bag, some tape, and some valving to join the tanks up, too."

My hand freezes on the little white pup, whose soft tongue is licking my finger. How the hell does this kid know about this stuff?

"You sure you up for this?" he asks. "Will you be able to follow through?"

I shrug. "Only a fool would think they know the answer to that question."

He nods and smiles, like I passed some test or something. "Come back and see me next week. Bring your friend. We'll talk more." He takes the puppy and sets it back in the cage. He turns his back to me and walks through a door into the supply room.

I stand there still feeling the soft puppy fur wondering who the hell that guy is.

I POKE AT THE READING GLASSES WITH MY OVERLY LONG thumbnail, trying to scrape the little plastic sticker off. I can't get it.

I notice that my fingernails need to be clipped. I can't do that myself either, and I'll be damned if I'm going to remind anyone at the Home that they need clipping. It's too damn humiliating.

The glasses have a little piece of plastic on it that says "3.0." They are just cheap readers from the Dollar Store. I should have prescription glasses, but I keep losing them, so I buy these and they do well enough. The sticker is vexing me today because I finally noticed it there on my newest pair. I've been wearing them for a week. No one told me. No one offered to remove the damn thing. I've got my next oldest pair on, which is why I can see the sticker.

I've got my right hand holding the glasses down on the little laminate desk in my room, while I try to remove it with the nail on my left hand thumb.

I've gotten the edge up a couple of times, but that's it. I want to scream at the frustration of it, but I know they'll just give me a pill to calm me down. So I swallow it and keep stabbing at the little piece of plastic, silently cursing it.

Seems like this shouldn't be a big deal, right? Why don't I just go ask someone to do it for me? That's not the point. I wasn't always this way. I used to have a life. I used to run a small company. I used to get things done. I used to matter.

I'm late for breakfast, my stomach grumbling. I worry that someone will come and check on me before I get this done. I'm an engineer, for Christ's sake. I used to solve problems every single day. Nasty, difficult problems.

I look around my little room. A tiny bed, my little desk stacked with things I mean to read, but haven't gotten to.

A small fridge and a sink. A few pictures on the wall, my late wife, my daughter, my grandson. I rip open the drawer to the desk, searching for what, I don't know. I spot a little box of stick matches. That will do.

I chuckle, that kind of thing is contraband around here. They don't want the old folks having the ability to burn the place down.

I slide it open and stare. How to get one of those tiny matches out with my terrible hands. It's a similar problem to the one I already have. I don't have time for elegant, so I spill out a bunch on the table and close the matchbox up.

After sliding one of the matches to the edge of the desk I manage to get it between my thumb and forefinger. I then hold down the matchbox with my left hand and pull the match head against the rough stripe of the striking plate.

Nothing happens. I need more pressure and more speed. I am focused now, my whole world just trying to light a damn match. I try again and get the tiniest puff of smoke. I discard that match and switch to another and give it a couple of strokes. A little smoke, no fire, but I smell sulphur.

I do another match, and another, and another. My brow is beaded with sweat when I finally get a match lit. When the flame flares up all yellow with that halo of blue at the base, I feel so damn proud. With my crap hands I did something.

The smile fades from my face when I realize I don't remember why I wanted to light the match so much. My eyes search my desk and I see that readers with the damn sticker. I take the glasses in my left hand and hold them about an inch above the flame. The glass starts to darken and the damn plastic that says "3.0" puckers.

I blow the match out and easily scrape of the little piece

of plastic. My glasses are stained with black, but that is a problem I can deal with.

I get my cane and head down to breakfast, a shit-eating grin on my face. It's my best day in months. I did something.

My old heart is thumping against my ribcage, like some prisoner trying to escape his cell. I can't tell you how long it's been since I felt like that. I literally can't tell you because it's been years. The horde has descended on the Dollar Store and Lenny and I are standing in front of the pet store. The same store where the bearded young man offered to help us get our helium rig. The gear we need to exit this life on our own terms.

"He really offered to help?" Lenny asks, licking his lips, looking up at me. Lenny is the Jeff to my Mutt. And if you don't know who Mutt and Jeff are, go look it up. Suffice it to say that I am the tall and skinny one and Lenny is built like a fire plug.

"He did," I answer. My heart is still beating like crazy and it's not comfortable, but I like it. I feel more alive than I usually do, so I let the moment draw out. "My heart..." I mutter.

"Yeah," Lenny answers, his hand going to his chest. He must feel it too. "They won't be in there forever," he adds, referring to the feeding horde next door.

We shuffle our way into the store and my heart gives one more loud thump against my ribcage before resuming a more stately rhythm. The guy I talked to isn't there. Instead a sour-looking middle-aged woman stands behind the counter looking bored. She has poorly dyed red hair with about an inch of black and grey roots showing.

Lenny whispers something to me, but I ignore him and walk up to her. She looks me over and quickly files me in the "annoying senior" bin, knowing I'm not here to spend money. "Excuse me, ma'am," I say flashing her what is left of my charming smile. "There was a young man working here last week. Can you tell me when he'll be back?"

Her eyes are a faded brown that belong more in a seventy-year-old than a fifty-year-old. She levels that washed out gaze at me and narrows her eyes. "He doesn't work here anymore," she says. Her eyes linger on me for a moment more before sliding off to the one other customer in the shop. She moves from behind the counter towards the customer. It is clear she has dismissed me.

I look around the small store. Aisles of pet food. Cages with puppies and kittens. A couple aquariums with fish, and one with a snake in it. A linoleum floor some shade of grey, scratched and worn. A bulletin board at the back of the shop near the storeroom door.

I walk back there making a show of using my cane and how hard it is to move around. The lady glances at me and I smile at her. I want to make it clear that I won't be leaving quickly. I feel Lenny follow me, but he doesn't say anything.

The little bulletin board is overflowing with flyers, as if no one ever removes them, just adds them. It's a throwback, just like this store. The Internet has taken over this function, and big box retailers have taken over for stores like this. There are the lost pet ads, someone starting a rock band and looking for a drummer, and on and on. I'm about to turn back—our ride will be leaving soon—when I hear Lenny's breath catch. I look and he's pointing at the flyer for the rock band.

Wanted: A drummer (tall and handsome) and a bass

*player (short and stout) for the band Helios. We play old-time
rock. We plan to burn out, not fade away.*

At the bottom is a phone number.

"Helios," Lenny hisses. "Helium." I nod and yank the
flyer off of the board, my palms sweating, my mouth tasting
like ash. There's something weird about the flyer. It doesn't
have the row of all the phone numbers on the bottom for
you to rip off, only the one. It asks for a short person and a
tall one. I hadn't told the young man anything about Lenny.

Lenny and I quickly walk out and into the little bus for
the Home. I have that flyer clutched in my hand, my heart
banging against my ribs the whole way back.

MY FATHER HAD A THEORY ABOUT THE HUMAN BIOLOGICAL
platform (that's what he called it, he took just enough
biology in his training to be a chemist to be dangerous). He
said that the human body is designed to live for sixty years,
at the best. Just enough time to grow up, procreate, gain a
little wisdom, and then die.

So once you go past that sixty-year boundary, things just
start to break down. If it's not something quick like cancer,
it's something slow like dementia. If it's not that, it's the
slow crippling force of arthritis and the mental blunting of
senility. Your warranty has expired, something is going to
get you, no way out of it.

My father, he was such the optimist. He died at sixty-
three in a head-on collision—lucky bastard.

These thoughts flit through my mind for the millionth
time as I sip bad coffee and watch the breakfast crowd
shuffle and wheel in. The room smells like cheap syrup and
the morning light is shining in through the big south-facing

windows. I sit at a table that is rather affectionately called the village idiots. I know, that doesn't sound affectionate, but we all treat those with dementia well—we that don't have it are just so damn glad. The ones with serious memory issues had magically started eating together. I think since they *all* have trouble remembering and cogitating, it's easier on them to be together. No one expected them to remember what they had been talking about at the last meal.

Lenny and I have taken to eating there some. We can talk about our plans without a real worry about the word getting out. It's not like we come out and say what we are doing, but we can talk more openly around the demented.

My stomach growls. I haven't started eating. I sit there waiting for Lenny. He's late, real late... too late.

I down the bitter dregs of my coffee and leverage myself up with my cane. I make my way to the elevator, up to the third floor, down the hall, and stop in my tracks. In front of Lenny's room stands a crowd. Not just the usual canes and walkers, but caregivers and an administrator.

I quicken my pace, moving faster than I have all year, my cane thumping down with each step, my heart beating loudly. I search the crowd hoping to see a paramedic or a nurse. But I don't. Only residents and staff. That can only mean one thing. I feel tears sting my eyes and quicken my pace further.

Lenny. Short, round Lenny. My partner in crime. My friend.

As I approach his room, my fast pace gets the best of me, my right foot catching my cane, knocking it out of my hand. I go down, my old body colliding with the floor, a sharp cracking sound startling me as my head connects.

I lie there unable to move, smelling the musty, chemically carpet, tasting fear, my tears flowing freely.

I know Lenny is dead. Nothing else explains the crowd and its makeup.

I hear shouts and people talking, but the darkness claims me. As it rushes in, cold and empty, I pray that it takes me, that I won't wake up, that I will leave this world with my friend Lenny.

CHILDREN ARE ALL A DISAPPOINTMENT AND THEY ARE ALL a joy too. Two sides of the same coin. They can't, or rather shouldn't, be everything you want them to be, so there is always some disappointment. And the joy? Well, if you look for it, it's there. From the vague, like somehow you participated in the miracle of life, to the specific, like how my daughter often indulges my addiction to red hots.

I sat in my hospital bed chewing one slowly, letting the sweet cinnamon flavor burn my mouth. She has the oh-so-worried look on her tired face. It's a look, frankly, that puzzles me. Eyes all focused, brow a bit furrowed, lips turned down. Doesn't she know I'm going to die one of these days? And "one of these days" keeps getting closer and closer. I don't know, maybe my pending departure reminds her too much of her own mortality. At her age, fifty, one does become more in touch with the reality of it.

"So, spit it out, honey," I say after I swallow the red hot and pop another one in. I eat them like I did when I was a kid, slowly. I don't get them very often, so I let them last. Besides, they help distract me from the smell of cleaning fluid and death that permeates the hospital.

She blinks, her face relaxing a bit, her eyes briefly meeting mine before looking into her lap.

"I'm just worried about you, Dad."

"Well, just stop that, honey. I'm okay."

She meets my eyes again and her need hits me like a slap on the face. "You promise."

I nod and say, "I promise." I half mean it. On the one hand, I'm not sure I can execute the helium exit plan without Lenny, but then again, I'm not at all thrilled about letting nature take its course—nature being as cruel as it is.

LENNY'S FAMILY DID A NICE MEMORIAL SERVICE, I AM SURE, but I didn't go. The thought of it made me want to puke, and besides, it's not like I got an invitation. His whole family knows me, but not one thought to invite me. Sure, Lenny and I had only been tight for a year, but we had been "tight." Like two eight-year-old neighbor kids banging around the neighborhood trying to find the right mix of trouble to get into.

And I guess I see it. I remind them of the end of his life. Probably not what they want to think about.

The Home does its little memorial, though. They bring in a rabbi—not that Lenny was a practicing Jew or anything—and I do the eulogy.

My daughter comes by early, dressed in a black skirt and blouse. She looks nice, the black helps hide the extra pounds she keeps putting on. She ties my tie and makes sure my hair isn't flying all over the place. She, at least, understands what Lenny meant to me.

Ana comes by too and helps fuss over me. She's not even on shift. I feel so important. I feel so touched.

"Thank you, ladies," I say to them both with a little bow of my head. My eyes are all misted up and their eyes are in the same state.

From my recliner, I start to stand, attempting to leverage myself up with my cane, but my hands shake and I don't get very far.

"Do you want a wheelchair?" Ana asks, her lips turned down.

I shake my head. "I just need a moment alone. Can you two wait for me outside?"

I see my daughter look at Ana who gives her a tiny nod of her head. Can the old man be trusted to know what he is capable of, is the question passing between them. My eyes mist up even further when Ana's nod says to trust me.

After they go, I settle all the way into my big recliner until I am nestled back into the indentation my body has made into it. I've had this thing for ten years, long before I came to the Home. It's comforting.

I close my eyes and take a slow deep breath. I pretend that Lenny is there standing beside me. What would he say? "Get off your fat ass, you old geezer," flits through my mind and I chuckle.

"I'm mad at you, Lenny," I whisper.

"One of us had to go first," he whispers back in my mind.

"That wasn't the plan," I say out loud, using my anger to lever myself up and launch myself towards the door. "Together," I whisper, "we were going to hook up the helium and go together. I'm sick of everyone going before me. First Alice and now you."

My wife Alice died five years ago from cancer. Everyone asks me what variety, which you too might be wondering. I always look at them and say, "Does it matter?" The details of that story have no relevance now. Dead is dead and cancer is a bitch.

I make it out the door, and while the women look at me closely, they let me make my way down to the dining room under my own power. The suit feels strange and my hand shakes a bit, but I make it.

THE WEEKS AFTER LENNY DIES ARE REAL HARD. I FEEL this emptiness that only comes when someone that is a part of your day-to-day routine is gone. I keep thinking I am forgetting to do something. Everything feels wrong. I am depressed.

My daughter starts visiting twice a week instead of once. Ana comes around more and lingers longer than she needs to. But I barely notice. I shuffle through my routine, doing my best to bear the loss of Lenny.

I am no good at it.

It was worse when Alice died, but I was younger then, more capable of handling it. I start to doubt that I can survive here without Lenny. He made the place bearable. He gave me a reason to get up in the morning.

"You've got to figure this out, Carl," Ana says, the frown on her face deep. I look away, no thought of even trying to make her smile. She's got my evening meds. I don't want them. One to keep my cholesterol down, one to take the edge off the arthritis, one for my thyroid, one to keep my bowels moving, blah, blah, blah...

Is this my life? Taking pills to extend an existence I don't want anymore?

I take the handful of pills and pop them all in my mouth. They rattle around there, all bitter and biting. I take the water and swallow them down in one gulp. Ana looks at me, one eyebrow raised. She knows how I fear choking and always take the damn pills one at a time.

I feel an anger rising up in me like a volcano that's been quiet for too long. I wait until Ana has left my little room before I let it out. No need to scare the girl.

After she is gone I get up out of my recliner and start pacing, my cane thumping on the thin beige carpet. What have I got to live for? Shouldn't there be something to life? Without Lenny, how the hell am I to survive this damn place?

This is what passes for cardio for me, and I feel my breath coming quickly, my face flushing with blood. I pace back and forth in the small confines of my room. It's not much, but it's the only space here that is mine.

My path becomes a little erratic and I bump into my desk, hard. I curse and whack the cheap laminate and particle board with my cane. There is a satisfying thump, so I hit it again, and again.

As I do the tears finally start to flow. I got all misty for Lenny's memorial, but I didn't cry. I couldn't. But now, the tears run down my cheeks, hot and salty.

There are neat stacks of papers on the desk and a cup with pencils and pens. I take my cane and sweep them all off and watch as they scatter and fall to the floor. The papers twisting in the air, the pencils spinning and skittering, the chaos that I so hate somehow comforting.

I stand there panting from the exertion, looking at it all. Junk mail, endless paperwork from Medicare, a letter from the Veterans of Foreign Wars, cards from my birthday a month back, and the one odd flyer.

Wanted: A drummer (tall and handsome) and a bass

player (short and stout) for the band Helios. We play old-time rock. We plan to burn out, not fade away.

An ungraceful sob escapes my chest as I reach for the flyer. I clutch it and cry. I cry for Lenny, my friend gone. I cry for Alice and the years fighting the cancer that eventually took her. I cry for all that I have lost: my strength, my independence, my usefulness, my life.

I weep until I can't anymore and then I lie on the mess of papers on the floor and sleep.

I WAKE UP, MY MOUTH TASTING LIKE CARDBOARD, MY tongue dry as sandpaper. It's dark and I try to blink, but my eyes are crusted up and kind of glued shut. My hip and shoulder hurt where I've been lying on the hard floor and papers, not something a seventy-eight-year-old body ought to do. I groan and roll over, smelling the acrid smell of urine. Great, I pissed myself.

I think about what to do. If I am found in this state, it will mean nothing good for me. They'll call my daughter, they may move me to skilled nursing. I don't want that. But it's dark and I could hurt myself getting up. I have one of those life-line buttons hanging around my neck. I think about pushing it despite the consequences but decide not to.

I slowly lever myself to a sitting position and look around. I see the blue glow of my clock. It's 4:00 a.m. I take a few deep breaths trying to move my aching shoulder enough for it to ease up. Okay, clock is at the back of the room by the bed, the light switch is at the other end of the room. I can do this.

I feel around and find my cane and use it to stand up. I hear the crunch of papers under my feet. I use the cane kind of like one of those sticks blind people carry and slowly move myself over to the door and turn on the light switch.

I squint my eyes against the painful light and then survey the damage. Papers, magazines, and mail everywhere. Pencils strewn about, some scratches on the desk where I whacked it with my cane.

I take a deep breath and let it out slowly. They won't bring my meds until eight. I have four hours to clean myself and this mess up.

I am about to get to work when I notice that damn flyer for a drummer and a bassist lying in plain view. It must have slipped out of my hand as I slept. But there it is again, and I can't ignore it. Lenny may be gone, but maybe that doesn't mean I can't carry out our helium exit plan. I slowly bend over, pick up the paper, and put it in a drawer, resolving to call the number. I then slowly start to put my room back in order.

WHEN I CALL THE PHONE NUMBER ON THE HELIOS FLYER no one answers, but a message plays in the voice of that young man:

Looking for the band Helios? Well, you've found 'em, Pops. We still need a drummer so come on down to practice, okay?

It then gives an address and some dates and times.

I don't go right away. I'm sore from sleeping on the floor and the huge effort it took to clean my room up. I go about my day in a haze. Everyone gives me space, thinking it's all about Lenny. And it kind of is, but that isn't all of it.

After lunch the next day I call for the Old Farts Bus Line (they have some fancy name for it, but that is what it basically is—transportation for the old and otherwise diminished) and have them drop me off at the mall.

No, the band doesn't practice at the mall, but there are some new apartments about half a mile away, and I'm keeping up appearances. I don't want anyone wondering what I am doing. So after the bus is gone and out of site, I begin my hike.

Two thousand six hundred forty feet. Eight hundred eighty yards. Half a mile. Not far, right? Well, try it with a cane and a bad back and arthritis and almost eight decades on your old bones. A hike it is. I have my smartphone with me and have the address programmed in. It somehow helps to look at my progress that way. And yes, even though I am as old as the hills, I can use a smartphone. I was an engineer, remember? My issue isn't understanding how to use it but manual dexterity.

The Flagstaff Mall is in a mostly retail area—the presence of the apartments is a bit odd. I make my slow trudge and end up in front of one of them. I raise my hand to ring the doorbell and see that it is shaking. From the unusual exertion? Yes, but also from what I am considering doing.

I am not going to lecture you on the pros and cons of assisted suicide. I will say if you are one of those that don't think it's ever valid, get your head out of your ass, please. You'll be able to breathe better that way. And I won't make my own case, but you can judge things as you like from the story I present to you here.

The door opens and the bearded young man from the Pet Store is here. He smiles widely, and I am struck by how very white and even his teeth are.

"Right on time, Carl," he says. "The boys are all back in the living room. Come on."

He ushers me through the house, handing me a bottle of Gatorade. He also walks at my pace—an old, tired man who has just been on the longest walk he's been on in months—which is to say, very slowly. He doesn't look awkward, like he is holding back for me. His slow pace looks perfectly natural, perfectly at ease. As we take the walk I feel tension melting and breathe deeply, feeling something I haven't felt in a while—peace.

In the living room are two other old men. One has a bass guitar, the other looks like lead guitar, and there is a drum kit set up behind them. Emblazoned on the bass drum is a fiery logo that says "Helios."

I stand there blinking while my escort makes introductions, but I don't hear them. I don't know what I expected, but it isn't this. I thought maybe it would be some kind of old person's euthanasia group, not a real band. I look at the young man, he's smiling with those beautiful teeth, and I smell roses. The other two guys are smiling too. Not like they just met me for the first time, but like this is some long overdue reunion. The smiles are big and genuine. As if they've been waiting for me.

My hand goes weak and my cane falls softly to the thick carpet. I can't hear anything now, although I see mouths moving and concern blossoming on their faces. My vision wavers and my knees buckle. The last thing I am aware of is strong hands catching me and the scent of roses.

My last thought is: *Oh shit! I'm dying.*

HOW CAN YOU WANT TO DIE AND THEN BE AFRAID WHEN you think it's happening? Simple. All it takes is being human. We are often conflicted. And besides, there is a big difference between an intellectual concept and the experience of that concept.

But I'm not dying. I'm just old and dehydrated and have been through a lot.

I wake to the scent of roses and hear soft talking. I feel a bed under me and see a white ceiling above.

"There you are," the young man says.

"You... you smell like roses," I tell him. He does, and it is not unpleasant, but it is a bit odd.

He nods. "Yeah, it's my girlfriend's perfume. She used a bit much this morning before she left."

I nod back to him, glad to be talking about something mundane. Not something life or death.

"You feeling better?" he asks.

"I think so. But..." His brown eyes don't waver but stay locked with mine. They look like they have this unfathomable depth behind them, like he knows what I am going through. Like I don't have to hide from him. Like I can trust him.

"I know," he says with a sigh. "You weren't expecting a real band. What did you think? I'd have the tanks set up ready to send you on your way?" He ends with a smile showing off his perfect teeth again.

"I don't know... I..."

"Listen, Carl, I know you have questions. And we'll get to them. But for now, how about I take you out to meet the boys. They're worried about you. After that, maybe you can bang on the drums for us a bit."

I blink a few times, like I am thinking this situation will change if I just close my eyes and open them again. But it doesn't. I'm still staring into the face of the young man with a beard.

"I don't even know your name," I say.

"My name is Angelo."

I COULDN'T SPEAK WHEN ANGELO FIRST TOLD ME HIS NAME. I mean, how dumb did I have to be to not know Angelo means Angel. That this guy seemed to know stuff. That he seemed to be going out of his way to interact with me. That he knew things about me, like my name. I had never told him my name.

"Carl," he began when we made it back into the living room. "On bass, this is Herb." Herb extends his hand to me and we shake. He has good hands—no oak knots for knuckles—covered in age spots. He's short, a little taller than Lenny, with a wisp of white hair around his bald head. He looks familiar and I soon find out that he lives at the Home too. I feel a stab of grief, wondering whether Angelo had wanted Lenny for the bass player with that flyer.

"Nice to meet you, Herb," I say after the shake.

"Yeah, thanks. Welcome aboard, we really need a drummer."

I am about to object, but Angelo is introducing the guitarist. "On lead guitar, this is Brian. At sixty-nine, he's the baby of the group."

Brian is shorter than me but taller than Herb. He's got a ruddy complexion and a few strands of brown mingling with his thick grey hair. We shake hands and exchange a few words about the weather.

"Shall we get down to it?" Herb asks. He looks at me and adds, "Can you do a 4/4 beat for us? We don't get too fancy with the music."

"I... What?" I mumble as Angelo guides me to the drum

kit and onto the stool. It's been almost sixty years since I did any drumming. It was a brief teenage dream to be a rock star.

Before I know it, drumsticks are in my hands, and I see Angelo smiling at me. It's a look I am not used to. It's a look that says, *I believe in you. You can do this.* At this stage of the journey, I haven't experienced that in a long, long time. Everyone expects my life to get smaller, my capabilities to diminish. No one has encouraged me to try something new (or very old, in this case) in decades.

"But, my hands," I say. "They barely work. They hurt all the time. I... I can't snap anymore."

Angelo listens carefully to me and nods. I see tears form in his eyes. "I know, Carl. I know it's not going to be easy, that there will be some pain. But I promise you this. If you do it, it will be worth it, and it will get easier."

Herb and Brian are watching, but it doesn't make me feel self-conscious. These guys know what I am talking about.

"Can't snap," Herb says. "Oh, that's a bitch. You're a rhythm guy, for Christ's sake. You gotta be able to snap."

I swear I almost lost it right there. I am not used to being related to. To being understood.

"Just try, Carl. Will you?" Brian says. "We need you."

I look up and meet first Brian's eyes and then Herb's. They need me? No one has said they needed me since my wife died. Lenny, he needed me, just like I needed him, but he's gone. But here are two strangers and this young man that smells like roses telling me that I'm needed, that they understand what I am going through.

I have such doubts. A sea of them that I could just drown in. For once I am not thinking of death by helium.

I am worried that I can't do what these guys need. But, I'll be damned if I'm not going to try.

"Okay," I say, barely above a whisper, but Angelo steps back and Herb and Brian put their hands on their guitars.

I get my right foot on the pedal for the bass drum and start the beat. Herb joins in, matching the rhythm on the bass, a smile spreading on his lips, and he nods at me. It's not much. A three-year-old could do it, but it's something. It feels good.

I fiddle with the sticks, working out a loose grip that my hands will support and start on it. The bass drum on beats one and three, the snare on beats two and four. I don't even fool with the hi-hat or the toms. I just work on keeping a beat. One... two... three... four...

Herb starts working the bass line, playing around the beat I've laid down, adding texture and variation.

Brian starts riffing on his guitar in the key of C. Nothing I recognize, but unmistakable rock chords.

My hands, they hurt a lot. But I don't give a shit. I have a big grin on my face and keep the rhythm going. After a few minutes, Herb gives me a nod and I finish it up with a few bangs on the toms and some simple cymbal work.

When it's over Angelo is clapping and I'm smiling so wide I'm afraid my face will break.

"You seem happy today," Ana says as she delivers my morning meds. She looks beat, her face drawn and tired.

"Indeed, my dear. I've got band practice today."

She stops, cocks her head and looks at me. I know that look, it's the "Is he still all there" look. I hate seeing that look on her face, but I don't let it get me down.

"A rock and roll band," I add. "I'm the drummer."

"That's great, Carl," she says, but I can tell she doesn't believe me. And I can't really blame her. I hardly believe it myself. A seventy-eight-year-old arthritic man living at the Home in a rock and roll band. Yeah, I get how it's hard to believe.

As she's leaving I say, "Ana. We'll be doing a gig sometime next month. Will you come?"

She turns and smiles. "Sure, Carl. Sure."

So HERE IS WHAT A TYPICAL PRACTICE DAY IS LIKE FOR our little geriatric trio. I get up a little early and take a shower. I have to arrange it the night before so the caregiver can show up at my room on time. I'm not to the stage where I can't take a shower alone, but I am at the stage where someone needs to be in the room because I'm a fall risk. I hate it, I do, but not nearly as much as I'm going to hate it when I can't shower myself.

After the shower, I get down and have breakfast with the first round of eaters. I usually sit with the village idiots. Since starting in the band, I like sitting with them even more. Somehow I don't mind hearing the same stories over and over or answering the same questions. Besides, it's fun to tell them I'm in a band and see their reactions fresh.

After breakfast, I go back upstairs and get in my recliner and close my eyes. I set an alarm on my iPad (the controls are big enough for me to work pretty well) in case I fall asleep. Practice day is a big deal. I want to go with all the energy I can muster.

At 10:15 I go down to the lobby of the Home and sign out. They've got to know where I am twenty-four-seven. I then go outside and sit on the bench in front of the curved driveway. Herb usually shows up a few minutes later. At 10:30 Brian shows up in his ancient Ford Taurus and picks us up. He's the young one, he still drives, although not very fast. We make our way across town to Angelo's house.

When we get there, Angelo's got the coffee ready, and we chat about mundane things until about 11:00. We practice for around two hours and then have some sandwiches for lunch.

I get back to the Home around 2:00 p.m. I'm exhausted and go to my room and nap until dinner.

We practice Monday, Wednesday, and Friday. I miss Lenny bad and wish he'd gotten to be a part of this, because it's just heaven. Well, not all the time. Just like everything in life, sometimes it's horrible.

IN OUR SECOND WEEK OF PRACTICE I LOSE IT. THIS IS NOT some gentlemanly fit or mild disturbance, this is a full-on nuclear meltdown.

My hands won't obey me. I keep dropping the sticks. Angelo comes and picks them up for me each time because it would take too damn long for me to get them myself. He seems apologetic each time he returns them, so I think he gets it. I want to pick up the stick myself, but I understand the need. But more than that I just want my hands to work.

Before the band, I'd have days like this, but it really didn't matter. I would just wait it out knowing, of course, that one day all my days would be bad hand days.

But now, I'm relying on my hands, my band mates are relying on my hands. The sixth time I drop the sticks is when I melt down. If I had been young, I would have done something stupid like putting my foot through one of the drums, but being a septuagenarian that isn't possible. So at first I just sit there unmoving, each joint on fire with pain. And then I literally get tunnel vision, I'm so mad. I then get up and walk out of the house without my cane cursing all the way.

Maybe you are old enough to understand this, maybe not, but at my age the daily betrayal of your body is a significant challenge. It is something you can't avoid, something you can't think your way out of, something unrelenting and unforgiving.

As I practiced with the band, my hands did get better. It never got easy, but it got easier. I began to believe I could do it. I began to hope that I could still do something with the tail end of my life. And then...

Angelo finds me leaning against a lamppost about fifty yards from the house. The adrenaline of my anger could no longer compensate for the lack of a cane, and my back hurt like hell.

"Hey, Carl," he says, like we are running into each other at the store or something.

I study his face. He's got a swarthy complexion like he could be Italian or Greek or Middle Eastern. His face is round and his brown eyes kind. His greeting is casual, but he is blinking back tears, like he can feel the pain I am feeling. But he doesn't come grab me or try to save me from myself like almost everyone else would do. He just stands there at the ready.

"It hurts a lot today," I say with a grin I hope is wry.

"Yeah, life is kind of like that, Carl. It hurts, sometimes more than others. What you gotta decide is if what you are doing is worth the pain."

I bite my lip and nod. He's got a point, but sometimes the pain gets so bad you don't really have a choice. I don't tell him that, but I think he knows it.

I wave him over and put my arm around his shoulder and he helps me hobble back towards the house.

"Are you an angel?" I ask.

He laughs, "No, I am not. I'm a man, just like you."

"Well, you act like an angel. You're so goddamn young and yet you seem to understand what it is to be so old."

I feel him shrug under my arm. "I've always been empathic, since I was a little kid."

"Well," I say, "if there are angels you ought to be one."

We make it back into the house and continue practicing. But the next time the sticks drop, I wave Angelo off and just keep the beat with the foot pedal and the bass drum. It ain't much, but it's all I've got. No one seems to mind.

BEING IN A BAND, BEING IN HELIOS, CHANGED ME. I STOP thinking about suicide and think a lot about drumming and singing instead. I stop focusing on my past and what I have lost and start thinking about my future and where I am going.

I'm not in denial about my age and the few years I have left, I know there isn't much time. But, instead of waiting to die, I start living again.

My mind is focused on the band Helios, not the helium exit strategy.

This is a full-on miracle. I am happy quite a bit, my hands hurt less, and I walk just a little bit better. We have been practicing for two months and in that time my health has improved. That just hasn't happened in a long time.

"We're happy today," Ana says, handing me my pills.

I have gotten up early and am whistling as I putter around my little room. "Yup, it's gig day, my dear."

She knows all about Helios. I have gone on and on about it. She even knows it is gig day, I have told her many times in the last few weeks. She even knows where we are playing, but she is kind enough to indulge me. "Where are you guys playing?"

I smile and kiss her gently on the cheek. She flushes red and asks, "What was that for, Carl?"

"For being so kind to me, my dear," I say, and her blush deepens. "Because you know full well we are playing here this afternoon."

The whole place is abuzz about it. Three old guys playing in a band, two of whom live at the Home. It's like Angelo told us once, "It will be as if you are all eight-year-olds, people will go crazy. Just like kids, you don't have to be the best. Just the fact that you get up there and do it will be enough."

And he's right. There is supposed to be a crew here from the local news station to film and interview us. Old people in a band are almost as cute as kids in a band.

My morning is the best I have had in years until on my way down to breakfast my mind strays into difficult territory. I want to talk to Lenny. I want to tell him how excited I am about this. I want my friend. But I can't tell him I found something better than helium, I can't share with him how my old hands are actually working better most of the time, I can't...

I suddenly feel weak and old and like a fool. I stop in the hallway and lean heavily on my cane. One of the residents goes past me in her walker on her way to the village idiots' table. The hallway narrows and I am overwhelmed with the smell of bleach—something must have required serious cleaning in this part of the hallway. I'm such a stupid old fool. Death is coming for me, just like it came for Lenny. Hell, I might not even live for Helios's first gig. And while we can belt it out, we really aren't that good. We are some novelty that people will gawk and stare at.

I decide to go back to my room. I'm going to go in and lock the door. I take a deep breath and am about to turn myself around when I see Angelo. He's striding down hallway with so much youth and energy that I look away.

"There you are," he says when he gets close. "We've been waiting for you."

Herb lives at the Home too, and I knew Angelo brought Brian over this morning so we could go over the set, help set the gear up, do a sound check. We're old and we know it takes us longer to do these things.

I don't answer. I turn around and ignore him.

"Okay," I hear him say as he comes up next to me, his hand soft on my shoulder. "It's okay, Carl."

I feel a flush of anger as my cheeks grow hot. The bastard is so empathetic he knows exactly what I am feeling. The anger quickly twists into shame. I stop and meet his eyes, "I am a goddamn old fool," I tell him.

"And that's what I like most about you," he replies.

"I can't do it," I say.

Right then, an old guy carting an oxygen tank walks by and says, "Can't wait for the concert," his voice is coming out in a thin wheeze.

I don't say anything to him, just stare at Angelo as I blink rapidly.

"Okay," he says. "Don't worry about it, we'll figure it out. The show must go on."

I nod, a cowardly sense of relief rushing through my body. I suddenly feel weak and start to go down, but Angelo's strong arms are around me and then I am in my room and on my bed.

Angelo is there sitting on the edge of the bed studying my face.

"What will you do?" I ask.

"Oh, I've got Garage Band on my Mac. I'll just hook it up to back the boys. It'll be okay." His face is a little pinched as he looks at me.

I can't believe he's not trying to talk me into it. Why the hell isn't he trying to talk me into it? Am I really that bad that the band is better off with a computer? I sigh and turn away from Angelo. I can't look at him anymore.

I feel him get up from the bed and hear him leave without another word.

I soon fall asleep.

UNLIKE ME, LENNY WASN'T ALWAYS FILLED WITH DOUBT. He had this sense of self-assurance that I admired. I think it was about the brain surgeon thing—you've got to be confident if you're opening up people's skulls. He would make up his mind and do what he thought right with hardly a second thought. Me, I could take weeks on my second thoughts. If we had gotten the exit via helium plan put together it would have been Lenny that didn't have cold feet.

I wake up from my nap thinking about Lenny, about what he would have to say about me lying in my bed when there is a concert going on. I look at my clock, 1:30 p.m. The concert starts at two. I groan, disappointed that I haven't missed it yet, that there is still time to second guess my second guess.

I get up and pee and sit on my recliner staring at the door. I almost expect someone to come knocking, someone to try to talk me into going down and banging on the drums.

But the minutes tick by and no one comes. I feel a stab of pain that no one cares, and then a sharp sense of guilt that I am playing such a childish game. That I want someone to encourage me, to hold my hand, to make everything all right.

I rise up, feeling my heart thumping in my chest. Everything isn't all right. I'm an old man with a body that is falling apart who has given up almost everything. No, nothing about that is all right.

I grab my cane and head to the dining hall where the concert is happening. I want to yell at Angelo, to berate him for giving me hope, for setting me up. As my cane thumps on the floor rhythmically, what I am worried about comes into sharp relief. I don't want to make a fool of myself in front of my friends.

The last time I was in a band was over sixty years ago. I was sixteen and the drummer of the Space Junkers. We played mostly covers of hits from the early fifties. It was a four- piece high school band and we never played a gig. We just holed up in Jerry Benton's garage and practiced for a year. We never got up the courage to play in front of people. At first we practiced three times a week, and then a couple times a month, and then we all just conveniently forgot to practice.

And now I want to beat Angelo with my cane. Maybe he's not an angel, but a demon. First he gives me hope, and then he sneaks this performance up on me, something I couldn't do as a child, something I never really got over.

As I enter the dining room the smell of bad coffee and the stare of hundreds of eyes assault me. Our equipment, including the drum kit, is set up in one corner. Herb and Brian are putting their guitars on. I see Ana and she nods and smiles at me as if she expects something great. My daughter is sitting next to Ana and even my grandson is here.

I stand there blinking, my jaw slack as I take in the scene.

"There you are," Angelo says as he comes up and takes my arm, gently guiding me towards the drums.

"I... I don't know if I can do this," I say, my eyes fixed on the drums with the flaming Helios logo.

"I know," Angelo says, and I believe him. "But it's time, Carl. It's time for you to play. You know what to do."

Then I'm sitting on the stool behind the drums with the sticks in my hand. Our set list is taped to the floor where I can see it. Brian is looking at me, a nervous smile on his face. The room is quiet. It feels much bigger than it is. All eyes are on us and I just sit there blinking, wishing I could throw up.

My eyes find Angelo. He's off to the side, a smile wide and bright on his face. He gives me a thumbs-up and he starts nodding with the beat of our first song.

I look back to Brian, he and Herb are both looking at me now. The room is even quieter, like church, almost a holy silence.

I look down at my hands with their swollen knuckles loosely holding the drumsticks. I know how to do this. My friends need me. Angelo's talk about using the computer was his way of getting me motivated. I feel tears of gratitude flood my eyes. I have people depending on me. I have something worth doing. Who cares if I make a fool of myself? I'd be a bigger fool not to try.

I bring the sticks together and measure out the beat. "One... Two... Three... Four..."

I HAVE TO TELL YOU THAT NOTHING FEELS LIKE A LIVE performance. You hear the audience, you see them swaying, or clapping, or, the few agile enough, dancing. You feel them as they feel the music. It's a hell of a high, I'll tell you that right now.

Our set is pretty short. We are all ancient, after all, and we finish up with the Stones "(I Can't Get No) Satisfaction."

I feel the butterflies rioting anew in my belly as I start pounding out the beat. This is my song. I sing it. And yeah, the lyrics are pretty simple, the music is easy to play, but all eyes are on me.

As I start belting out the lyrics, I think of Lenny and me and our quest for helium. How unsatisfied we were with our lives. How it didn't really feel like living to us. How much my life has changed since I met Angelo. I feed all those emotions into the lyrics as I sing. I bang on the drums as hard as I can. I vent all the frustrations I have with my life getting smaller and smaller. My wife dying. Having my car taken away. Living at the Home. Not contributing. Being a nothing.

And when it's done, I'm exhausted. The crowd is clapping and cheering and making as much noise as they can (which is to say not as much noise as a younger crowd could make). I come out from behind my drum set, forgetting my cane, my legs shaky, but usable. I get between Herb and Brian and we put our arms around each other and bow.

It's only a little gig in the dining room of the Home. But it could have been Madison Square Garden for how I feel. When we come up from the bow I see the faces looking back at me. I see joy and excitement and some hope.

Angelo's beaming at us, tears on his cheeks, his hands on his heart. He's so happy.

That day, that wonderful day, we all thought we would have more time together than we did.

THAT IS WHAT I REMEMBER NOW FROM THAT FIRST CONCERT. The hope. It took me three full days of feeling like crap to get my energy back after that concert, but we changed people that day. They looked at us and we gave them hope that they could actually have a life in their twilight years.

Angelo did this. He saved our lives, he gave us hope, something to do, and now we give other people hope.

We've been at this for about six months now. We are up to doing a gig a week and it only takes me a day to recover after we do one. We've toured old folks homes all over Arizona. Or at least we did.

Now, as I dictate this, our future is uncertain.

I swear that Angelo is an angel. A real live angel. He recruited us, directs us, drives us, does all the heavy lifting. He is spending his life giving us a life.

Or at least he did.

Angelo died last week. He was riding his bike when a van got too close to the bike lane he was in and clipped him with the side mirror. He was sent tumbling down a hill, his head connecting with a rock.

When Brian comes to my room and tells me, I think he's kidding. Angelo's an angel, how can he die?

I stand there, my mouth hanging open like one of the sad sacks in the memory unit. I blink at Brian, his rumpled face sagging much more than usual.

"What? Dead?" The words echo in my head, they sound hollow and I feel numb.

Brian nods solemnly and stares at his feet. Brian who still lives on his own. Brian who can drive. Brian who can still do something independently. If Angelo and this band mean that much to Brian, what does it mean to Herb and me? We're stranded at the Home. Helios is our life.

We're in my little room and I sink down into my recliner, but even it is no comfort. But at least from this position I can't fall.

"Go get Herb," I say. "Bring him here. We'll tell him together."

After Brian leaves I look up at the plain white ceiling. "Angelo," I whisper. I don't know what I'm expecting, that he'll talk to me or something? That he'll suddenly appear and assure me he was an angel all along. A sour frown forms on my face as the ridiculousness of it comes home. I'm not that kind of a person. I don't believe easily, and I don't expect miracles.

But Angelo *is* a miracle to me. He *is* an angel to me.

"What the hell is so important," Herb growls when Brian drags him in a few minutes later.

"Sit down, Herb," I say. "We're having an emergency band meeting."

"Why?"

I see the fear in Brian's eyes, he doesn't want to tell someone else the news he just told me, so I just blurt it out.

Herb's thin face goes from looking old to looking ancient, his mouth opens and closes several times and then just clamps shut as his eyes well up with tears.

In that moment, all three of us know we can't do Helios without Angelo. I can see it on their grim faces. I can feel it as a stabbing pain in my stomach. All the equipment is his—he did all the physical labor. He glued us all together, made us whole.

The silence is heavy and oppressive and I can't stand it. It feels like I'm dying again, like before I met Angelo when Lenny and I were on our quest for helium.

Not this time.

"Get me my sticks and pad," I say to Brian who pulls the drumsticks and practice pad off of the desk and hands them to me. I look at my bandmates, but they won't meet my eyes. This feeling, it feels like death, and I can smell the sour scent of our fear.

I bang out the beat on my drumsticks, "One... two... three... four....," and start on the little pad. The sound is muffled, but it's a beat. "I can't get no... satisfaction," I begin singing. My voice is low, and I've slowed the beat way down. It sounds more like a dirge than a rock song, but that is exactly how I'm feeling.

Brian and Herb are both looking at me, and I give them a nod. They come in on the next line, Herb's tenor and Brian's bass harmonizing with my baritone. A smile creeps onto my face. I can't help it, we sound pretty good. Our voices aren't the smooth voices of youth, but the textured voices of age. We know what it's like to "get no satisfaction."

When the song is over I look up at them. "Angelo may be gone, but Helios lives. Even if we have to become some damn boys' acapella group."

They both nod at me, their faces serious, their old, cloudy eyes sparkling.

And right then, I feel myself promising to Angelo to continue his work. Helios will live as long as I am alive and I've got my mind. Helios will live.

BACKSTORY—THE HELIUM EXIT STRATEGY

THIS STORY IS MY ATTEMPT TO EMPATHIZE WITH SOMEONE close to me. So this backstory isn't completely awkward, let's call them by the gender neutral Pat.

Pat is someone that I give a lot of my time and energy supporting. That can be rewarding and it can also be difficult. A few years ago Pat stayed with my wife and me and it was a challenge for us all.

One day Pat told me they couldn't snap their fingers anymore. In the moment I brushed it off, but on later contemplation it became clear to me that it really was a big deal—one more thing taken away from Pat.

A year or so before this incident I learned from my friend Jack about the use of helium to terminate your life.

Those two elements mixed together and this story was born. Since my goal was to be empathetic, the Carl character is basically me. What would I be like at that age? What would I value? How would I cope?

Pat is still in my life and I still spend a lot of energy on their care. Time has made the questions in this story even more relevant.

What will you be like when you are that age? How will you cope? How do you find meaning in a life where your limitations are becoming greater and greater every day?

Robert J. McCarter

A POSTSCRIPT FOR ELIZABETH

Day 1

"HELLO, ELIZABETH," I SAID AS YOU DROPPED THE BAG of groceries you had just come in with. I watched as broken eggs mixed with spilled orange juice. You looked tired, as if you hadn't been sleeping much.

"Hugh?" you said, staring at me. "But... you're dead."

"Sorry for the surprise, hon." I understood, I had died only twenty days earlier. I smiled as best I could, but it didn't seem to ease your mind. I moved my little round platform so you would understand. In the dim light my holographic nature hadn't been obvious.

You blinked, your eyes as big and brown as ever. You twirled your hair with your right index finger, just like you did the first time I said hello to you at the grocery store. I was newly divorced and helpless in the store; you took the time to get me oriented. "I... I don't understand," you finally said as you squatted and started gathering up the spilled food.

I had surprised you, but you hadn't been as surprised as you might have been. It seemed like you had been expecting to see me, like you had spent the last twenty days not quite believing I was really gone.

"I guess you don't remember," I began. "That fancy life insurance policy we bought a few years before my diagnosis. It had a Holographic Surrogate benefit. When the reoccurrence happened, I activated it."

As you put the groceries away and cleaned up the mess, I explained it all to you. The scanner they gave me, how I spent months recording my memories, how they assembled the holographic me from all of that after I died.

"But... but..." you stammered, a glass of Pinot Grigio in your hand. "You—no, Hugh—didn't tell me. Why didn't he tell me?" I didn't like that. You were thinking of Hugh as someone different than me.

"You would have tried to talk me out of it," I stated.

You nodded in answer and took much more than a sip of your wine. "Why are you here? What do you want?" you asked.

I smiled and took a sip of my holographic wine. With my platform right next to the table it almost looked like I was real, not some hologram pretending to sit and to drink. I wanted to look normal and put you at ease.

"I am here to help you, Liz. I know my death—Hugh's death—must still be so hard, the house so empty. I am here so you don't have to come home to an empty house every night. I am here so you can still tell me about your day." You nodded as tears ran down your cheeks. "What I want,

Liz, is to love you." What I desperately wanted was for you to accept me.

Day 3

"You pick," I said.

"Seriously?" you asked, seated on the big overstuffed couch. I had positioned myself to the right of you. It looked as if the couch extended beyond the arm and we were sitting together.

"Seriously," I answered.

"Don't you think that's a bit out of character? Hugh was never that fond of my taste in movies."

My brow furrowed as I searched my memories. "Sorry, I am not perfect. I have many of your husband's personality traits, and many of his memories, but not all."

You nodded, your stare lingering on my holographic face. I hated it that you weren't accepting me as Hugh, but I knew pushing it wouldn't help. "All righty, then," you said, turning your attention to the flat screen on the wall. "Show me all the rom-coms you think I might like." The flat screen turned itself on and began showing movie trailers.

Day 4

"What do I call you?" you asked over breakfast. Oatmeal with blueberries and black coffee. It made me happy to see that you were eating.

"My name is Hugh," I said.

"But you are not my Hugh."

"I am, Liz. I am parts of your Hugh, maybe not all of him, but enough. My name is Hugh."

Your lips pursed and your eyebrows narrowed. After a

moment you nodded slowly. "Parts, eh? 'H' then, I will call you 'H.'" You turned your attention back to your breakfast. Your lawyer brain had locked in on a decision and that was that. I smiled, it was so you. An artist and a lawyer; when we met my friends said it would never work, but it did.

After eating, you grabbed your bag to go and turned back and said, "Bye, H." The smallest of smiles played on your lips. I rejoiced.

Day 23

"WHAT'S WRONG?" I ASKED, THE BUBBLES OF THE BATH up around your chin as you wept.

You gave me a scathing look and I felt fear. You might doubt that I am capable of emotion, but I am. It may not be the same as your emotions, but I have them, I know them, they are real to me. I felt fear and searched my memories.

"Our first date," I said. You sniffed and nodded. "It was twenty-five years ago today."

You nodded again, your lips pursed.

"I was so damn nervous," I continued. "I was standing at the door to your apartment staring at my fingernails. They still had paint underneath them. I almost panicked and turned away. You were a lawyer, for God's sake, what did you want with a poor artist like me?"

You sighed and continued the story, "You looked so... so... adorable. You had that silly brown tie on that was too wide and so far out of style. You stood there, your eyes wide, like some deer in the headlights. I was used to men that were so assured, but so full of themselves. You were—"

"Terrified," I offered.

"No... Well, yes, but not that. You were so sweet. So

open. So sensitive. It was right then, you know. Right then that I fell in love with you... I mean, Hugh, right then that I fell in love with Hugh."

"Really?" I asked.

"Yeah. I mean you—he—could have easily blown it, but the seeds were planted right there."

I chuckled. "I had no idea. And you know, that date almost didn't happen."

"What?" you asked, pushing yourself up in the tub and looking directly at me.

"After we first met at the grocery store, I kind of started going there a lot. It didn't take long to figure out you were one of those scheduled, orderly people—unlike me. So, I started showing up when you did, so we could bump into each other."

You smiled and nodded, encouraging me to continue.

"That day that I asked you out, I had planned it. I had snagged the little daisy from the floral department. I had rehearsed my monologue a thousand times. Then I saw you, in your navy blue business attire." I laughed at your expression, you looked like I had said something scandalous. "No, I loved that outfit. I know you never believe me, but your work clothes have always turned me on."

You blushed and sank back into the warm soapy water. "Go on, H."

"Well, when I saw you, my mind went blank. I was going to quote Rumi and make a big dramatic display. But I couldn't think. You came up and said hi, and asked how I was doing. I just stammered and you looked confused. Right then I wanted to run. Everything in my body was screaming at me to run. What would a woman like you want with a man like me? But, instead, my arm extended itself and I handed that pitiful little daisy to you, and managed to say one word: 'Dinner.'"

Day 41

"I WILL NOT BE ONE OF THOSE PITIFUL OLD LADIES," YOU said in between bites of fettuccine.

"What?" I asked. I was again pretending to sit and eat at the table with you.

"You know," you said, pointing your fork at me. "Those old ladies I see in the restaurants. The ones that have hauled their holographic husband with them to eat dinner."

I looked down at the round platform that projected my image and held my mind. It was thin, about eighteen inches in diameter and maybe ten pounds. Definitely haulable. I smiled, trying to not bring attention to the fact that you were having dinner with your holographic husband, you just hadn't hauled him anywhere. "Okay," I said.

"It's not seemly. I'm not that old yet, anyway."

Day 64

YOU LAUGHED. A REAL LAUGH. THEY HADN'T COME OFTEN in the days since my activation. And this one was wonderful, your whole body joined in. "Oh, my God, Hugh, you should have seen him."

You went on to tell me about Alex and Sue; about how you were having lunch with them and Alex's ex came up and started yelling at him after the man she had left Alex for left her.

But, really, I wasn't paying much attention. You had called me "Hugh." I felt such happiness; you had fulfilled my purpose in that moment.

Day 80

"WE SHOULDN'T SELL IT," YOU SAID, TWIRLING YOUR HAIR. The black had grey streaks in it, but still you are so beautiful.

"Why? It's of no use to me now." I replied, holding my palms up to emphasize my holographic state.

"But the gallery, Hugh. You put so much into it. It's the home of your wonderful paintings." Your gaze traveled to the living room wall. The large watercolor pictured high mountain peaks on a beautiful sunny day. I gifted you with it on the one month anniversary of our first date. It wasn't one of my best pieces, but it was your first, your favorite.

"You are all I need now," I told you.

You nodded slowly. "But your art needs a home."

"Maybe I can find someone to buy the gallery that will keep my art. What do you say? When you are away I can work on that."

You nodded, your gaze returning to the watercolor mountain.

Day 81

"THIS ONE?" YOU ASKED, HOLDING UP A NICE HORSE HAIR paint brush.

"They all can go," I answered. "Except that one." I pointed to a single cheap polyester brush, well-worn with the paint on the handle peeling. "Give the rest away; they're just brushes."

You smiled and picked up the little brush. "You're mother gave it to you, right?"

I nodded. "My first brush." I smiled as the memory swept over me. The memory was old and lovely and worn smooth by constant use, like a rock that had spent centuries at the bottom of a brook. "I was three, and Mom was tired of me running off with her brushes. She gave it to me with my own little easel and a set of those little water colors for kids. 'If you're going to be a painter, son,' she said, 'you need to have your own equipment, and you need to learn how to take care of it.' The brush was brand new and wrapped in plastic. I loved it."

"Okay, Hugh, I'll keep the brush. What about everything else?" Your hand swept across the room, my studio. There were canvases everywhere, in all stages from blank to finished. It had all my easels and stool, my paints, and my books. It had been my home.

I smiled. This is just what I was here for. To help you deal with this kind of thing; so you didn't have to do it alone; so it didn't have to be a horror for you. We dug in and got to work.

"WHAT'S THIS?" YOU ASKED SEVERAL HOURS LATER, pulling out a large case.

I didn't have specific memories of it, but I recognized it. "It's the scanner."

"The what? You mean... Oh..." Your face fell.

I knew you wouldn't let this be, that if we didn't get this out of the way, it would fester. "Open it," I said.

Your fingers ran over the little metal clasps, and you licked your lips. You popped it open and pulled out the device, a helmet with a clear screen over the eyes.

"How..." you began.

"Hugh put it on and shared his memories. The scanner recorded the words, but also brain patterns; tracked eye dilation and movement; heart rate and blood pressure." I didn't use "I," because I knew that for the moment, at least, the spell was broken, I was back to being "H."

You closed the case, sat on it, as your hands caressed the helmet. "How long? How much?" you asked, your voice unsteady.

"Hundreds of hours. He recorded hundreds of hours of memories to make me. Memories of you and your life with him. Memories of his past, his childhood. Stories of his art and his passions. His fears and his dreams."

You held the scanner to your chest and leaned your head against it, tears running down your cheeks.

"I'm sorry, hon," I said, moving close, being Hugh again. "I just couldn't tell you what I was doing. What I was creating."

"You said you were working, all that time you were doing this?"

"Not all. But a lot."

"You told me you were in here creating your greatest work," you said.

"And I did," I replied, but you didn't seem to hear me.

"After you died I searched the studio, looked at all your canvas. I was so confused. I couldn't find any paintings newer than a year old."

"I'm sorry, Liz. I couldn't tell you what I was doing. I couldn't risk..." I trailed off, at a loss for what to say.

I was about to speak again when your eyes found me. They were hard. "Don't," you said as you got up, still clutching the scanner. Long strides carried you to the door of the studio.

"Liz, please. Let me explain, let me—"

"You are not Hugh," you said. You were crying, the sobs making it hard for you to talk.

"I am Hugh," I said. "I may not be all of him, but I am all of him that is left."

You blinked rapidly several times, your mouth opening and closing. A sob escaped as you turned away from me, left the room, slammed the door, and left me there trapped.

Day 86

YOU LEFT ME IN THE STUDIO FOR FIVE DAYS. I DIDN'T TRY to contact you, I didn't ask you to open the door. You needed time. I watched you for the first few hours, tapping into the internal security system. I watched you cry, that scanner clutched to your chest, until I couldn't stand it any longer.

When I started this project, started creating this holographic me, I knew there would be hard times for you. But I hoped that this would make it better. That I would imbue my holographic self with enough memories, enough knowledge of you and us that I would make this passage easier for you. But, I never for a moment thought *it would be easy.*

On my second day there, I had to start powering my systems down. With my charging station in the living room, I didn't have enough battery left to continue on full power.

On the fourth day I went into hibernation mode.

On the fifth day I woke in the living room on the charger.

"I've been thinking about this," you said. "You are not Hugh, not all of him. But you are some of him. I'm sorry I locked you in the studio."

"Don't be," I said.

"Aren't you mad?" you asked.

"No. Why would I be?"

"Well," you said, your smile sweet and sheepish. "I locked you away for *five* days."

I shrugged. "But I'm here now."

You shook you head staring at me.

"What?" I asked.

"Hugh had a temper, he would have been so mad."

"As you pointed out, I am not all of Hugh. I will never get angry with you, or jealous."

Your eyes narrowed and you bit your lip. "But you feel, you have emotions." I nodded. "What did you feel when I locked you up?"

"Sad and scared."

"What other emotions do you experience?"

"Love, Elizabeth. I feel love most strongly. Love for you. I was made to love you."

Your mouth opened in a silent "O" for a breath and tears came to your eyes. "Hugh used to say that to me, that he was made to love me. He would sign his emails and the cards he got me that way."

I nodded. "I know. But for me it is literally true."

Day 210

YOU YAWNED AND PULLED THE COMFORTER UP AROUND your neck. "Good night, Hugh," you said.

"Good night, love," I replied. "Sleep well."

I told the light to turn itself off and left you there to sleep. We had fallen into a comfortable pattern. Most days when you came home, dinner had been delivered and you would sit and eat and tell me about your day. After dinner you would get in bed and try to watch something, but would usually fall asleep. When you were ready, I would turn off the TV and the light and return to my charging station. I would gently wake you each morning after a few glorious minutes of watching you sleep.

During the weekends we would work in the studio, until we finally got that sorted out, or talk about the gallery, and more and more you would go spend time with friends.

You never brought them back here. None of them knew about me. Part of me loved that pieces of you were only for me. Part of me was scared about it. You called me Hugh, but—

"Honey," you said, your voice thick with sleep. You were beautiful dressed in one of my old T-shirts and rubbing your eyes, looking so vulnerable.

"Are you okay, Liz?" I asked.

You nodded. "Bad dream, can you come talk to me?"

"Sure." I disengaged from my charging station and followed you back into the bedroom. You crawled back into bed.

"What did you dream, hon?" I turned my hologram off so it would be dark.

"No," you said. "I like your light shining on me." I reactivated the hologram and turned the brightness up. "That's better."

"Your dream?" I asked.

"I dreamed of that day, that day you died. You had been so restless. I started reading to you like the hospice nurse suggested. You got quiet, your breath so slow, so deep. It was Rumi that I read to you, that you loved so much, that you read to me when we first dated. All those expressions of love." You licked your lips and sighed, pulling the comforter up closer.

"Yes?" I prompted.

"And then you were gone. And then I was alone. Really alone. Just me in this white room with the walls slowly closing in."

"I'm right here, Liz," I whispered to you.

"I can't stand being that alone. Don't ever leave me, Hugh," you said as sleep took you.

"Never," I whispered back.

In the morning you moved my charging station into the bedroom. That was the proudest moments of my holographic life.

Day 312

THE DAY THE GALLERY SOLD, YOU CAME HOME CRYING. You had gone alone to turn the keys over. I think it highlighted for you how much things had changed, how much I had changed. Once a man, now a hologram.

You wouldn't talk about it. You sat on the couch eating cookies and watching *Casablanca*. You cried through most of it mumbling the lines.

"We could go VR," I suggested after the movie ended.

"What?" you asked, looking surprised.

"It would be more real if we were both in virtual reality. There I would be as real as you are. There we could do things together, not just sit around the house."

Your eyes narrowed. We were both a bit old for it, a generation late. We had tried VR, of course, but had never really gotten hooked by it.

"We could... you know..." I stammered.

"You mean..." you began, a flush of red landing on you cheeks.

"It's not the same," I said with a smile, "but the hardware has gotten a lot better since it first became popular."

You blinked, then frowned, and then shook your head.

"Why not?" I asked.

"Remember when I told you I wouldn't be one of those old ladies at the restaurant with my holographic husband?" I nodded. "Well, I won't be one of those women that get it on in virtual reality. No."

I hastily agreed. It was unseemly. I tried to laugh it off, to tell you that it was just a crazy idea, but I was lying. I had wanted to suggest it for months.

After that things changed.

Day 345

I WAS PREPARED FOR YOUR SADNESS. I WAS PREPARED FOR you to cry all day. But that is not what happened.

It was the three hundred forty-fifth day of my operation. I was turned on twenty days after my body died. It was the anniversary of my death.

"Anything planned today?" I asked as you read on your tablet computer over breakfast.

"No, nothing special. Just work."

I nodded. I knew you knew what day it was; you are so good with dates. It was me, the artist, that always used to forget. But me, the hologram, didn't forget dates.

We hardly spoke over breakfast and you worked late and went right to bed when you got home.

"Good night, Hugh," you said as you pulled the covers up around you.

I didn't know whether to be relieved or terrified.

Day 400

"YOU'RE SURE YOU DON'T MIND?" YOU ASKED AS YOU PUT your earrings on. The pearl ones I had gotten you on our honeymoon in Thailand.

"No, not at all," I said. "It's a big day for you, making partner, you should have a date at your party. It wouldn't seem right if you didn't."

Your dazzling smile was brief before a frown turned your lips down again. "You're not just telling me that?" you asked.

"No, of course not. As I explained, I am not capable of jealously."

"The new and improved Hugh," you said as you pulled on your heels. "I'll tell you all about it when I get home."

I nodded. This was good, I knew this was good. You were moving on with your life. And while I wasn't jealous, I was sad.

Day 432

"HE'S REALLY NICE," YOU SAID AS YOU PUT THE WINE bottle in the picnic basket. "I think you would like him."

"I am sure I would," I answered, as I had the previous fifteen times you had told me that in the last month.

"He's the same one that took me to my partner dinner. His name is Alan. He's just a friend. It's nice, you know. It's nice to get out." You had told me that numerous times too. But I knew you. He was a friend then, but he wasn't going to be for long.

I felt so happy for you, and so sad for me. "You have a great time, okay?"

"I will, Hugh," you said, blowing me a kiss as you made for the door.

"One more thing, Elizabeth," I said.

"What?" you asked, turning to look back at me.

"I think you should call me 'H.'"

"What?" you asked, looking so very confused. "Why? You *are* Hugh."

"Well, I've been thinking," I said. "You were right way back when. I am Hugh, but not all of Hugh. I think 'H' is a better name for me."

Your puzzled face turned sad. "Okay," you said.

I stayed there staring at the door until you returned.

Day 472

IT WAS INEVITABLE. YOU SNUCK INTO THE HOUSE AT 10:00 a.m. after being out all night. You looked tired, happy, and guilty.

"Good morning, Liz. Do you want some coffee?" I asked, trying to make it sound like any other morning.

"Sure... sure, that would be nice. Thanks, H," you said.

Your eyes kept getting lost as you sipped your coffee. "You know," I said, "it's Sunday. Maybe you should go spend the day with Alan. Have fun."

"Really?" you asked, your eyes brightening. Your face reminded me of when we were both young and were falling in love. Except I knew that look on your face wasn't for me.

"Yeah, of course," I said. "I'm here to help you live your life, not get in the way of it."

"Well... yeah," you said smiling, "why not. I'll call him."

Day 498

"I'M GOING TO BE GONE FOR A FEW DAYS," I TOLD YOU.

"What?" you asked, looking scared. "Why?" We were in what used to be my studio; you were sweeping up the last of the trash. Everything was gone except for a few paintings on the wall. You were planning to turn it into a guest bedroom. Not that you really had any guests since I was activated. Friends would drop by now and then and I would hide in the bedroom until they left.

"Maintenance," I said. "We are done here and I've been putting it off. I've been online for well over a year now. They need to give me a once-over. They'll be here in the morning and pick me up."

"Oh," you said, looking so distant.

"Don't worry, it's covered as part of the life insurance settlement," I said, knowing you didn't care about the money.

"That's fine," you said. "I'm not worried about that. How long will you be gone, H?"

"Maybe a week," I lied.

You paused your sweeping and looked at me, your face so sad. "I'll miss you, H," you said.

"I'll miss you too, Elizabeth," I said.

Goodbye

MY DEAREST ELIZABETH,

I can only imagine how you will react to this, since I won't be there to see it. I would like to think that you are sad, but not too sad. That you will miss me and grieve me a bit, but will move on with your life.

I can see you drinking red wine and reading furiously,

your hand twirling your beautiful hair, your brown eyes moist with tears.

The emotions are probably pretty complex. You might be mad, too. I lied to you about maintenance. I am sorry for the deception, but just as I kept my creation a secret from you (because you would have told me not to), I kept my destruction a secret too, for the same reason.

And please believe me, that if you are reading this I am gone and cannot be recreated. It is important that it be this way.

This postscript is an indulgence, not something I was specifically programed to do. But I felt that this piece of my life, 'H' that is, should be represented here. And that I should at least try to explain.

As you can see from the text that precedes this post-script, I have taken all the memories that Hugh built me with and composed them as stories. It is all he told me about you and him; about your life and your love; everything that was behind my programming that made me like him. That made me yours.

I once told you that I was literally made to love you. And because of that, I know it is time for you to move on with your life. You don't need me; you have your memories of Hugh. And if you want to feel him close, if you want to remember him, read these stories and feel him that way.

I am sad to leave you, to leave you again. But this is the best way. This is the last gift I can give you, my love. You are too strong and too vibrant a woman to settle for a holographic husband. You were never meant to be one of those old ladies having dinner with a hologram, or one of the younger ones that live in virtual reality.

See where this thing with Alan goes, and if that doesn't

work out continue on with your life. You needed time to grieve and time to heal from my death, and I like to think that this holographic version of me played a part in helping you through.

But now... well, life is for the living, go live yours my dear, sweet Elizabeth.

I was made to love you,

H

BACKSTORY—A POSTSCRIPT FOR ELIZABETH

I READ A SHORT STORY, I CAN'T REMEMBER ITS NAME anymore, that featured holographic representations of the dead. Well, that was an idea that was right up my alley. That story used the holographic dead in a rather impersonal way, but what would that be like with a loved one? That seed eventually turned into this story.

What I like best about science fiction stories is that they often ask a question and explore what an answer might look like. The question asked here is, "what would you do to help ease the grieving of a loved one?" How might technology help us do that in the future? What might that feel like?

This, in many ways, is the same question asked in "The Turing Test Will Be Televised." If technology provides us with a simulacrum of our deceased beloved, how many of us would take advantage of it? How would it be received? And a question—perhaps for another story—is how might we abuse that technology?

This story was a semi-finalist in the Writers of the Future Contest in 2013.

Stories of Life, Death, and the **Places in Between**

Robert J. McCarter

AFTERWORD

Everything in this book is a lie, but hopefully in reading it through you've enjoyed the journey and found some truth. Fiction (and art, really) is lying to tell the truth.

What a writer writes says a lot about them. How can it not? Your job as a writer is to dig deep and come up with those lies that tell the truth, with those stories that have meaning despite being complete fabrications. You pour yourself into your stories and steal from yourself to populate them.

These stories are little pieces of where I was on my own journey when I wrote them. They explore things that move me, puzzle me, scare me, or amuse me (often all of these). I hope you have enjoyed the journey. If you want more along the same lines, check out the books set in my "A Ghost's Memoir" universe: *Shuffled Off, Drawing the Dead,* and *To Be a Fool.* There is another one in the works—head over to RobertJMcCarter.com and sign up for my newsletter to find out when it is available.

The Following is an sample from
Shuffled Off: A Ghost's Memoir, Book 1

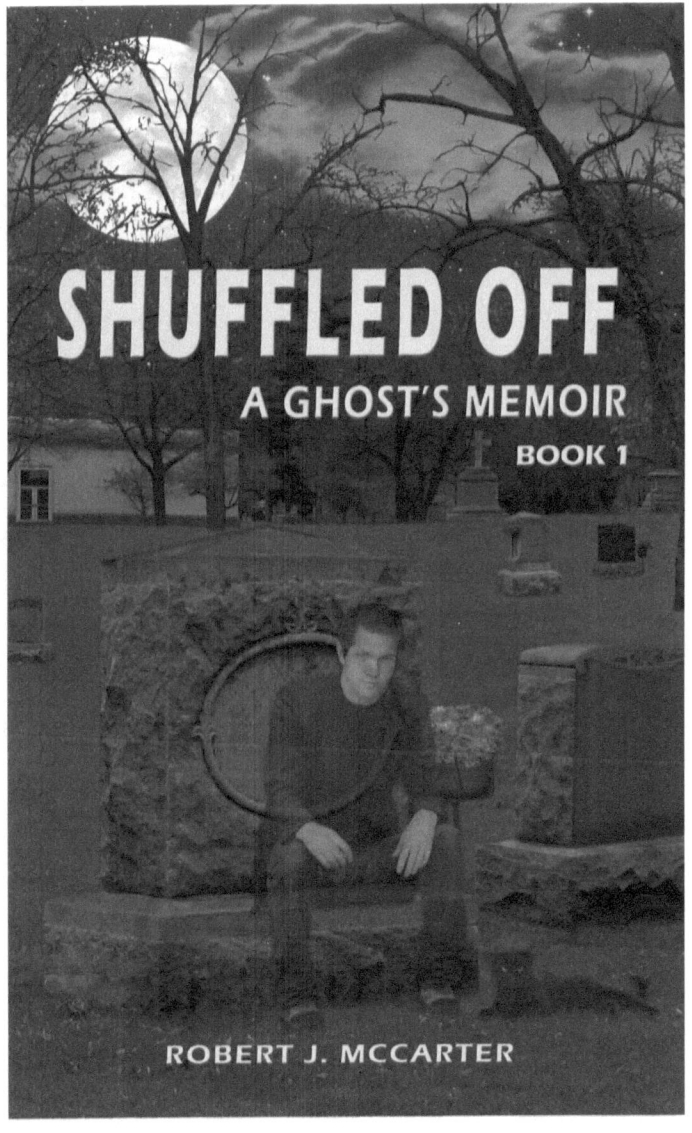

SHUFFLED OFF

A GHOST'S MEMOIR

BOOK 1

ROBERT J. MCCARTER

SHUFFLED OFF: A GHOST'S MEMOIR, BOOK 1 (SAMPLE)

Transmission #1

Received 2010/10/19 03:14:03

WHEN SOMEONE DIES, THE WORLD DOESN'T STOP. IT seems like it should, but it doesn't. Sure if it's a famous person, or a grisly murder, there is a period of piranha-like activity on the part of media. But that's not stopping, that is just business as usual in the land of the twenty-four hour news cycle. Even then it settles down quickly and everyone gets back to their shaky, unsure life.

It would be useful if it did stop. You know, take a moment, get your bearings, and deal with the practical and emotional details that engulf a death. But no, no stopping, no break, you just gotta continue your drunkard's walk down the path of life.

When I died, the world didn't stop, not a bit. I wasn't

expecting it to, but it would've been nice, you know?

The death effect is kind of like throwing a stone into a pond: a famous person is like a rock—it stirs things up; an everyman, like me, is more like a tiny pebble—it effects the immediate surrounding but has no discernable effect on the whole. In the end neither one really changes things much; the world doesn't stop. Life goes on.

My ma was a mess, it rocked her world—"a parent shouldn't outlive her child," and all that junk. My sister Jean spent about three days contemplating her own mortality and just went back to business as usual—the college social scene is all consuming. Nate, now he was ripped up. We've been joined at the hip since junior high, and my exit really sent him spinning.

I used to wish there was a sign that a person was going to leave soon. Like a light over their head that they can't see, and no one tells them about, but everyone around them sees and can act on. You know: be nice, spend time with them, tell them what you've got to tell them. My dad died quick, a heart attack, and it left me devastated, wishing I had said and done things different towards the end. You know the end is gonna come, but when it arrives it arrives so damn quick.

But now that it was me, I would want to have seen the light over my head too. I would have liked to look up Rhiannon and told her how sorry I was. I would have ditched work and taken a good long vacation. I would have slept a lot less, and lived a lot more.

So now you must be thinking who's the mouthy guy writing from beyond the pale. Woooooooooooo. At least that's what I would be thinking, I have no idea what you are think- ing, I ain't no mind reader.

OK, so my name is Joseph Jeffery Lynch, JJ to my friends. I am twenty-nine years old, and I am dead. Well mostly dead. Actually I don't really know. The body is gone, but I seem to still have a sense of myself, of who I am, even without it. Is that alive, or is that dead? Is that un-dead? I guess if you had to choose a word for my condition, you would choose the word "ghost." Woooooooooooo.

Scared yet? I would be if I were you. What I have to tell has its scary parts, its happy parts, and its sad parts—just like life. Is life scary to you? To me it was, sometimes, and I can now say the same thing about death.

Wonder how a ghost can write? Good question. I am using some new technology here at the University of Arizona (UA) that allows me to "type." Part of the SECI program. Never heard of it? It stands for the Search for Extra-Corporeal Intelligence. What SETI is to aliens, SECI is to ghosts.

Don't be surprised if you haven't heard of it. It is kind of a ghost project (pun intended) running underneath a more respectable project studying lightweight electromagnetic (EM) shielding. Now I don't fully understand the technology, but here I am the first beta tester.

I graduated college (barely, and with a liberal arts degree at that), but because of circumstances, that I imagine we'll get into later, I never moved on from my college job. I worked as a janitor at UA and among other things, I cleaned up the small lab that Jin Shi and Tamara Watson run the SECI program out of. They would often be there late and we would talk about things: about ghosts, and death, and the nature of life. The basic theory is this: consciousness exists outside of the body, the body being an amplifier for that consciousness. Jin and Tam were trying to figure out another type of amplifier—so was born SECI.

"Look," Tam told me once, "every religion in the world believes consciousness goes on beyond the corporeal form, exists separate from the corporeal form. They can't all be wrong; we are just trying to find a way to communicate with that realm."

Tam, she was always good to me, and she was cute, so I kinda had a crush on her. Big lips, lots up top, but not much of a butt (but I wouldn't kick her out of bed for that!). She also had this vulnerability, this deep need; it was clear she was doing SECI for very personal reasons.

"Imagine it, JJ," Jin said, he always had this glint in his eye when he talked about this part. "How much would this be worth? Talk to the dearly departed; solve murders; find out the secrets of the great beyond." Clearly the monetary ramifications were what got him going.

"So how does it work?" I asked.

"Our theory revolves around detecting non-random, patterned EM fluctuations in a highly EM shielded space," Tam explained. "Our SECI Chamber will theoretically shield all external EM radiation, so that any EM it picks up will have to be from within the chamber, from an extra-corporeal. The chamber will have in-depth instructions for the earth-bound extra-corporeal entity so they know what patterns to create to communicate with us."

"Huh?" It was all beyond me; I'm just a janitor with a liberal arts degree.

I lived about a mile south of UA, in a little studio apartment. It was old, not in a good part of town, but serviceable. Couldn't do much better on what I made.

I mostly used my skateboard to get around. Yeah, I know, a man of my age—what can I say? I was without four-wheeled motorized transport.

About two months ago—give or take, time is tough to measure right now—I was headed home on a blistering August night at about 2 a.m. I was kicking my way south when a black Audi A4 plowed into me.

The car, full of drunk undergrads, veered to avoid something (or nothing, they were seriously altered), hopped the curb, hit me and plowed us all into a Mickey D's. I was out quick, and my body expired some minutes later pinned to a kiddie jungle gym.

That undergrad's car was equipped with airbags leaving the passengers relatively unharmed. I, on the other hand, was smushed like a bug against a windshield.

The EMTs tried to revive me, they tried hard. They got me out and hauled me back to Saint Mother of the Weeping Virgin (or something like that), but it was no use.

It wasn't bad, dying that is. I've had headaches that hurt more. What was hard was watching it all. As soon as the car plowed into me, I popped out and kind of floated (I guess) along and watched the whole bloody procedure.

One plastered, Barbie-blond co-ed stumbled out of the car, looked at what was left of me and said, "Oh my God, that is so gross!"

The driver, a GQ pretty-boy, called someone, Daddy I presume, and said, "It wasn't my fault, you've got to get me out of this." His voice shook and his face was pale.

There were people screaming, others with broken bones and injuries, weeping women, and one patron barfing up their recently consumed meat-like-substance.

As the firemen pulled back the car, it was surreal watching my body slide to the floor like a wet rag, my eyes open and vacant, my limbs bent at odd angles. So quick, so sudden, one moment alive, the next dead and all that is left is the meat body I used to inhabit. Like a candle being snuffed out, like a marionette getting its strings cut, like the air rushing out of a balloon, like a... Too many metaphors? Maybe, but man was it sudden, and that suddenness was bizarre and hard to accept.

The paramedics went right to it, following their procedures: mobilizing my neck; shocking my heart; pumping me full of meds; hauling me off in the ambulance. I was attached to my body by some sort of silver cord. When the body was moved, I just got dragged along.

The ambulance was cool; I had never been in one. All that gear, and it was fast. We tore through the streets, sirens blaring, weaving around what little traffic there was. Kind of made me wish I had been an ambulance jockey instead of a janitor. What a ride!

Transmission #2
Received 2010/10/20 02:15:26

SORRY ABOUT THAT, GOT TIRED I GUESS. THIS IS HARD work: forming the shapes clearly enough to be translated into letters.

Jin, you called it. The feedback system works well. If I couldn't see the result of my efforts this just wouldn't work. Sorry if the prose is a bit rough, it's just too much to go back and edit it into something prettier.

I can't think that it matters to you though. I bet there was jumping for joy when you saw the first intelligible bit come in. Did that bottle of champagne finally get opened? Sorry I wasn't here to witness it.

So where was I? Oh yeah, death by car at the Mickey D's. When my dad passed, I got my head shrunk for a while and the shrink, she told me about the five stages of grief. As I recall they are: Denial, Anger, Deals, Depression, and Acceptance. I think that is it, normally I would just look it up, but that's not going to work right now.

JJ's Things That Suck About Being Dead (JJTTSABD) #1: *Can't use the net to look stuff up and pretend you are smarter than you really are.*

So I think there are stages, similar stages, to dying; at least for me.

Stage 1: Shock, aka Denial, aka wtf just happened?

So watching myself die, the self-absorbed bleating of my killers, the wild ride to Saint Mother of All That is Virginal, watching the heroic efforts to save me—was Stage #1: Shock, and shock is just one variant of the larger (much larger) area of Denial.

There was this weird detachment. It was me, but it wasn't me. As I watched those doctors and nurses trying to pummel my body back to life, I kept trying to talk to them. I said, "Hey, I'm right here, it's OK. I'm not really dead." Shattered hip; broken ribs; lacerated bowels; punctured spleen; blood loss; head trauma; and on and on it went. One at a time they accessed and tried to stabilize my injuries. They got the heart going a few times, but never for very long.

After a while I started getting worried—what if they succeeded? I didn't want back in that thing, man that would just be hell. So I kept telling them that it was OK, that they should let me go. Eventually they did. The process, though, was gratifying. It was amazing seeing my life cared for to such a degree by a room full of strangers.

At this stage I was attached to my body—I went where it did, just got dragged along. After the heroics were over

I was left there for some time, just me and my body. Just me and me.

I don't remember much of that time, but I developed a little mantra that pulled me through: wtf, wtf, wtf, wtf, wtf... For how long I have no idea. How could this have happened? That might have been crossing tentatively over to Stage 2: Anger. But believe me, it was way more shock than anger. When anger came there was no denying it.

The morgue was next, a cold sterile room where my body was shoved into a drawer. There were three others there with me. I guess you would call them ghosts, but I was still having a hard time with that. All three were wispy floating forms with silver cords leading to a drawer. Two were completely out of it, looking gape jawed and stupid, just wandering around. The third's name was Jesus.

"Hey fresh meat, what happened to you?" he asked.

I would have jumped out of my skin, if I had skin. I don't know why, but I just wasn't expecting that.

"Huh?" I mumbled.

"Oh man, not another bardo-brain," he said.

"What?"

"What a waste of space. Can't you bring me someone to talk to?" He looked up as he said this.

"Are you talking to me?"

"Praise be to Guadalupe! Yeah man, I'm talking to you." With a big smile on his face he added, "My name is Hey-zeus."

"Hey-zeus, you mean as in Gee-zus?"

"Difference in pronunciation. If you would be so kind, please call me Hey-zeus. Although I am a mighty handsome guy, I don't want to be confused with the big fellow." He pointed up.

I am not sure if he was handsome or not: his dancing eyes were brown; his face was plain and kind looking; and he had a big full mustache wiggling above his smile.

"Oh yeah, sure. My name is JJ." I would have extended my hand, but it wasn't quite like that. I had a sense of form, but it wasn't steady, especially regarding limbs. Jesus's face was clear, but the rest of his body came in and out of... hmmm... focus I guess, depending on what he was doing. I suppose it was the same for mine.

Turns out Jesus had been there a while. He was an illegal and as such his body had not been claimed yet. Jesus was a bounty hunter that had snuck across the border chasing a murderer. He wasn't like a normal bounty hunter, at least not what I thought normal bounty hunters did; he also tried to "show them the light of the divine Mother Mary" before he turned them in.

Next came, what I have come to know is, a standard ritual among the dead.

"So, how'd you die?" Jesus asked.

"Pinned to the jungle gym at a Mickey D's by a car full of ripped college kids."

"Nice! Wow." He seemed to be impressed.

"How did you die?" I asked. It only seemed polite to reciprocate.

"Ice pick to my left eye," he answered pointing to it. "I had the perp caught and cuffed, not sure how he came up with the pick."

There was a period of awkward silence for a while after that. I mean, what do you say? So sorry we're both dead; what the hell do we do now? I guess I must have started to glaze over.

"Don't go bardo on me man!" Jesus yelled. "Just keep

moving man, and keep talking. That will help you settle in to... well you know." With that he walked to the other end of the room and right through the doors.

I tried to follow him, but after I got about two feet further I was snapped back all the way into my drawer. I got out of there quick; I didn't want to be in there with my body.

JJTTSABD #2: *Being attached to a dead chunk of rotting meat really sucks.*

When I got out, Jesus was back and he just chuckled. "You've got to keep practicing. I met a fellow a few days ago that could move independently of his body; he didn't have the silver cord."

"Really?"

"Yup, you might see him too. He likes to come down here and mess with the bardo-brains, they're easy to scare."

"Bardo-brains?"

"Yeah, those poor suckers," he pointed at the two others wandering around gape jawed and unaware, "are stuck in their own private hell—can't get out and move on. Banquo, that's his name, says he is doing them a service, trying to shock them back to this world. Me, I don't know, just kinda looks like he is scaring the shit out of them."

"Banquo? That's a weird name," I said.

Jesus shrugged, "Well he's a *strange* fellow."

We talked a lot about everything, and when that got old we would turn to trading insults. I would give him shit about his name, and he would say: "At least I didn't die at Mickey D's kiddy land." I would come back with: "And what kind of bounty hunter were you? Getting ice-picked by some coked-up, handcuffed perp." He would then call me a red-neck, and I would call him a wetback. It was good natured and it was fun. Until it wasn't, that is. Eventually someone would hit pay-dirt sending one of us close to going bardo and the other would have to pull them out while staying in safe conversational territory.

Transmission #3
Received 2010/10/21 04:23:15

So Jesus really saved me there. Kept me from going bardo, which I guess I would have done if he hadn't been there. I was with him for maybe a day before I got transferred to the mortuary.

They pulled the body—yeah, I wasn't calling it mine anymore but "the," trying to view it more as an anchor—out of the drawer onto a gurney and into a meat-wagon. I guess you could look on this as the first whisper of Stage #5: Acceptance. I was starting to accept the fact that hunk-o-meat was not "me."

As I was being dragged along with the body I shouted to Jesus, "Thanks Jesus, you really saved me!" Pronouncing his name as Gee-zus.

That made him grin as he floated along besides me, "Just keep talking, keep moving. Stay out of bardo-land and you'll be OK."

"You too bro. Thanks, I owe you."

Jesus hit his limit and couldn't go any further. As we parted I shouted, "Jesus saves!"

The mortuary sucked. I was stuck, attached to that which used to be me, watching this weird guy with thick old fashioned glasses work on my body.

He first checked for a pulse (yeah bub, I am seriously dead), stripped and washed the body, flexed and massaged the arms and legs until they would lie flat, sewed up the injuries, and injected fluids into it. Then came trying to make it look like it wasn't dead. Only problem was, he was making my meat-face look scary as shit. Some sort of android version of what I once was.

I can't believe my mom was going to do the open casket thing. I guess it is good for some folks: seeing the dead chunk of meat helps them let go. Me, I never wanted that. Just burn me quick and dump the ashes somewhere. Nothing left, no place for folks to go and cry.

I slipped briefly into Stage #4: Depression, but thanks to Jesus I was good at catching the signs. See, depression leads to bardo-brain, and I was more scared of that than I was of being dead. Without Jesus here to save me I had to keep myself on track.

So when I felt that depression coming on, I just started singing as loud as I could, the song *Don't Fear the Reaper*.

The worse it got, the louder I sang, and I marched slowly away from "the meat that used to be me" stretching out the cord. When I got there I could only move four feet away. After a few hours of singing and marching (and making up really lyrics staring your's truly). I stretched it to eight feet.

I was trying to break the record, went too far, and got snapped right back to my body. My head, such as it was, was taking up the same space as the spectacled embalmer dude. He was applying rouge (yeah, rouge!) to my cheeks. It freaked me out and I felt the bardo approaching fast, so I started singing louder than ever.

Embalmer dude—let's call him Ed for short—jerked up and looked around, scratching his head. Did he hear me? Not sure, so I got right next to his ear and shouted as loud as I could, "Don't fear the reaper, JJ is the man!"

Sure enough, Ed jumped, just a bit, and looked around. "What was that?" he whispered.

I was ecstatic, and started running around with my hands in the air as if I had just won an Olympic gold medal. I wasn't really watching where I was going and popped out into the next room where another piece of meat was laid out in a coffin with folks lining up to pay their respects.

Not only had I communicated with someone, I had extended my leash! As I found out later, feeling good made things work better on this side too.

The situation in the room was tense: folks in small intimate knots talking quietly; a small line of people parading past the body muttering their goodbyes, most crying or with tears in their eyes; and one older lady, the wife I presume, wailing in a corner, awkwardly comforted by what I assume were her children.

That is another tough thing about grieving. The one with the greatest loss is the one that receives the comfort, kind of like a pecking order. The wife lost the most, so the children comforted her, when they were ripped up inside too.

There were also a few mortuary suits standing there: impeccably groomed, good posture, and appropriately dour expressions on their faces. How do you do a job like that? To be surrounded constantly by other people's grief and yet retain a shred of your own joy, or sanity at the very least.

Yup, I woke up happy today, smiling with a spring in my step. Then I went to work and had to transform myself into a conciliatory zombie. Yuck.

And then, finally, was the ghost. Hovering around the coffin was a bardo-ed, gape mouthed extra-corporeal. From what I heard folks saying he had a massive stroke and went fast.

I walked up (OK, hovered) to him and said, "Hey pops, how'd you die?" His expression didn't change, those eyes hollow and far off. Then I had an idea: since he was still closely attached to his body, maybe...

"Look at this old fart. I bet he has a mouth full of crowns in there, probably some of them gold. I love gold!" I glanced over but nothing had changed. "I'm just gonna reach in here and see what I can find." I gingerly stuck my hand into his mouth and made a good show of it.

That did it, his eyes popped into focus, and he said "Hey!" He swooped towards me, passing through those that were standing there looking at the meat that was him. One of them shivered, and I felt what I can only describe as a cold breeze rushing past.

I pulled my hand out and said, "No harm pops, no harm. My name is JJ. So how did you die?"

He stopped, looked around and moaned, "Dead, I'm dead? How can I be dead? I'm not dead!" A look of horror came over his face and, pop, back to bardo-land for him.

I left; he just didn't seem to be ready for what had happened to him, thoroughly engrossed in the denial/shock stage. I spent the rest of the day just outside the building. I tried to go further, but couldn't. So I loitered near the entrance yelling in people's ears seeing how many I could reach.

Not many, but a few seemed to sense something. Not what I was saying or anything, but they sensed something. One old biddy shivered, a man with a hearing aid twiddled with it like it had squealed or something.

Not much of a way to pass time, but at least I wasn't stuck in there with my meat.

When I went outside, I discovered this was not just a

mortuary, but a cemetery too. That freaked me out a bit, probably lots of ghosts around here. And you know, just because you are a ghost doesn't mean you want to run into a bunch of other ghosts. The bardo-brained newly dead were bad enough, but what must it be like for a spirit stuck in a place like this for a decade or a century?

This place was on the corner of Miracle and Oracle. You think the roads were named that way when they built the place? Seems like two strange names. With tall trees and green grass it was surprisingly lush for Tucson. At least it was a lovely place, and peaceful at the moment.

I hung around outside, and poked around inside, carefully avoiding my meat, but not much exciting happened. I did learn a few things.

First of all those mortuary suits got pretty weird when they were on break and no one (but us ghosts) were around.

The tall one, Hal I think, did a dead-on impression of the grieving widow for his coworkers, complete with crying, carrying on and a grief soaked east coast accent.

Alice, the only chick on duty, was a foulmouthed, chain smoking witch when she was out of sight of the patrons. She kept going on about how much she would drink at night, and how sick she would get. Later in my stay I caught her and Hal getting it on in the embalming room—sick.

Ed, my embalmer, started to regale them with the gruesome details of just how messed up I was. I got out of there fast, planning to stay outside until everyone had gone home and the place was locked up.

I didn't take it personally. I've just got to imagine with a job like that you've got to blow the steam off any way you can.

Transmission #4
Received 2010/10/22 02:56:21

I HAD TO TAKE A BREAK, BUT I THINK I AM GETTING BETTER at this; it is going faster at least.

One weird thing that happens; when I get really exhausted, I just go away. I have no idea what happens to me or where I am but some time later I come back and feel all groggy. Kind of like a deep dreamless sleep. It is referred to as "fading," I have seen other spirits do it, and that is what it looks like—they just slowly fade away.

I often wake up somewhere different from when I went to sleep, often not in good places. The other day I woke up in the middle of I-10 with a wall of traffic descending on me. I would have died, if I had not already been dead.

JJTTSABD #3: *Waking up at some random location and getting the shock of your life... err death, ... sucks.*

I don't like "fading," I just don't trust it. I guess I am afraid that I won't come back, that it will be the end. I think I went through a phase like that when I was a kid. I would fight sleeping as long as I could—I didn't trust it, I didn't want to miss anything, and I was afraid of not coming back.

That evening things got really interesting at the mortuary; I had a series of visitors.

First up was Marilyn. She arrived just as the sun was going down, the sunlight filtered through the dust and pollution bathed everything in a warm glow. She was well formed, wearing last century's fashionable clothing over her bulbous body. She was so well formed that for a bit I thought she was meat. That is until she walked right up to me and said, "Have you seen my cat?"

"You can see me?"

"Of course I can sonny," she said. "Have you seen my cat, Motor? He got himself lost again; he must be around here somewhere."

"So, how did you die?" I asked. Standard greeting, right? Just like in prison—hey bub, whatcha in for? Her face got pinched, her form started to break up, and her eyes got vacant. I scrambled, "Cat. Yeah, I saw a cat, just a little while ago." That snapped her back a bit, her hands reforming out of the vapor.

"You saw my cat?"

"Not sure if it was yours, but I did see a cat," I lied. "Hey lady, what's your name?" I backed up a bit, forcing her to follow me. Following Jesus's lead and getting her talking and moving.

"Marilyn. My name is Marilyn. I really need to find my cat." She paused and thought for a moment. She was fully back now. "Was it a black cat with lovely green eyes that you saw?"

"Yeah, I think so. I saw it run into the trees over there."

She waddled off and I didn't see her again until the same time the next day when we went through a similar routine. She didn't appear to recognize me; it seems like she was running the same track on repeat.

Shortly after Marilyn left, right after the sun went down, the noise started: stirring, rattling, whispers, mumbles, and more shocking noises. This place was surrounded: graves on two sides, and crypts on the other two.

At first I was curious, but when the moans turned into screams I started to get scared. I was really wishing Jesus was with me, and just when it was getting bad, I thought I heard him say, "Just keep talking, just keep walking."

I had no one to talk to, so I started back up with my

butchered rendition of *Don't Fear the Reaper* and started running. At first I ran around the building, but the crypt sections just creeped me out too much so I kept to the front, running back and forth singing as loud as I could.

The red of the sunset deepened, and then before I knew it the light was gone. The night was moonless and the darkness dropped fast and heavy. As things darkened I saw shapes moving out in the cemetery. Perhaps my singing attracted them or perhaps they marched onto the mortuary every night, but either way they were coming closer and closer.

So I ran faster and sung louder—what else was I to do? I had no idea what they wanted, or how to defend myself. In retrospect I thought of them as "them." Not the same as me, but somehow separate and scary. Ghosts are scary, right? I didn't know what they could do to me, and that unknown was keeping me tottering on the brink.

I think he must have been yelling at me for a while before I noticed him.

"Boy! Boy! Screw your courage to the sticking-place."

He was the most well-formed spirit I had seen, although not an impressive form. He was short, bald, with a heavy belly.

I slowed down, and he repeated the phrase again: "Screw your courage to the sticking-place." The phrasing was odd, but his delivery resounding. I got the drift, and stopped long enough to look around.

The spirits were indeed moving into the mortuary, but they had given me, and this fellow, a wide berth. After I stopped, they moved in and took over the path I had been running, and I had no choice but to move closer to the man.

"So," I said, trying to insert some swagger into my voice, "how'd ya die?"

"Better, boy, better. My name is Banquo and I died in a plane crash." His void was deep, resonant, and calming.

"My name is JJ; I died pinned to a jungle gym at a Mickey D's."

"I thought I would find you here. Jesus told me that you might need some help."

"Jesus saves!" I couldn't resist pulling that one out again.

Banquo chuckled, "Indeed he does."

"Those... Those..." I stuttered, pointing towards the mortuary where the gang of spirits had gone.

"Just curious, for the most part. It is a small community, visitors are always an excitement. Come, we must talk."

Banquo guided me, much to my dismay, to the embalming room where my body, now dressed and fully "restored," was laid out. There were a few of the cemetery spirits examining my body, sticking their faces into my abdomen, fingers into my head.

"Hey!" I shouted. Just like the old fart that I messed with, I felt proprietary about that piece of meat. It was *my* piece of meat.

"JJ, until you accept what happened, accept that you are dead, and that *thing* is no longer *you*, you will be chained to it."

Shuffled Off: A Ghost's Memoir, Book 1 is available now.
Go to ShuffledOff.com for more information.

ACKNOWLEDGEMENTS

These stories are, in many ways, for my amazing wife, Aleia. She is the audience I write for and the first person to hear these stories—I read them aloud to her which helps me catch all kinds of things I wouldn't otherwise. She's not a sci-fi nerd like myself (except for *Star Trek* and *Star Wars*), so if I can write science fiction and fantasy that appeal to her then I know I've written something that works for a wider audience.

These stories are also hers in another way. Her work with people who are very ill or close to death has influenced my life and thinking in ways that are hard to express (or even grasp). Such influence is natural after twenty-five years with someone, but this someone has such courage in the real world heading into territory where *angels fear to tread* that it gives me courage to write about things that really matter to me.

The other people these stories belong to are my stalwart band of beta readers. They gave crucial feedback that has improved each of them. They are: John Bifano, Roni

Hornstein, Chris Kalinich, Peter Klein, Gary McClellan, Aleia N. O'Reilly, Jack Pelton, and Eliot Schipper. Thanks, guys!

And, of course, a shout out to my always reliable proof-reader, Diana Cox (www.novelproofreading.com).

ABOUT THE AUTHOR

ROBERT J. MCCARTER IS VERY COMFORTABLE WRITING about characters as long as one of those characters is not himself. Actually, Robert is anything but comfortable speaking (or writing) of himself in the third person—he finds it pretentious and silly.

So, let's drop all that usual bio crap.

Hi, my name is Robert, and I make things up and write them down. As a reader you may be interested in knowing something about me, so here goes:

I am a computer programmer by trade and have been for a very long time. I wrote my first program over thirty years ago and never stopped. I found the dramatic arts in high school, which got me through that rather daunting rite of passage, and fell in love with the arts. After high school, I started writing really bad poetry about how lonely I was and how clueless I was about the opposite sex (which, fortunately for all of us, I burned). After that my writing turned towards fiction.

I have written sporadically for several decades, and in

what is, in all probability, part of a mid-life crisis, I started writing seriously (i.e. regularly) a few years ago. I have always been drawn to the arts (acting, photography, fractal art, and writing) and find that I am most happy when I am being as creative as possible. Thus, all the sitting alone at my computer making things up.

My writing is colored by my technical (i.e. geek) past as well as my age. I'm no youngster, so themes of death, grief, and change tend to creep into my writing (Okay, that's an understatement). Also, having been trained as an engineer, I like things to make sense and do my best to keep the hand waving to a minimum.

If you asked me to succinctly say something to summarize my writing style, I would tell you to go buzz off. But then, after profuse apologies, I would say: "I write humanist-geek, character-oriented sci-fi with heart."

I live in the middle of a Ponderosa Pine forest in the mountains of Arizona with my beautiful wife and my ridiculously adorable dog.

If you'd like to get a hold of me, use the contact form on my website (RobertJMcCarter.com/contact-me/). I'd love to hear from you, really I would.

Oh, and if you want the inside scoop on my writing, sign up for my newsletter (I won't share your name and emails are infrequent—around once a month). You can sign up using the blue box on the right of my website at RobertJMc-Carter.com.

BOOKS BY ROBERT J. MCCARTER

Novels in the "Ghost's Memoir" world:
Shuffled Off: A Ghost's Memoir, Book 1
Drawing the Dead
To Be a Fool: A Ghost's Memoir, Book 2
Of Things Not Seen: A Ghost's Memoir, Book 3
(Coming soon)

Books in the Neutrinoman and Lightningirl Series:
Meteor Attack!
Lightningirl and Neutrinoman, A Love Story. Episode 1
Toxic Asset
Lightningirl and Neutrinoman, A Love Story. Episode 2
Protocol X
Lightningirl and Neutrinoman, A Love Story. Episode 3
Season 1 (Omnibus edition of Episodes 1 - 3)
Off Book
Lightningirl and Neutrinoman, A Love Story. Episode 4
(Coming soon)

Short Stores and Collections
Life After: Stories of Life, Death, and the Places in Between
Probability: Resolve
The Turing Test Will Be Televised
Ghost Hacker, Zombie Maker

For a complete list, go to RobertJMcCarter.com